For The Girls

A SAPPHIC CONTEMPORARY ROMANCE COLLECTION

R.L. MERRILL

Foreword

Welcome to *For The Girls: A Sapphic Romance Collection*. Over the past ten years, I have contributed stories to multiple anthologies and group projects, and I often used those opportunities to write stories about women loving women. I've collected the contemporary romance tales in this volume for the first time, and all proceeds will go to support Planned Parenthood. I have been a volunteer with the organization for the past two years in order to give back during these tumultuous times.

During my college years (1990-94) I lived in Iowa, far from my home in the San Francisco Bay Area and the medical professionals I was accustomed to. I had been on birth control for several months before I left for school as I was taking the acne drug Accutane, a treatment which required those with uteruses to be on contraception as it was guaranteed to cause birth defects. The doctors showed my mother and I pictures of what would happen if I were to get pregnant—as if I weren't already terrified of getting pregnant at seventeen years old.

Once in Iowa, I found myself in need of a reliable place to get my birth control pills, so my mom suggested I look for a Planned Parenthood.

I'd spent the eighties as a young person equating the clinics as places to get abortions, and I recalled they were constantly under threat of bombings from pro-life organizations. The nearest clinic was more than an hour's drive from where I went to school, but I made the trip. I was in an unsafe relationship at the time with a partner who threatened me when my period was late. I could not take a chance of becoming pregnant.

Planned Parenthood does more than provide abortion services. During my college years, I also took friends to the clinic for HIV and pregnancy tests. It was a life-saving haven for many of us. After having an unbearably uncomfortable pelvic exam experience with the male "family doctor" in town, I went to the clinic exclusively for my health needs. I will never forget the kindness the clinicians showed to all of us who needed their help.

After college, I returned to the San Francisco Bay Area. I became a high school social studies teacher, and then a school counselor. I taught parenting and sex education programs to students and always kept a volume of *Our Bodies, Our Selves* in my classroom. I gave birth to two children and made sure they had a thorough understanding of sexual and reproductive health. When they left for college, I quit teaching so that I could take care of my health and my aging parents, however I wanted to find a way to continue supporting young people. I joined the Planned Parenthood Mar Monte Speaker's Bureau and attended Capitol Day in Sacramento, where we met with legislators and their staff to discuss the importance of protecting reproductive health for all Californians. Since then, I've tabled at community events and at Pride celebrations, and we've received so much support from folks. I'm proud to stand with Planned Parenthood, and I look forward to donating proceeds from this collection to the important work that they do.

For The Girls

The following stories are included in this volume of Sapphic Contemporary Romance

Salty and Sweet – Previously published in the Summer Fair Anthology

Pinups and Puppies – Previously published in Love Is All: Volume Two

Joy Is A Phone Call Away – Previously published in the A More Perfect Union Anthology

Let Me Stand Next To Your Fire – Previously published in Love Is All: Volume Five

Love And Pride – Previously published in Love Is All: Volume Four

The Maiden and the Crone – Previously published in Love Is All: Volume Seven

❀ Created with Vellum

Salty and Sweet

About the story...

Heather Wright is embarking on a new journey this summer: Musical Theater. Why not? She needs the credits to clear her teaching credential, and maybe she'll learn something along the way. When she meets the fascinating and lovely Naomi Oliver, that backbone she's been working on is put to the test. Heather will have to learn that love can be both salty and sweet, and being confident is the key to getting what you want.

Chapter One

Join the theater. It'll be fun. It's just for the summer.

I'd had some bright ideas in my life, but joining a summer theater program at the local university was shaping up to not be one of them. I imagined I'd be dancing in a production, maybe learning how to act like something other than a snarky high school teacher, and maybe even learning how not to shatter glass when I sang. I needed credits if I wanted to keep my teaching job, and it didn't matter where I got them, so theater seemed like a great option. It was only the middle of the first day and I'd already figured out I was in over my head.

Singing was definitely not going to lead to stardom for me. That I figured out in my first class of the day, Musical Theater. The instructor appeared to be sorry she didn't take me at my word that my voice sounded remarkably like a dying cat. I was informed I was an alto dying cat, so hey, I learned something!

My second class was Monologues, where I would soon learn whether I had any acting ability or not. Our instructor, a young Black gentleman not much older than me dressed in a suit with long locs pulled back in a hair tie, gave us a couple of examples of the kinds of monologues we might perform. I was thoroughly intimidated by his stellar performance. Acting seemed to come so naturally to Alfonso

Tremaine. He ended the class by sharing some advice about choosing the best piece to perform.

"Pick something that can be easily memorized and is easy for you to relate to. You want to be able to live inside this monologue, breathe it. Feel it in your bones and on your skin before you're through with it."

I loved his energy and passion for acting. I thought just maybe I could learn something from this class that would be helpful in teaching as well.

Shop was the third class, and I figured we'd learn about set building, painting, and working with tools. Instead, I sat crammed between a Filipina woman in her thirties and a Latine teenager with way too much fragrance on trying to pay attention to the instructor who was supervising our Shop class.

"Our job in this portion of the summer program is to not only construct the sets for the two plays, but also to outfit the performers. Each of you will be required to put in four hours per week in the workshop to earn your credits. This is a pass-fail course, so no one is going to ding you if you aren't the best stagecraft person ever, but you will want to do your best for yourself and your classmates. At the end of the five weeks, you'll be putting on a three-day festival, which includes a performance of Shakespeare's *Othello*, the monologue showcase, and then a big stage version of the Broadway hit *Kiss Me, Kate*."

The latter I'd been looking forward to since the advisor I'd registered with told me about the program. I would get to dance. That was my only known talent in the trifecta of Musical Theater Performance.

Naomi Oliver was our supervisor for the Shop session. After her introduction, she gave us a tour of the workshop and stage areas. She was a lovely statuesque Black woman who was stern but kind, and the sound of her voice gave me chills. The good kind. I could picture her acting onstage, which she told us she'd been doing for nearly thirty years. But she'd be a great audiobook narrator as well. The tone of her voice was deep and rich, smooth and powerful. The perfect kind to get lost listening to. I loved audiobooks. I probably spent way too much time listening to them and daydreaming about the glamorous lives of other people while my own was recovering from another kind of drama.

Shop was going to be my weak point, a fact I realized when she handed out various assignments. I got sewing.

"I can't sew, Ms. Oliver."

She gave me a skeptical look.

"You're kidding, right?"

"Nope. I avoided sewing like the plague at home, and I even failed it in Home Ec. Along with cooking. I failed that, too."

Her expression changed to disbelief. "Is there anything you *can* do, Ms. Wright?"

I swallowed hard. I found myself attracted to this woman, and for some reason, I didn't want to screw up my first impression with her. I feared whatever I said was going to do exactly that.

"Well, I'm willing to try anything. I just don't have any experience in this area."

"Can you hammer a nail?" She enunciated every word clearly and with plenty of sarcasm.

I grinned, and my cheeks were hot. She may have been annoyed, but her reaction only encouraged me. "Yeah. I'm experienced with tools."

She smirked. "I bet you are. I'll come back to you, Ms. Wright. Is there anyone who *can* sew?"

A couple of the other younger women in the class raised their hands. This program was upper division but still undergrad, and was open to high schoolers as well, so the age group ranged from late teens to middle-aged folks just looking for a good time this summer. I'd been out of college for four years already and none of my classmates appeared to be my age. *Awesome.*

After Ms. Oliver had everyone working on their projects, she came back to me.

"I swear, I can help in here. Just show me what to do and I'll gladly do whatever you ask."

She raised an eyebrow at me as though she were trying to decide what use I might be to her. At this point I'd sweep the floors if it would make her happy. "When you say you can't sew, do you mean at all? Can you, like, sew a button on?"

"Yes! Yes, I can do that. Totally."

She narrowed her eyes and then lifted a finger to beckon me over to a station.

"Here," she said, handing me a sewing kit. "How about we start you with ripping seams and taking *off* buttons? These are old costumes we're going to repurpose for the show, and I need this fabric. I don't think you can screw this up too bad."

"Probably not, but you never know." I immediately wished I could take that back. I knew how frustrating it was to have a class full of students waiting for my attention and having to spend all my time with one student.

She gave me side-eye. "Let's hope not."

Nice one, Heather. I had a terrible habit of messing with people. My coworkers either avoided me like the plague at staff meetings or they fought to sit with me because they knew they'd be entertained. My classroom was always loud and boisterous, and despite the disdain of my administrator, my AP classes had the highest test scores last year on the state exams, so they left me to my own devices.

Ms. Oliver taught me how to use the seam ripper, making sure I did it correctly and wasn't in danger of stabbing anyone other than myself. I got to work on a pile of big poofy skirts and ripped to my heart's delight. There was a satisfaction that came from the feel of the fabric separating and the sounds had me feeling rather Hulk-ish. I might have been a little too enthusiastic about it. I'd just finished cutting a row of stitches and was about to pull it apart with yet another *hiyeeeeaaaahhh* when a strong hand gripped my arm.

I squealed and spun around, only to crash into Ms. Oliver's chest. "Oh! I'm sorry."

The workshop was empty save the two of us. Ms. Oliver held my arm for a second more, her grip relaxing a bit.

"Class is over. It's time for you to head to Musical Theater Performance. Are you finished here?"

I gulped and then laughed nervously. "Halfway. Sorry. I guess I was in my own little world over here."

"Uh huh."

I couldn't tell if she was annoyed or amused by me at that point. I guess I'd made some sort of impression at least. *What does it matter?* It wasn't like I was back in college. I needed the credits from this class to help clear my credential, not to become a full-time thespian. I shouldn't care what she thought.

"Well, thank you. I'll see you tomorrow."

"Yes, you will." She didn't exactly smile, but her expression seemed to indicate she was more on the amused end of the spectrum than annoyed. She gave me a once over and pursed her lips before walking away.

I grabbed my backpack and left the shop stunned. *Did she just flirt with me?*

No. It didn't matter. I intended to have fun with this summer program, not to find companionship. Nope. Didn't need any more of that.

Performance class was in the evenings four days a week. I ended up cast in the chorus, thanks to my amazing singing ability, and we began learning the opening song as well as the stage blocking. Toward the end of the first class, the director, an older Black woman with silver hair named Maureen Jackson, went through her overall vision for the show and the history of *Kiss Me, Kate*. It sounded like a fun mixture of Shakespeare and camp. My kind of show.

"And since the original production was in nineteen forty-eight, there was a tap number featured prominently in the show. I'd love to include this, but I'd need to know if we have any tappers."

My hand shot up excitedly.

"Ms. Wright! Wonderful. What kind of experience do you have?"

I shrugged. "Sixteen years of lessons? I've also been to New York and Los Angeles for master classes."

Some *ooos* and *aaas* were heard from the group.

"Would you have any interest in choreographing the number for us?"

"I'd love to!"

I had a hard time concentrating the rest of the night and only vaguely remembered driving home. My thoughts traveled from the songs I needed to learn, which I put on repeat on my iTunes the minute I got in the car, and what monologue I might end up performing.

Then I thought about Ms. Oliver.

Naomi.

The woman was fascinating, and though I knew she probably wouldn't give me a second thought, that wasn't enough to douse the flames of attraction. Even when she'd been sarcastic with me, I hadn't been able to look away from her full lips, her deep brown eyes that curved up just a little at the edges, and her silky skin. I couldn't gauge her exact age, but I could tell she was older than me. The fact that she wasn't actually evaluating my performance made me even more eager to see whether or not the attraction I was feeling was mutual. When she smiled at something a more capable student said, I'd felt a little flutter in my chest. Somehow, I told myself, I would make her smile at me like that.

Somewhere between the university and home, I stopped for fries and a chocolate shake, but I was so distracted, I missed my turn and had to wind my way back around the block to reenter the one-way street.

I climbed the stairs and stumbled into my apartment, tripping over a package on my doorstep.

It contained the last of the items left behind when the woman I thought I would marry evicted me from her life. She FedExed them. That seemed appropriate. She got fed up with me and I was exed.

Laura had wanted a more polished partner. Professional. Reserved. Not someone who always got food on her clothes when they went out to eat. Not someone whose boobs were always popping out of something. And definitely not someone who thought Beavis and Butthead were appropriate humor for birthday cakes.

Laura was an executive with a company that specialized in, let's be honest, fat removal for rich folk. The last straw for me was when she'd called me on the carpet in front of her colleagues for refusing to take part in a test study.

I happened to think my figure was as God intended it to be. Curvy like the Bay Area foothills, luscious as a hot fudge sundae, and strong as the brand-new Bay Bridge. Cold lasers or weight loss supplements need not apply.

Laura hadn't appreciated my very flamboyant exit from that particular dinner party. I'd gone into the bathroom, unbuttoned my blouse and tied it under my boobs old-school style, and rolled down the waistband of my slacks, showing off the vast expanse of my abdomen, including the tattoo I'd gotten last year—against her wishes—of two mermaids swimming together below my navel.

"Honey, so sorry I have to leave you," I said, flicking my long blonde hair over my shoulder. "But I'm off to the hot dog eating contest at Cindy's. I'm going to win this year for sure. Shoving all those wieners in my face will be orgasmic. Toodles!"

Okay, I really had gone to my friend Cindy's bar from there, but I'd gotten wasted and bawled like a baby while men climbed all over themselves to buy me drinks, hand me tissues, and persuade me that they liked me the way I was. They claimed they would appreciate me way more than my girlfriend, however, if I wanted to bring her along, they'd be fine with that, too.

As if.

When I got home that night, she was in the middle of packing my shit. She cordially invited me to get the fuck out. I don't know what else I expected after my performance. It hurt, but at the same time I was relieved. Deep down, I'd always known I was a pleaser, and I'd fallen all over myself to make Laura love me and approve of me. Somewhere along the way, I'd grown a backbone, I thought, and lost that need to please. I took her invitation and got the fuck on with my life.

Ever since that night I'd been all about Heather and what makes Heather happy, which is possibly what this adventure in theater was all about. I ate what I wanted, wore what I wanted, and gave no fucks about anyone but me.

But then Naomi Oliver's face popped into my mind, and while I was still working on that backbone, I loooved a challenge, and she was one beautiful challenge if I'd ever seen one.

Chapter Two

A week into classes I still hadn't managed to make her smile, but she had given me a slight nod of approval when I showed her all the fabric had been seam-split, laundered and pressed, and all of the buttons were now sorted by size and colors into trays.

"Great," she'd said. "Now you can go use those tools you're so good with over on the set-building station."

Huh. Still sarcastic, but was there some humor in there?

"Awesome. Let me know if there's anything else I can do. I can't run a machine, but I can organize like you heard about."

She raised an eyebrow at me, and one corner of her lips curved slightly upwards. "I'll keep that in mind, Heather."

That was better. We were past *Miz* Wright.

I couldn't help admiring the way her long legs, the color of dark amber, disappeared into a pair of denim shorts. The length was definitely appropriate for school, it was really fucking hot in these buildings this summer, but the length of her legs and the way the fabric hugged her muscular ass captivated me. Her work in the shop required a lot of movement—reaching up high, bending over to look for something in a low cabinet, lifting heavy objects. Each action accentuated another part of her powerful, yet very feminine anatomy. I was worse than a teenage boy, watching her and hoping for a peek at more skin. What had started out as my least favorite class turned out to be the one with the best scenery.

I still hadn't settled on a monologue, but I'd found so many that I loved and was having fun going over them again and again. I probably would have four or five memorized by the end rather than just one.

The dancing was coming together slowly but surely. There were only four of us who had dance experience in the cast, so the rehearsals required lots of patience. I often stayed after and worked on the tap piece in the small studio behind the stage. Maureen wanted me to start teaching it the following week, so I needed to put the finishing touches on it. It was a short combination, but I wanted to showcase the talent of the other women who, like me, probably hadn't been on stage since our teen years. We deserved our moment to shine.

I reported to the shop for my costume fitting at the beginning of the second week and waited in line to have my measurements taken. When I got to the front, Naomi was working alongside two other students. She took one look at me and grabbed the tape measure from the one doing the measurements. *Huh.*

I stepped up to her and raised my arms out to the sides. She moved around behind me and measured from my neck to wrist.

"Arm, twenty-nine and a half." She walked around to my front, looking everywhere but my eyes.

Her lemon chiffon scent hit me as soon as she reached around behind me, and I sucked in a breath. *God, she smells good.*

"Bust, thirty-eight," she called out, and I had to fight to keep from panting as her fingers grazed my nipples. They instantly came to life, and I had to look away from her.

"Waist, thirty-six," she said, her hands lingering for a moment on my waist.

Oh God, and then it was time to do my hips. She squatted in front of me and whipped her tape behind me, wrapping it around the widest part of my hips. Her hands met just over my pubic bone, and I squirmed. I couldn't help it. Her nearness was making my body swoon. I had such a crush on her.

"Hips, thirty-eight. Now let's get your inseam—"

"It's thirty-two," I squeaked, backing away from her, my cheeks hot. No way she was getting her hands that close to my happy place. I'd melt into a pool of lust on the floor.

"Alright, then. Inseam, thirty-two. Next."

Her pursed lips told me she knew exactly what my problem was and that she'd enjoyed making me squirm.

The Thursday night of the second week, I was dancing my ass off and having way too much fun in the little studio by myself. The rest of the cast had left at least an hour before and I was still there, stomping away. The mirrors were such a kick, and I pretended like a whole audience was watching me. I did my Ann Miller turns, showed off my killer high kicks, and even threw in a wild jump split at the end.

You can imagine my surprise when I actually heard clapping.

"I wondered who was making all that racket in here. Shoulda known it was you."

Naomi Oliver stood in the doorway, her arms crossed over her chest and a close-lipped smile on her face.

"Maureen said I could use the studio. I'm choreographing the tap section for *Kiss Me, Kate*."

"I gathered," she said. She entered the room, her boots squeaking on the hardwood floor. She walked over to the sound system and turned off the music. "I was just coming to turn out the lights and lock up. Mind showing me what you got?"

I scrambled to my feet and stood in the middle of the floor. "Yeah? You really want to see?"

"Uh huh." Still not the smile I was hoping for.

But that eyebrow, though.

I lifted my chin, ready to face the challenge she'd just dropped in front of me. "Sure. Why not? Can you start it over? It's track nine."

She clicked the buttons on the stereo and then sat on a stool, kicking her legs out in front of her. "Show me."

I swallowed hard, that fluttering back in my chest, but I wasn't nervous about dancing. I knew I had talent. I could have kept going and had a career, but after college, I decided I wanted to have dance be something I continued to enjoy, and if it became a job, it wouldn't be stress-free any longer. Plus, there was the whole starving-myself thing, and I wasn't having that.

The music reached the beginning point to the combination and I threw my arms out to the sides.

Stomp.

Stomp.

Stomp stomp stomp clap!

I broke into some time steps and then made a high-speed turn around the floor, spinning so fast my taps practically kicked up sparks. I returned to the front, threw my shoulders back and added some sass before throwing in some wings and toe-backs. For a big girl, I was light on my feet and my leaps caught some air. I wrapped up the combination with a windmill turn and a flick of my imaginary skirt, ending with my toe popped in front of me.

"That's it," I said, pulling my booty shorts down a little. I'd assumed I'd be alone, so I'd stripped down to just the black spandex and a sports bra as the AC wasn't very powerful back here. I was a sweaty mess, my blonde hair piled haphazardly on my head and held in place with a scrunchie.

And Naomi was staring at me.

When she didn't speak, I walked over to my stuff in front of the mirror and bent to pick up my water bottle. I was draining the last bit when she spoke.

"Where'd you learn to dance like that?"

Water spilled out of my mouth on one side and poured down my front.

"Whew! That's cold! Um, at a studio in Fremont? It's not there anymore. I've taken classes other places, too."

She stood and walked over to me slowly. "You look good."

I pulled my hair free and shook it out so I could restyle it. Then it hit me. She hadn't said, "you dance well," she'd said, "you look good."

Hmmm. Interesting word choice.

"Thanks. I can do some things, I guess."

"And you didn't even require a tool," she said, stopping about two feet away. Close for the situation but not so close as to be inappropriate.

I smiled. "Nope. All me."

"Mmm hmm."

The music ended and all that could be heard was my heavy breathing.

Naomi crossed her arms again. "What's your story?"

I frowned. "My story?"

"Yeah. Why are you here?"

I barked out a laugh. "I told you. Maureen said—"

"Not *here* here. Why are you in this program?"

"Oh," I said, feeling a little silly, but honestly, she made me nervous. Excited nervous. "I'm a teacher. I came from out of state, and California requires a fifth year of college to clear a teaching credential. I'm starting a master's program in September, but I needed more credits, and this looked like fun."

She frowned. "And how old are you?"

"Twenty-six. Why?"

She shook her head. "Nothing. I was just wondering, if you aren't, like, a theater person, why you'd give up your summer for this gig."

"Oh, I don't know. It's fun. I get to hang out with whiny teenagers, get insulted by teachers. It's just like work but I'm not getting paid."

Naomi barked out a laugh. "Insulted? No. Teased, maybe. I'm sorry if you thought I insulted you. You caught me on a bad day that first class. I don't normally teach this program. I'm in the theater department here, but I take the summers off. The Shop gal had an opportunity to take a costuming workshop in Italy this summer, so they suckered me into it."

"Sounds like a teacher's lament."

"Yeah."

"Yeah."

Silence. I bent to take off my tap shoes and pull on my yoga pants. When I stood, her whole demeanor changed. Instead of her arms firmly crossed over her chest in an uninviting manner, she had one thumbnail hooked behind her teeth and an unsure smile behind it.

"Hey, Heather?"

I slipped on my Vans and picked up my purse. "Yeah?"

She paused for a moment, then dropped her hands to her hips and rocked on her toes. "You want to go out? Get something to eat?"

Oh, those flutters were back. Was she serious?

I looked down at myself. "Uh, I'm kind of a mess. You mean like *out* out?"

She hesitated and then took a step away. "Never mind. You're probably busy."

"The only thing I'm going to be busy doing is swinging through the Wendy's drive-thru to grab a chocolate Frosty and French fry. My favorite late-night snack. You ever try dipping your fries in your shake? Mmmm. Heaven."

She frowned and tucked her chin in. "You mean to tell me you take a perfectly good milkshake and dip French fries in it? Are you mad?"

I shrugged. "Probably, but then I figured you'd guessed that already." I narrowed my eyes at her and took a wild stab in the dark. "You want to follow me? Come over to my place for a while? I just need to shower real quick and then we can hang out. Visit. Share stories."

Naomi rubbed at the back of her neck and looked around. "I should probably—"

"We don't have class tomorrow. Do you still have to work?"

She shook her head. "But you probably have things—"

"I've got brownies, too. I baked them last night."

She chuckled. "You've got a sweet tooth, don't you?"

"Yep. Come on. I want to hear *your* story, and don't tell me there isn't one. Mr. Tremaine can't stop talking about how amazing you were onstage in *Rent*."

Her eyes bugged out, and then she sighed. "That boy, I tell you. Alright. Let's go."

She followed me out, locking the doors and setting the alarm for the building with a keypad in the foyer. Her shiny blue Jeep Rubicon was parked two rows over from my beat-up Ford Ranger pickup. I gave her my address in case we got separated and asked her for her order from Wendy's.

"Whatever you're having. Oh, and a Diet Coke."

I didn't know where I got the guts to invite her to my house, but I was so excited I could barely stand it. It was after ten o'clock, so our eating choices would have been limited to Denny's or my sister's bar in downtown Hayward, just a couple of miles from the university. But honestly, I was so gross. I needed a shower before I could be chatty with anyone and not have them run away.

I swung through the drive-thru and ordered double my usual and Naomi's Diet Coke, making it back to my apartment about the time Naomi was pulling up. We had to park in the lot behind my building and walk up the back stairs.

"How'd you end up here?" she asked me. "I didn't know anyone lived above these shops anymore."

"Yeah, well, my friend's friend owns the building, and he rented this place to me. I had to, uh, move quickly seven months ago. There weren't many apartments available in the city at Christmas time, so…"

"Ah."

I unlocked the door and led her into my very interesting place. The ceilings were massively high and unfinished with giant fluorescent lights suspended above. The space used to be used for storage. There were several weird closets that partitioned off the back hallway from the main space. My bed was shoved in one corner, I had a couch in front of a flat-screen TV near the front windows looking down over B Street, and there was a kitchenette at the other end. There was a hallway off of the kitchen that led to more closets and a big bathroom with an industrial-size shower. No tub. Sadly. But at least I had a place to live. The walls that were finished were painted a green that reminded me of my elementary school, and the floor was very worn hardwood.

"I'd say take off your shoes and make yourself comfortable, but you might get splinters from this floor. Aaron, my landlord, says he's going to get the floors redone when the other tenant, his friend Schroeder, goes to Europe next month."

Naomi was looking around in wonder. I'd added a few homey touches, but it was kind of a dump.

"Yeah, it's not much to look at, I know. And I apologize for the heat, but I only have a portable AC unit and I don't run it when I'm gone." Speaking of which, I rolled it out of the corner and hooked up the vent to the window and turned it on. It would take all night to get this place to a bearable temperature, but it would be worth it tomorrow morning.

"Gotta live somewhere," she said.

We sat at my wood picnic table in the middle of the space, which was half covered in mail and junk I didn't want to deal with including the box Laura sent and ate our fries and Frosties. I took the lid off my Frosty and dipped my fries in one at a time.

"Where did you ever get the idea that was a good thing? I'm serious," she said when I started laughing. "I've never seen anyone do that before in my life."

I shrugged. "You get your salty and sweet together this way. And I would argue that ice cream and French fries are basically the top choice in either of those categories."

Naomi chewed thoughtfully for a moment. "Bacon."

"Hmm?"

"Bacon," she repeated. "I'd argue that bacon is the top choice for salty foods."

"Oooo, you have a point. I've never tried bacon and ice cream though. I wonder—"

"Oh, no. No no, don't you go ruining bacon."

"Just try it," I urged. I dipped a long fry and held it out to her. To my surprise, she bent and took it between her lips. Oh, the flutters, the flutters.

"That is surprisingly good, Blondie. You might just be onto something."

"Blondie? We've gone from Miz Wright to Heather to Blondie now?"

Naomi shrugged. "If the hair fits."

I had to ask, no matter what the outcome. "Why did you ask me to get something to eat tonight?"

She leaned back and pulled one of her long legs up, resting an elbow on her knee. "Just trying to figure you out. And after watching you dance, I was more curious."

She took a draw on her straw, but nothing would come up.

"You gotta let it melt more before you can suck it."

Her eyes flew up to mine, and I laughed out loud. "Ha! Oops.

Okay, I'm going to take a quick shower. Make yourself...well, as comfortable as you can. The couch is comfy at least."

I went down the hallway and tried to calm my crazy heartbeat. I couldn't believe she was sitting at my table in my apartment. I pulled a sundress out of my closet just outside the bathroom and hopped inside to take the fastest cool shower in the history of showers. I worried she might leave if I took too long.

When I returned, she was eating her Frosty with the spoon and holding my newly arrived DVD of *Kiss Me, Kate.*

"Have you seen it?" I asked her, wrapping my hair in a towel. It was down to the middle of my back and would take forever to dry. I didn't want to be bothered with it.

She turned to look at me and took in my appearance. Fuck makeup or dressing up. This was my house...and by the way she was looking at me, she was more than happy.

"I haven't. I know it's a retelling of *Taming of the Shrew,* which is one of my least favorite Shakespeares."

"Why is it a least favorite?"

I walked around her and sat on the couch. Her eyes followed me and when I kicked my feet up on the coffee table, she came over as well.

"I get it, fathers and suitors did some shady shit to marry off women, but having it thrown in my face, and to have the 'shrew' actually accept it in the end, pissed me off."

"Oh, I don't know. Maybe after the play, she poisoned him and was free of all the men *and* had her money."

Naomi looked at me wide-eyed. "You're dangerous."

"Maybe. You mind if I pop this in? I just want to hear what professionals sound like singing the music."

"Go right ahead."

I put the disk in and sat back on the couch next to her. Maybe a little closer than previously. The movie started up and it was not at all what I thought it would be.

"You go to bed with wet hair?" she asked me.

"Huh? Oh. Yeah, sometimes." I pulled the towel off and ran my fingers through it. "I'll do something with it. Right now, it's cooling me off."

"Want me to braid it for you?" she asked.

OMG her hands on me? Could I handle it?

"Sure. Thank you. I can't do it very well myself. Never could."

I handed her a comb and a hair tie that I'd brought with me.

"Years of theater. You get used to doing all kinds of hair."

I moved to sit on the floor in front of her. I had a nice fluffy shag rug that covered this part of the floor, at least, so no splinters.

"I love your hair, by the way. I keep telling myself someday I'll cut mine off." It was true. She had her tight curls cut close to her scalp, a style that accentuated her high cheekbones. She was truly stunning.

"It's easier," she said, interrupting my latest fantasy. She divided up my hair into three sections with the comb. "But yours is gorgeous."

Her fingers on my scalp made it tough to stay upright, and I found myself sinking into the floor. I might have moaned a little.

"Glad you're not tender-headed. Some of the women I've had to work on for shows bitch the whole time."

"Dancing gets you over that quick. I learned after getting smacked with a hairbrush two or three times. Notice I didn't say the first time. I'm not that quick of a learner."

She laughed. "I don't know. You were pretty quick with that seam ripper."

"Yeah, well, I didn't want to piss off the teacher any more than I had already."

She worked quietly on my hair for a few long moments. I let myself relax against her legs and sighed happily. This was heaven.

"I'd had a fight with my daughter that morning."

A daughter? "I'm sorry."

"Yeah. She's living with her dad in L.A. while she goes to college. I wanted her to stay here. Since I work for the school, we wouldn't have to pay tuition, but no. She just had to be stubborn. I don't even remember what we fought about that morning, to be honest. All our calls have been drama lately."

"She's asserting her independence all up in your face, huh?"

"That's right. And I don't like it one bit. Oh, that's right! We were fighting because I couldn't go down to her gallery opening because of this summer gig."

"That suck. I'm sorry you had to miss it."

"Me, too, but based on the rave reviews she's gotten, it won't be her last. The selfish part of me wanted to say, 'well, you decided to move away,' but then I know she'll have more opportunities down there."

"True. My mom didn't want me to leave Iowa, but then, I was in *loooove*."

She laughed at that. She'd finished one row of French braids and was working on the next. I couldn't wait to see what it looked like.

"Iowa, huh? Yeah, you couldn't pay me to stay in Iowa."

"It was okay. But when my girlfriend got a job out here in Silicon Valley, I came with. Got a job teaching in Fremont. She made a fuck-ton of money. Life was good."

"And now you're living in the Haystack. How'd that happen?"

I thought about myself storming out of that dinner in all my big girl glory and laughed. "I was tired of trying to live up to her expectations. I wanted to be me. I like me."

"I like you, too."

Flutters. "I was a little intimidated by you," I admitted.

"Nah. My bark is worse than my bite. You should know that. Teachers have to be all gruff on the first day, isn't that right?"

She finished the braid she was working on and started the next. My skin broke out in goose bumps as her fingers grazed the back of my neck. I was going to have three braids when she was finished and then… What would happen when she finished?

"I guess so."

"I'm glad you stuck it out, though."

I smiled to myself. "Me, too."

We made jokes about the movie for a bit. I sang along to "Tom, Dick or Harry," and she cracked up at my horrible singing. It felt good to hear her laugh, to know I'd made her happy. When I started to bounce along to the music, she tapped my shoulder with the comb and we both laughed.

"Were you married to your daughter's father?"

"Yeah. My parents kinda made me. I wanted to do it on my own, but they were worried about appearances. It was the early nineties in Orange County, and I was only twenty. I got married, she was born, and I insisted on going back to college, which my ex-husband Clarence hated. He wanted me to stay home and be the trophy wife. He was starting his MBA program and already looking into internships with big business. I was like, 'nah. I'm going to graduate and act.' We split when she was still a baby. I continued acting, he made, how'd you say it? A fuck-ton of money. He was really good about supporting her, and when I got a job up here about twelve years ago, he made regular trips to visit her. She spent time down there with him on breaks and fell in love with it. As far as ex-husbands go, he's pretty great. But I never loved him, so he was always going to be an ex."

"And no one currently?" I asked, peeking over my shoulder. I didn't want to be getting involved with someone who had someone.

"Nope. You?"

"Nope."

She smiled and turned my head back around so she could work on the last braid.

Then she was finished. I was very aware of her bare legs against my shoulders, her hands resting on the sides of my neck, and I wanted to feel more of her skin, but was that what she came over for? After that story, I wasn't sure.

I couldn't stand it anymore. I had to know.

I turned my body and rested my arms on her knees. "Thank you," I said, smiling up at her.

"It's going to look gorgeous when you take them out after it dries."

"You're gorgeous," I whispered.

Her eyes widened, but she didn't pull away.

I got up onto my knees, facing her, my hands on her thighs. "Is it wrong that I've been thinking about kissing you since that first day in class?"

"Not as wrong as me thinking about getting you naked after I saw you dance."

"That's not wrong. Naked is never wrong. It's our natural state, right?"

I leaned closer and she smiled.

"I wasn't wrong asking you out, then?"

"Not wrong."

And damn, but I wanted her. I kissed her. I kissed her long and deep. And she didn't pull away. And I didn't want to stop there.

I must have taken her a little by surprise, but it didn't take her long to reciprocate. She sat up and ran her hands up my thighs, under my sundress, where I was naked as the day I was born.

She smiled against my lips as her fingers grazed the tops of my hips and then curved around my ass.

"Naked's never wrong, huh?"

I shook my head and smiled at her in invitation.

She lifted my dress over my head, careful not to muss up my braids. I reached for the hem of her t-shirt and lifted it over her head. She wore a black lacy bra that beckoned for me to play before removing it. Something about lace just drove me crazy.

I nibbled and sucked at her breasts through the fabric while I undid the buttons on her shorts. I slid them down her legs that went on forever. I was tall at 5'9", but she had a couple of inches on me, and it was all in her legs. God, I wanted to lick and suck all the way up them both, and that's exactly what I did. When I got to her center, she was already trembling.

She reached for my head, and I grabbed her hands.

"Uh uh. Don't muss my braids."

She laughed, throwing her head back as I brought both of our hands down to touch her. I wanted to watch how she touched herself, to see what brought her pleasure. She slid her fingers along the sides of her clit. I was mesmerized, watching them slide up and down, up and down. I pressed my tongue between them, and she continued to rub, just like that.

Between watching and tasting and feeling the smooth skin of her inner thighs against me as she lifted them over my shoulders, my excitement built into a lovely ache in my lower belly. Her legs began to shake, and she moaned a really long sound of release that sent shivers straight down to my core. I licked and licked, drawing out every last wave of her orgasm, pleased she'd responded so well to my touch.

"When I invited you out to eat, I certainly wasn't expecting that," she said, her hand over her eyes as she tried to catch her breath.

I kissed my way up her body, taking time to remove her bra along the way. Her breasts were large and heavy like mine, and I loved the feel of them against my skin.

"I was hungry," I said, sucking her nipple into my mouth, causing her to arch into me. "I have a big appetite."

She laughed and flipped me over onto my back. "We'll see about your appetite when I'm finished with you."

Chapter Three

I'd never had as much fun with sex as I had with Naomi. We had several rounds that got really messy when we brought food into the equation. We tried more salty and sweet combinations after midnight. Cheese and strawberries, which tasted delicious off of her breasts, and then we even made bacon to test with some ice cream I had in the fridge. We decided the fries and Frosty was a much better combination. Around four in the morning, we fell into my bed, exhausted and ready for some rest.

"It's been a long time since I've had so much fun with someone. Thank you for being so fun."

"You're welcome," I said, kissing her one last time before curling into her side and closing my eyes. "Thank you for being hungry."

She laughed and kissed my hair, careful not to muss my braids, and we fell asleep in each other's arms.

She was gone when I woke up. No note, no nothing. I didn't have her number, nor did I have any way to contact her other than her work email, but that seemed inappropriate. Despite the fact that I was very much an adult, and she was only supervising the Shop time, she was still an instructor at the college. I didn't want to make trouble for her.

I spent the weekend working on the monologues, but I wasn't

feeling it. I was feeling sad. Why hadn't she left me a note? Anything? I thought…

Whatever. It had been fun. I guess that happened to folks, right? They had mind-blowing sex with someone they were insanely attracted to and never heard from them again. *Awesome.*

I immediately understood that she'd left without saying anything intentionally when I reported to Shop. I approached her with a tentative smile and was greeted with a glare.

Fuck.

I still had three more weeks of this. She sent me with the set-building half of the class, and she stayed behind in the shop to sew costumes, ensuring we'd have no further contact.

Fine. I'd just dance my ass off, memorize my fucking monologue—which I still couldn't decide on, despite the fact I knew like six or seven by now—and I'd work the set for the damn Shakespeare show. Then it would be time to prepare to go back to work and to start graduate school. Probably didn't need the awesomeness of a new relationship or the excitement of exploring with a new partner, or the joy of waking up in someone's arms, or having someone braid my hair.

Fuckety-fuck fucking fuck.

Chapter Four

"I need your final choice for your monologue, Heather."

I looked up from my notebook to find Mr. Tremaine standing in front of me expectantly.

I tossed down my pen. "I don't know which one to choose. I've memorized six different ones, and I can't decide! I was thinking Viola's monologue from *Twelfth Night,* but I'm not sure."

He stared down at me. "You memorized six? In three weeks?"

I nodded but looked away. "But none of them feel right."

"What's the message you're trying to convey?"

"That's the problem."

Mr. Tremaine heard my sordid tale of love lost, found and lost again, of questioning my self-worth, of not living up to the expectations of others and trying to find the real me...All the pressures both internal and external. He listened well and offered to help me. He brought me a couple of options and I fell in love with one of them. I only had a week before the monologue performance at the festival to perfect it.

The festival started with the Friday afternoon performance of *Othello,* followed by the first half of the monologues, and then a nighttime performance of *Kiss Me, Kate.* We nailed it and my tap number even got a standing O. I was so friggin' excited…until I ran into Naomi offstage.

"Nice moves, Ms. Wright."

She walked away before I could say anything other than "thanks."

What was that for?

Saturday, we flipped the schedule. The musical was first, in the afternoon, then the monologues were in the evening followed by *Othello*. The show went well, not as well as the first night, but I was happy with the dance parts.

Before the monologues, I took extra care to do my hair in braids, just like she'd done them, and I wore the sundress I'd worn that night. I might have been overdoing it, but I intended to let her, and everyone else, see that I liked me just fine, and despite whatever reason she'd left that morning and refused to speak to me, I was going to *be* just fine.

Maybe. Probably. *Shit.*

I was scheduled to go last, and by the time I took the stage, my stomach was in knots. I stood up there in front of several hundred friends, family members and community people here to watch everyone else but me, and I took a deep breath for strength. The one person I wanted to hear what I was about to say was nowhere in sight, and that was probably good, I supposed.

I launched into Meryl Streep's rant from *Postcards From The Edge*, where she's just had a day of criticism of everything from her performance to her cellulite to her enjoyment levels and the shape of her tits. I even brought along the bag of Fritos just as she had in the film. It was everything I'd heard for years, and everything I'd internalized and then rid myself of. No more would I let those messages define me.

The cheers heard in the theater when I finished were louder than my students on the last day of school. That was something. I left the stage and went backstage to the lockers to get my things. I wasn't scheduled to help that night with teardown, and I had no other reason to stick around.

As I was walking by the shop, I heard a string of superlatives that would have made a trucker blush.

I stuck my head in the workshop and found Naomi staring at a pile of fabric.

"Everything okay in here?"

She turned to glare at whoever was disturbing her temper tantrum.

"Hey," she said. "The after-show crew just tossed all the costumes in a heap and left. Nothing got hung up. These all need to be pressed before tomorrow. Fuck! This is not how I wanted to spend my Saturday night."

I walked closer and dropped my bag. "I'll help you."

She waved a hand at me. "Don't worry about it. You have better things to do."

"I don't."

She gave me one more glance and then we both got to work. We divided up the pile, turned on the irons and got to work pressing the long skirts and bodices of the dozens of dresses needed for the cast of *Kiss Me, Kate.* It took us over an hour, and we didn't talk the whole time. The silence was deafening.

As I finished the last dress, Naomi came up and placed a hand on my arm. "Thank you for staying," she said.

I looked down at her hand and then back up at her. "Why did you leave?"

She dropped her hand.

She walked over to the cabinet where the dresses now hung neatly. She fussed with them for a minute. I thought she was done talking, so I bent to pick up my bag and was ready to go.

"You said you weren't seeing anyone."

I turned back to face her. "What?"

She stood with her hands on her beautiful hips. Her eyes looked wet. "You said you weren't seeing anyone else. Why didn't you just tell me the truth?"

"I did. I wasn't seeing anyone else. I'm *not!* Why would you think—"

"The box. On your table. Someone obviously knows you like tools."

"The box? What box?"

Oh. *Shit.* The package from Laura. After I'd tripped over it, I'd opened it and had one last laugh, then left it on the picnic table. The box with the panties I'd left behind, hidden all over the house and the dildos I left in all of her drawers that would turn on every time she opened them. I wanted her to miss me, miss what she'd been too bitchy and pretentious to realize she had.

"That package was my ex telling me she didn't appreciate my idea of a joke. I left that shit at her house to piss her off. Seven months ago. I hadn't been out with anyone before the night I spent with you, and I haven't seen anyone since."

Naomi looked down at her feet and cursed to herself. I waited, but she said nothing else.

"Yeah, well…I'll see you—"

"You were great today."

"What?"

"Your monologue." She came closer to me and leaned her hips against a worktable. "I envy you that at such a young age, you're able to tell people to go to hell for criticizing you. I love that you have such strength about you. It took me a lot longer. Sometimes I still let it get to me, and I'm thirty-eight."

I shrugged. "I just got sick of people telling me I wasn't enough the way I am. I am enough. I deserve better."

"You do deserve better."

And cue more awkward silence.

"Well, thank you. I should—"

"Want to go get something to eat?"

I could only blink at her. Was this for real? This time?

"I'm craving something salty and sweet."

My mouth watered as I remembered what we'd done with salty and sweet together not too long ago.

"I could go for that. As long as this time you at least leave a note when you leave."

"Heather, I'm sorry."

I held up a hand. "It's fine. I can imagine I might have been suspicious if I found a box of dildos and panties at my girl's house."

"Your girl, huh?"

"Mmm hmm."

"Right. Well, I'm hungry, and I want to see if you're really that good with tools."

I burst out laughing. "You doubt me?"

Naomi stepped closer and placed her hands on my waist. "I just want to see for myself. Maybe you can teach me something, Blondie."

Her kiss reminded me of what I'd been missing about her, and what I'd realized I wanted after we'd made love. A start. A new relationship. A partner to explore with. A pair of arms to wake up in each morning.

Naomi fingered my braids and tugged on one lightly. "You mussed up these braids."

I kissed her once more, pulling her body flush with mine. "I guess you'll have to fix them in the morning."

Acknowledgments

I'd like to sincerely thank Savannah Frierson and Shannon Monroe for your candid advice and encouragement. I admire both of you ladies more than you know.

To the real "Ms. Oliver" and to the teachers I've worked with over the years who encouraged everyone to seek within themselves that something special and run with it. I'm still running!

To Laurie for inviting me to join in on the Summer Fair Anthology. Thank you so much for having faith in me.

Pinups and Puppies

About the story...

Marianne Cross has lived a life of structure and purpose for the past twenty-four years. Now reluctantly retired from the Air Force, her life is missing those two things that have always defined her. As she struggles to decide where her future lies, she finds peace and solitude flying her vintage airplane. When an opportunity with the organization Pawsitive Flight comes along, allowing her to combine flying with a purpose, she's interested in the possibilities—especially those concerning the owner of Goth Dog Rescue, Dinah Shaw. She's tough, beautiful, and she makes Marianne want things she hasn't allowed herself to want in a long time.

Dinah Shaw is happy with her life's mission, connecting needy pups with families that will love them. It's hard but fulfilling work that completely satisfies her—until she meets Marianne Cross. Part of Dinah is more than ready to hop in the jump seat and show the shy pilot a good time, but the other part isn't interested in another woman who's just passing through, looking for Ms. Right-For-Now. She's been there and done that. Until she discovers what she wants to do with her life, Marianne is a possible flight risk Dinah can't afford to trust.

Flying rescue dogs to their furever homes may give Marianne new purpose, and even a home of her own in the process…if Dinah can risk her heart on a little fly-by-night romance.

To Smokey Young…

Your expertise and joie de vivre are much appreciated.
Thank you for your dedication to ensuring quality romantic fiction.

Chapter One

The wheels of my Cessna touched down gently on the tarmac at Hayward Executive Airport and I sighed happily. *I'll never get tired of this…* Flying on my terms, on my time schedule, in my own plane. There's just something exhilarating about taking off from a small municipal airport, flipping the bird to The Man, and taking a break from the exhausting requirement of talking to people and telling them again, "I'm fine."

Really, I was. Or so I'd told myself every day for the past five months as the career I'd worked for my entire adult life came to a premature end.

It hadn't been my choice to retire from the Air Force at age forty-six, but moping around wasn't going to change anything. I had feelers out for jobs, but nothing sounded interesting. I definitely didn't want to fly people around anymore—too many memories—and I certainly didn't want to teach people to fly. I needed to find a purpose, and find it fast, so my family would leave me alone and I could get on with my life.

I taxied around to the hangar I'd rented and found a visitor. I shook my head with a smile. I pulled the plane into the hangar and turned off the engine.

"Aunty Em!" Nell bounced on her toes while clutching her tablet to her chest.

"I see giving you the codes and keys to get in was a mistake."

"You're just saying that because you're a crotchety old lady."

Nell was an adorable, if a little pushy, nineteen-year-old college student. I was grateful to have her in my life. My brother and his husband had done well raising her to be a talented, outgoing, and persistent young woman. I'd just hoped for a little more time in solitude this afternoon before making conversation.

"Not as old as your dad. Now, what brings you out to my, ahem, private lair?"

I'd been thrilled to find this space. When Dad and I came to look at the plane, the owner said they'd be giving up their hangar as well, since they were moving to the desert for retirement. It was exactly what I needed so we were able to take over the rent.

When my retirement was made official two months ago, I'd returned to the Bay Area to live with my photographer brother Matt, his wickedly funny husband, Zack, and their daughter, and though I loved being with them after twenty-four years of living the nomadic military life, I needed a place to hide. The hangar was big enough for my new baby—Siouxsie, a 1950 Cessna 140A—and a workspace. Matt gave me one of the couches they'd recently replaced, and I bought a small fridge and microwave. All I needed to do was bring some of my art supplies out here and I'd be set. Well, that, and figure out what the hell to do now that I had no job.

"I heard about this program today while I was at the shelter and I thought it would be perfect for you, now that you've got Siouxsie. Come look."

Nell plopped down on the sofa and booted up her tablet, her dark brown curls bouncing around her face. "My supervisor got a call from a friend of hers that works at a shelter down near Visalia, and they were looking for someone to take this mom and her puppies before they have to put the mom down, and a local rescue volunteered. They don't have room there. I would've offered to drive down to Visalia myself, but I've got finals tomorrow."

Nell turned her big brown eyes on me and proceeded to blink back manufactured tears, a tactic that had worked many times since she'd first joined our family.

"I can't believe they wouldn't be able to adopt out the puppies." I reached for the tablet, my curiosity piqued. Sure enough, the listing said they only had until tomorrow. Most days, I figured people could eat dirt, but I'd do just about anything for an animal in need.

"Tammy, my supervisor, said they have a program they've used before called Pawsitive Flight. Pilots volunteer their time to fly out, pick up the animals, and take them to a place that has room for them or, in some cases, a veterinarian who volunteers their services or a sanctuary for the dogs no one will adopt. I thought maybe you could take a look."

I scanned the site Nell had pulled up with interest. It seemed pretty straightforward. Pawsitive Flight provided a service connecting pilots with rescues and shelters in need of transportation, and they worked out the details via text. Pilots were responsible for their own fuel, a representative from the shelter met the pilot at the nearest airport with the animal, and the pilot flew the precious cargo to the specified airport, where a rescue worker met them to make the exchange.

The pilots entered in the range they were willing to fly, their payload limit, as well as other pertinent details, and got to pick and choose which transport requests they wanted to take.

"I know we can find fosters for the pups and the mom until they're all able to be adopted. We work with a great rescue organization that takes on situations like this. What do you think? Is this something you and Siouxsie could do?"

I paused to think for a minute. I didn't want to fly people anymore, but dogs? I loved dogs. I hadn't been able to have one of my own since high school.

Matt and Zack had always had cats, but when Nell started working at the shelter in high school, they couldn't resist her plea to foster a dog. That led to the first of several senior dogs they'd rescued and given love to in their final years. Currently, Milo and Bruno—a pair of elderly dachshunds—held the places of honor in the Cross household. I admired my brother and his husband for it, and fell in love with each and every dog, spoiling them rotten. As soon as I was ready to settle down somewhere, I'd already planned to get a rescue dog.

But that meant making decisions I wasn't ready to make.

"I could probably do it. Let me check the weather."

Siouxsie could only be flown during the day using visual flight rules. The weather would have to be clear with good visibility. I checked out the weather app on my phone and, sure enough, tomorrow was going to be a gorgeous day. The flight down to the Fresno Chandler Airport would only take about an hour and a half, I could refuel there and get back up to Hayward all in an afternoon. Piece of cake.

Nell entered all of the information needed into the tablet as I gave it to her, and before I knew it, I'd accepted the job.

"Thank you so much, Aunty Em! This will be awesome! It says the rescue people will contact you to set up the times."

I readied the plane for leaving again in the morning and closed the hangar door. I followed Nell home to the split-level place in the Hayward hills I'd bought with my brother back before the housing boom, when you could still buy a house in the hills for under half a million bucks. I tried not to roll my eyes on the walk up the driveway as Nell gushed about how cool it was that her aunty was going to be flying rescue dogs.

"Not a bad gig, eh?" Matt asked as we cut up vegetables together for dinner.

"Nah. Plus it earns me 'cool aunty points.' Does that get me anything?"

Matt bumped me with his hip. "It gets you the undying admiration of your niece, the appreciation of dogs everywhere, and a mission, Lieutenant Colonel Marianne Cross." He saluted me. I threw a hunk of onion at him.

"I'll keep all that in mind."

Dinner was chatty that night as our parents joined us, back from their latest cruise.

"C'mon, Marianne," General Mason Cross said, shaking his head in frustration. "I told you I could set up interviews for you with any number of consulting jobs, or hell, you could take that job with FedEx flying cargo. I know Dave wants to hire you, he's just waiting on you. What are you fooling around with this for?"

"Alexa," Matt shouted. "Play 'C'mon Marianne' on Apple Music."

"Playing 'C'mon Marianne' by Frankie Valli and the Four Seasons on Apple Music," the pleasantly creepy robotic-voiced device called back. The old tune never failed to make Matt laugh hysterically.

"Dad, give her some time to breathe. The Air Force owned her for twenty-four years! She deserves a vacation, not some job in an office with a bunch of stuffed shirts." Matt patted my hand. "You're always welcome to come manage the gallery. My current manager is a pain in the ass—ow!"

His current manager, who also happened to be his husband, kicked him under the table.

"For your information, I am the best manager you'll ever have. Besides, being a manager means dealing with…*ew*…people." Zack winked at me.

"You could maybe come hang up some of those fantastic paintings you've been working on," Matt added. "I saw the ones you did of the bay. They're beautiful."

It had taken me a while to pick the brushes back up after coming home, but I'd started with some of the old magazines Dad gave me. I loved the old B-17 Flying Fortress and B-25 Mitchell bombers. I'd built models of them as a kid and then, when the painting bug caught me, I learned to paint them. The planes drew me in, and the pinups frequently painted on them continued to hold my interest.

"Thanks, Mattie." My brother was always my cheerleader. His support meant the world to me, especially when things went south.

"Yeah, well, she's gotta do something with herself. Something that makes money. It's not like she has—"

Wendy Cross kicked her husband under the table this time and shut him up.

No one needed to remind me that I didn't have a significant other. Dad had been thrilled I'd followed him into the Air Force Academy and into the service, but he'd fully expected me to take a job in support services rather than flying. He'd been less than thrilled when my career choices left me single and without children. Thankfully, Matt and Zack had adopted Nell, which gave our parents someone to fuss over and dote on.

It left me kind of out in left field, though. What the hell was I supposed to do now? Retired at forty-six? Kinda young to be a spinster and yet too old to give a shit. Part of me was itching to rebel a bit. Not so much against my beloved father, but against expectations of who I was supposed to be.

My phone buzzed in the pocket of my black cargo shorts.

"Aunty Em!" Nell threw a cherry tomato at me. "No phones at the table."

"Sorry." I threw the tomato back as I glanced down at my phone. "It's someone about the flight tomorrow."

That got me off the hook with her. "Well, go answer it!"

"Excuse me," I said as I pushed back from the table and walked into the other room.

Thank you for taking the transport request! I'm Dinah with Goth Dog Rescue. I've contacted Billie at the Visalia shelter and told her we'd like to take in the terrier and her pups. Please let me know what time I should be at the Hayward Executive Airport. Looking forward to meeting you. Tammy from the Hayward Shelter says your niece can't stop raving about you.

I turned on my nosey niece hovering behind me and shoved my phone in her face. "'Raving' about me?"

"What?" She stepped back and then forward to read it. "Well, duh! Of course, I'm proud of you."

She had no idea the effect her words had on me. I never thought I'd hear anyone in my family say that again. Thank God I'd been wrong.

"Auntie Em?" She gave me a questioning look.

"I'm okay," I said with a fake smile.

Nell frowned at me and went to the kitchen.

Interesting name for the rescue. Matt and I had fallen into the Goth category in high school. The Goth subculture in the '80s had been made up of kids who hadn't fit in anywhere else. You could spot us by our outrageous appearance and our alternative music. Our group went to shows every weekend at The Edge in Palo Alto, The Omni in Oakland or the Berkeley Square, and reveled in our outcast status. I still had my Doc Martens, although they'd seen better days, and my leather jacket with the band patches on the back. Depeche Mode, Oingo Boingo, The Cure and, my all-time favorite, Siouxsie and the Banshees. I had such a crush on Siouxsie.

We'd done each other's hair in Siouxsie Sue/Robert Smith styles or mohawks, and then left black hair dye all over the bathroom. The General had been royally pissed when we'd pooled our allowance to buy clippers.

Being out of the service meant I could wear my hair how I wanted, so Matt took over my hair care when I came home, and now the back and sides were buzzed, with the top growing out. It was down to my cheekbone and mostly covered my left eye when left hanging. I was contemplating dyeing it some fun color or black again.

Goth Dog. Cool name. It will be early afternoon. Around 2.

I went back into the dining room to help clear the table and was chased out of the kitchen to see off our parents. I hugged them goodbye, and Dad held on for an extra-long moment.

"I just want you to be happy, pumpkin."

I cringed inwardly at the old nickname he'd taken to calling me again ever since "the trouble."

"I am, Daddy. Just give me some time to get my bearings. I promise, I won't disappoint you again."

He pulled back with a frown. "Baby, you know better—"

I kissed his cheek. "Gotta get to bed. I've got a mission tomorrow, General."

I clicked my heels together and saluted him, causing him to groan and salute back. Old habits die hard.

"Have a safe flight," Mom said as we hugged.

"Will do. I'll text you when I land at each stop."

It made Mom less nervous that way. She'd been horrified that I'd insisted on buying "that death trap," but Dad had assured her we'd work on it together and he wouldn't let me fly it if it wasn't safe. It was kind of nice having Daddy back again, rather than General Cross. Even at forty-six, a girl needed her father.

I went in to say goodnight to Matt and Zack and found them smooching in the kitchen while Nell made retching noises.

"Haven't you learned by now, dear niece, that only encourages them?"

Nell groaned.

My phone buzzed again, and I paused at the top of the stairs leading down to my place.

Yeah. I'm an unapologetic Goth girl. Still have my entire vinyl collection and Doc Martens.

Dinah's response surprised me. It wasn't often that people freely admitted being a part of what Matt and I used to call the Artistically Sarcastic Assembly, or the Melancholy Morose Muses. We changed our Goth gang name frequently, much to the amusement of our friends.

Matt had worn way more makeup than I did and got into more trouble. I earned straight As, eventually trading in my fishnets for a flygirl uniform and joining the Air Force to make Daddy proud. And proud he still claimed to be, despite the circumstances that ended my career.

Same. I'll text you when I'm leaving Fresno.

"Is everything all set?"

Nell leaned over my shoulder to see my texts. The little snoop.

"Yeah, I guess so."

Nell hugged me from behind. "Thank you, Aunty! This is gonna be so cool!"

"Thanks, babe. Night."

Huh. Tomorrow I'd be flying dogs in my little plane. Taking them to start a new life somewhere. There was a metaphor there, I just couldn't find it yet. Anyhow, it was a piece-of-cake flight, and it would give me something productive to do. Nice, uncomplicated way of spending the day.

Famous last words.

Chapter Two

The flight down to Fresno was uneventful, but I grew more anxious the closer I came to landing. I should have asked a few more questions. Would the dogs bark the whole time? Would they be in a crate? What if they got sick? Maybe I should have contacted one of the other pilots first…

But then I called on my years of flying newbie soldiers around and all the times I'd dealt with puke on my transports, fainting, whining…I could handle a couple of mutts.

Once I landed at Fresno/Chandler Airport, I refueled Siouxsie before cruising over to the area where the website said I could park her in the tie-downs. When she was secured, I went into the airport lounge. I needed to pee like a—

"Are you Marianne Cross?"

I turned to find an older woman standing next to a small crate. Guess I'd have to wait for that bathroom break.

"I am. Billie?"

She approached and we shook hands.

"Thanks for picking up the transport request. I think if we had a little more time, we could have found a home for Prudence and the pups here, but they need to be fostered together for a bit before they can be adopted out and all of our rescue partners are full up."

"That's so sad." I crouched down and caught a glimpse of a white and tan wire-haired terrier mix of some kind and a bundle of blankets that probably hid her pups. Prudence looked fierce, guarding the babies. Plus, she was pretty stinkin' cute. The kind of dog that borders on so ugly you can't help but love them.

"Goth Dog is great. I'm so glad Dinah was able to work with us."

I peered around the crate trying to get an idea if it would fit in Siouxsie's cargo space, thinking it just might.

"Would you excuse me for just a minute? I need to—"

"Oh sure! Go right ahead. I'll take Prudence out on a leash and see if she needs to potty."

I thanked her and ducked into the women's restroom to take care of business and wash up. I grabbed a soda and a protein bar from the vending machine and found Billie just outside the door with the crate at her feet, letting Prudence prance around in the grass. She did her business and Billie picked it up with a baggie over her hand like a pro.

"There. That should make your trip more pleasant."

"Thanks. Um, I didn't think to bring a crate. This is my first time."

Billie's smile grew wider. "That's no problem. Maybe bring it on back next time?"

I breathed a sigh of relief. "I knew I didn't ask enough questions. Thank you. Even if I don't do another run, I'll make arrangements to get this back to you."

Billie nodded and handed me the leash. "Mind holding this for a minute?"

Prudence stood on her hind legs, tapping my shins with her dainty paws. I got down on her level and Prudence licked my chin hesitantly, as if asking permission to love me. I was a goner. One look in her scruffy little face and I wanted to scoop her up and assure her I'd never let her go.

"She's a sweetheart," Billie said, watching us knowingly. "I'll have to be sure to ask Dinah to keep me updated."

"I bet it's hard to see them go and not know what happens to them." I know I'd forever wonder who this little pup ended up with.

"At least now I know she's *going* to end up with someone." Billie's smile was sad as she opened the crate door and Prudence walked right in, sniffing around to be sure her babies were still there. I could hear the tiny whimpering sounds, but I'd yet to see the puppies. It had to be tough knowing you could only save so many of them.

"Nice plane you got there," Billie said as she lifted a hand to shade her eyes. "You been flying long?"

"Twenty-four years. Air Force. Just retired. This was my gift to myself."

Billie smiled. "Active four years. Reserves for eight. Tough times but a great experience."

"Same." We shook hands. "Right on. I'll be sure to let you know when I've made the handoff."

Billie thanked me again and handed me the crate.

My stomach dropped. I'd flown sensitive missions into Afghanistan, refueled jets in midflight over a war zone, and yet this felt like an equally important mission. My precious cargo needed a new home, and I intended to make sure these puppies arrived safely back in Hayward.

Thankfully the crate fit in the tiny cargo space behind the seat. Before I lowered the lid, Prudence gave a tiny woof and licked her snout.

"You just hold on there, dear Prudence."

I untied Siouxsie and hopped in. Her engine started right up, and we taxied around to the airstrip. I called into the tower and was given the go ahead for takeoff. Once we reached a comfortable nine thousand feet, I rolled my head around on my neck and peeked behind the seat at my little passengers.

"You guys want some music? How about I play your song?"

Prudence's little nose poked through the slats of the crate and then disappeared. No whining or yarking noises came from the crate. I prayed they were doing fine. I turned on my iPod and my Bluetooth speaker, filling the cockpit with the sweet sounds of Siouxsie and the Banshees' cover of the Beatles' song "Dear Prudence."

"I think it's kind of kismet that you're my first canine passengers." I thought maybe my voice might soothe them if they were nervous.

"Don't worry, I'll make sure this Dinah chick is cool. I won't leave you with just anybody."

This chick better be on the up and up, or I'm talking to Nell's boss. No way would I put dear Prudence and her babies in harm's way.

The flight went quickly. I couldn't help but check on the pups frequently. I worried when they didn't make any noises yet was grateful they weren't losing their shit.

The landing went smooth at Hayward. We taxied around to the terminal and parked before I pulled out my phone to find a text from Dinah.

I'll be waiting for you in the lounge at 3:00.

The round-trip flight took less time than I'd imagined, so I took the plane over to the hangar and let Prudence out for a stretch. I figured I'd drive her and the pups over to the terminal when it was time.

"Want to stretch your legs, Mama?" Billie had loaned me the leash along with the crate. I was already beginning to compile a list of things I'd need if I did this again. Which I just might. I decided to reserve judgement until the handoff was complete.

As much as I loved flying Siouxsie, it was nice to have a plan or a reason to take her out. So far, I'd flown her to Vacaville to meet some folks I'd served with who were now stationed at Travis, and I'd taken her up a few times just to cruise around the Bay Area. Flying the rescue dogs would give me a plan, a mission…a reason to get out of the house. As each day passed, not knowing what I was going to do with my future weighed on me even more.

I owned half of the split-level. I had my own entrance and a master suite in the lower level of the house, as well as access to the hot tub in the backyard. We shared the kitchen, and that was fine, but did I want this type of arrangement forever? Of course, I couldn't afford to buy anything else in the Bay Area, and I did want to stay close to Matt's family and my parents…

God, I hated everything being up in the air, which was pretty ironic. Up in the air was my favorite place to be, but on the ground, I liked order and structure. After four years at the academy and twenty-four years in the Air Force, I was struggling to adjust to being a civilian, and I couldn't make a damn decision to save my damn life.

Inside the hangar, I opened the crate carefully and hooked the leash onto Prudence's collar. Once I let her down, Prudence pranced around in a circle and sat down, her tail wagging. I was so taken with her scruffy face and big brown eyes. I wondered what her pups looked like. I carefully lifted the blanket and saw two lumps of white curled up together, their little bellies rising and falling in sleep.

Prudence tapped at my leg with her paws, alerting me that my attention was misplaced.

"Yes, ma'am. Let's take you for a walk."

We strolled on over to the restroom and back and Prudence seemed content to look and sniff around. She had really long legs for her tiny size. I got a kick out of watching her.

It was nearly three, so I loaded her back into the crate with her pups and into the passenger seat of my beat-up Ford Ranger. I pulled down the hangar's metal door and snapped the lock shut. I drove around and parked in the lot by the terminal and carried Prudence and company inside, suddenly feeling quite reluctant to hand her over.

If only I knew what the hell I was doing with my life, maybe I could foster the dog and her puppies. Not that I knew anything about caring for puppies, though Nell could always help, right? But when it was time for them to be adopted, could I give them up? And then what if I ended up taking one of the consulting jobs down south Dad was pushing me to do? What if I had to move to a place that didn't accept dogs? All of this uncertainty had me feeling quite surly.

Until I turned the corner inside the terminal and spotted Dinah.

Chapter Three

The moment the redhead stood from her seat and smiled, I nearly forgot I was supposed to be putting one foot in front of the other.

Dinah Shaw was the kind of woman who looked as though nothing could control her free spirit. Her dyed-red hair was pulled back and held in place by a navy-blue bandanna, and she wore a white t-shirt with a black bra clearly visible beneath it. The shirt was tucked into the waist of wide-legged jeans rolled up at the ankles, with red-and-white-striped socks visible above the tops of her Doc Marten shoes. Her slender arms and neck were covered in tattoos, and she had several piercings in her ears, septum, and one in her cheek that sparkled as she walked toward me.

My heart seemed to stop in its tracks and then stutter back to life.

"Is that the little mama?"

I could not for the life of me move my mouth to form words. I looked down at the crate I was carrying in my right hand and then back up at the bombshell.

"Dinah?"

Lips painted dark red split to expose a bright smile. "Marianne, right?" She stuck out her hand and I shook it firmly. Dinah looked me up and down with interest evident in her deep brown eyes. "I was hoping to see your plane."

I looked outside and back. "Oh. Sorry. I got in a little earlier than I thought and parked it in the hangar."

"What do you fly?"

I noticed one of Dinah's pale pink arms was covered in a full sleeve of pinup girls. "Um, a 1950 C-140A. I just bought it a couple of weeks ago."

Dinah did a little excited shimmy. "Oh, that's awesome! I'm a sucker for vintage planes. I used to go to the Reno Air Races every year. Did some modeling with the planes."

Hell yeah, I bet you did. Modeling made perfect sense. Dinah had the perfect pinup look going on herself. She had a youthful energy that lit up the room. Only the faint lines on her face told me she might be close to my age.

"She peed. When we got here. I took her for a walk."

I smiled awkwardly and prayed she didn't think I was a complete moron. I hated how stupid shy I sometimes got around people I was attracted to, and this woman had just wiped out any chance I had of making coherent speech.

Dinah's smile went straight to businesslike. "That's good. Are the pups pretty small?"

I set the carrier on top of the back of the couch so Dinah could peek inside.

"They seem to be okay, but I'm sure this was stressful for them. She's a good little mom though. She was really good on the trip and on the leash." *And I don't want to give her up.*

Dinah bent at the waist and wiggled a finger at the terrier mix. "You are a cute one, little girl."

Dinah was taller than me by about three inches. At five foot seven, I probably outweighed her waifish figure by about twenty pounds. I liked to work out and, right now, given I had nothing better to do, I was probably at my largest size. My tank and cargo pants had felt a little snug this morning when I got dressed. Dinah seemed to be appreciating me, though.

"We'll get you back to my place and decide where you're going to be fostered."

I tightened my grip on the handle. "She's going to someone else's house?"

"Yes, my business partner, Carla, has a lot of experience fostering moms and their puppies. They'll either stay with me or her until the puppies are old enough to adopt out or we find a home for the mother."

"Her name's Prudence."

Dinah cocked a hip out. My eyes were involuntarily drawn to the faded jeans that clung to her hips, and the way the loose-fitting material outlined her hipbone and the juncture of her thighs.

"Dear Prudence," Dinah said with a laugh. "You a Siouxsie fan?"

"Named my plane after her." I shifted my gaze to Prudence in the cage, too nervous to make eye contact with Dinah in case my emotions were showing. *I can't do this. I can't walk away from this dog.*

"That's so cool," Dinah said. "How'd you get into flying?"

I wondered if she was really curious or if she was just making small talk.

"Air Force. Retired two months ago."

"Wow," Dinah said, her eyes wide. "Really? That's impressive."

I shrugged off her reaction. "It was a job." People tended to be more excited about my job than I was. It had been a great career, but it wasn't like the movies made it out to be, all pulse-pounding terror, nail-biting suspense.

"And now, what? You go fly for the airlines?"

I shifted my weight and frowned. *Why must everyone need an answer about what's next?* "I haven't really decided yet, but no. I have no plans to fly for the airlines."

Dinah blinked. "I didn't mean to pry. It's just that most of the people I've met in aviation are either commercial pilots or retired military that end up flying commercial."

"It's okay. I'm taking a little time to decide. This volunteer gig was perfect."

"Great. I hope you'll consider doing it again. We have lots of people willing to foster and adopt up here, but it's hard to ask anyone to take time out of their busy schedules to drive ten hours in a day to go pick up a dog." She ran a hand lightly over the top of the crate. "I do it whenever I can, but Pawsitive Flight has been a great resource for us."

Prudence pawed at the door of the carrier and my chest tightened. *I know, little one. I don't know what to do.*

"She won't go back to the shelter?"

Dinah cocked her head to the side. "Are you interested in her?"

"I… She's great, like *really* great, but I'm not quite settled yet. I just feel…"

"It's hard, I know. But I promise you, we will find her the perfect furever home."

I scoffed. "That sounds like something you say to ease guilt."

Dinah stepped back and her confident smile slipped a little. "I don't know, maybe? I don't want volunteers to worry, but I'm honest about what we can and can't do. It's hard. Sometimes volunteers get attached to the dogs."

"I can see that. I'm sorry, I didn't mean—"

"It's fine," Dinah said, and I felt like more and more of an ass. "Rescue work is full of feels, I get it. It's not for everyone. My business partner and I started it together after she'd gotten a divorce, and it was a long time before she didn't cry over every foster we adopted out."

"I bet. My niece volunteers at the shelter. She convinced her dads to take in a couple of seniors three years ago. Now they're on their third set of seniors. I admire them for that."

Dinah smiled, and then her body snapped to attention. "Oh! I need to have you sign the transport form."

She reached into a *Nightmare Before Christmas* messenger bag and pulled out a clipboard. "We both sign this, and then you can keep a copy for your records."

I stepped closer and caught a whiff of Dinah's scent. Fresh lavender, so heady it nearly bowled me over. Sort of like when you smell smoke and your whole body jumps to attention, only this scent didn't warn of danger…it was sensual. Alluring.

I inhaled deeply and Dinah chuckled.

"Smell something you like?"

"Oh God." I was completely mortified. I'd just sniffed the woman like a serial killer! "I'm…wow." I laughed nervously and took the pen she was offering, then filled out my information with a shaky hand. I had to cross out my phone number twice because I kept screwing it up.

"It's fine. I know, it's strong when I first put it on. I make my own essential oils. I live on an organic farm with my sisters. Do you like lavender?"

When I glanced up, Dinah was watching me with interest, as though she were trying to solve a puzzle. I handed her the clipboard, making deliberate eye contact.

Screw it. I was done being awkward. I was my own woman now. The Air Force was no longer breathing down my neck about who I spent time with. If I met a woman I liked—and I liked this one already —I could sure as hell be up front about it. The only consequence now was rejection, and honestly? I had nothing to lose. Not anymore.

I rolled my shoulders back and stood at my full height. "Yeah. I really like lavender. It's…enticing."

Dinah's eyes flared and she sucked in a breath. "Hmmm. Enticing. Yes. Do you ever use oils?"

"I have a couple of blends one of my former officers' wives made me for injuries and for sleep. Tangerine and other citrus. Chamomile. Tea Tree. I'm out, though. I haven't needed it in a while."

"Injuries. Working out?"

"Yes, ma'am." I'd loved that aspect of the service and I intended to remain in shape. I had weights and a bar for sit-ups and pull-ups in my place, and I liked to run trails in the area.

Dinah's eyes traveled over my toned arms, and she grinned.

"I'd be happy to whip something up for you if you ever need it. Or," she said, smiling wider, "if you're ever downtown on a Saturday, we have a booth at the farmers' market. Organic dog treats, oils, eggs, soaps, fresh flowers. Whatever we're experimenting with at the time." There was no mistaking the invitation in her smile.

Why not? I didn't know anyone around here. I'd grown up on the move. Daddy's last post had been at Travis Air Force Base in Vacaville, which is where I graduated from. Matt went to college in the nearby Bay Area and, after graduating, he'd stayed. We'd bought the house in Hayward because it was close enough to our parents, who'd decided to remain in Vacaville, and to Oakland, where Matt's gallery was. If I was going to stay in the area permanently, it might be nice to have some friends. And Dinah sure seemed friendly.

"Sounds good." Smelled good, sounded good. Looked good. I'd definitely be visiting her booth.

Dinah licked her bottom lip and narrowed her eyes. "Am I going to see you again? Transports, I mean," she laughed, her cheeks going red. "That was a little forward. I meant will you be available for transports in the future?"

Dinah was flirting with me. Truthfully, I was kind of thrilled and felt myself slipping back into that awkward space where I probably looked like Patrick from SpongeBob when he meets the undersea princess. It was also refreshing. My time in the service had been a series of covert missions to meet up with women. I'd been very careful.

Or so I'd thought.

"Yeah, I think so. This was fun."

I bent down once more, and Prudence put her paw up to the crate door. "Take care, dear Prudence." I put my finger up to the cage and Prudence licked it through the bars. It broke my heart to walk away, but I honestly didn't know which end was up right now. It wasn't the right time. And that just sucked.

This is it. There was no more delaying the transfer of my precious cargo. I offered to carry the crate out to Dinah's car, and she thanked me. We exited the terminal doors, and I followed her over to a light blue Subaru Crosstrek. Dinah popped the hatch, and I saw she had a dog area cordoned off in back with a couple of small crates.

"Oh, here," she said. "Let me transfer her so I can give you back your crate."

"Sure. The lady in Fresno, Billie, she let me take it. I should probably get my own if I'm going to keep this up."

Dinah smiled and took the leash from me. She clipped it onto Prudence's collar and carefully lifted her out, setting her gently in the cargo area.

"So, you're thinking about it?"

I grinned. "I'm thinking about it."

"Great." Her smile…it did…*things* to me. I couldn't believe I was a grown-ass woman getting butterflies from her smile.

Turning to look at Prudence sobered me. I might have been reading too much into the situation, but she seemed to be watching me as though she was waiting expectantly for me to take her home. Part of me said I should be.

"Let's get a look at these little puppies, shall we?"

I swallowed back my sadness as I watched Dinah carefully lift the two pups out. "Awwww, look at you two," she said in a voice full of wonder.

She turned around and showed me the bundle. Inside were two tiny pups, no bigger than a handful each. They made little puppy squeaks and Prudence pranced over to supervise.

"Don't worry, little Mama. I've got just the thing."

Dinah opened one of the small crates and inside, she had several little fabric boxes. "These little dividers work perfectly with cloth diapers. That way, they're snug as a bug when we take the corners in the car." She placed the puppies together in one of the dividers and then carefully placed it into the back of the other crate, then she led Prudence inside to check out the arrangements. She folded up the blanket and put it back inside the borrowed crate, handing it to me.

"If you ever want to check in on her, you've got my number," Dinah said as she handed me the borrowed crate. "Thanks again, Marianne. It was great to meet you."

"You, too. See ya around." *Way to go, Cross. Total loser.*

Dinah held eye contact as I walked backwards toward my pickup. I waved before turning to unlock the door, my heart pounding.

It was going to be a long week waiting for that farmers' market and an excuse to see her again.

Chapter Four

Dinah texted me the next day, which set off a series of exchanges that made her all the more attractive to me.

You had me a little flustered yesterday, and I forgot to take a picture of you with Prudence for our website. She says hi, by the way.

She sent a picture of Prudence with her puppies, who looked a little more awake than they had yesterday.

"Oh, my heart."

The little scruffy mama sat up proud as if to say, "These are my children, and I will fight to the death to protect them!" She was such a tough little cookie. I wished I'd given in to my desire to pick her up and snuggle her in my arms, but I'd been trying not to get too attached.

I showed Nell the picture. Big mistake.

"She's so *cute*! Auntie, how could you let her go?"

I'd been asking myself the same question for the past twenty-four hours.

"I know, but is it fair for me to adopt a dog now when I don't know where I'm going to end up?"

Nell rolled her eyes and went back to her homework.

"What?"

She slammed her pencil down. "Didn't you always used to say, 'where there's a will, there's a way?' Because the way I see it, if you want something, you can make it happen." She gave me a hurt look and picked up her pencil as if to say the conversation was over.

Uh-uh. There was more going on here than the dog.

"Nell, babe, what if I have to take a job away from here? Would that be fair?"

"You don't have to leave. There are jobs here. Grandpa said so." She didn't look up from her work, and her voice was barely above a whisper.

I sat down next to her at the table where she was studying and rested my chin on her shoulder. "Even if I took a job here, babe, flying often means being away overnight. What would I do with her then?"

She sat up and stared me down. "If you stay here, you have *me,*" she said. Her chin trembled as she spoke, and I recognized the look of fear.

Nell had struggled with abandonment issues for a long time after Matt and Zack adopted her. She'd been in and out of foster homes for two years prior to her adoption as her mom struggled with addiction and mental health issues. She'd specifically had a hard time with *my* visits. For the first year, every time I left, she'd be a sobbing mess at home, and at school she'd end up in the office for starting trouble in class. Matt shared it all with me, and Nell and I had instituted our Sunday Night Skype sessions so wherever I was, we could talk. If I had to miss one, I'd give her notice and we'd catch up as soon as we could afterward.

I hadn't realized just how important I was to her, but when I did, I worked hard to assure her that she was just as important to me, too, and made sure to be there for her when she needed me. Like now.

I opened my arms to Nell, and she gave me a tentative hug at first, then once the tears started, she held on tighter.

"I'm sorry," I said and squeezed her.

"I love having you here. I don't want you to go away again."

I took a deep breath and realized my little existential crisis was affecting more than just me. "I don't want to go away either. I promise, I'll keep looking for something here, okay?"

She took a couple of deep breaths and wiped her tears. I recognized it the moment her mood shifted from sad to crafty.

"What about Prudence?"

I put her in a headlock until she started squealing loud enough to bring Zack running in.

"Man, you scared me. I thought Milo had finally had enough of your suffocating snuggles and was eating your face off."

"I'm just fighting back against her evil powers of persuasion here," I said, letting her go and running away to escape retribution.

"Daddy, tell her she needs to adopt that cute little mutt. Look—oooo wait, who's this?"

I snatched the phone away from her and looked. Dinah had sent another picture, this one with her holding the puppies up next to her face.

"Wait! Is that the lady from Goth Dog? I think I've seen her with Tammy before. Damn, Auntie. She's hot."

A wrestling match ensued between the three of us that only stopped when Matt came in and pulled us apart with the announcement of dinner. The Cross family never hesitated to run for the table at chow time.

Thanks for the pictures. I really appreciate it. Please keep me posted. I miss that little mutt already.

I'd made arrangements with Billie to bring her back the crate on Wednesday, but the weather wasn't ideal for flying, so we postponed until after the storm blew through. The change in plans left my days open for contemplation, which failed to be productive.

I took my easel and some paints out to the hangar, turned on my space heater and listened to SiriusXM 1st Wave while I set up a little art corner. The rain came down steadily and the pitter-patter sound of it hitting the metal building eased some of my stress. There in my little hideaway, I could forget about what I was supposed to be doing—

starting a new life—and just be myself. I could paint, listen to my music, and commune with Siouxsie.

I'd also brought a small bookcase and some periodicals and reference books to keep here, including a book Dad bought me with stories about people and their love affairs with their Cessnas. As I was setting the books on the shelf, a magazine slid out. I set down the stack I'd been working with and picked up the one that had fallen.

A wave of warmth rolled through me, giving me a pleasurable jolt.

It was a program from the Reno Air Races. Dad had given me a bunch of his old magazines to use for painting inspiration, and this one in particular provided a whole lot of it right now.

The cover had two P-51s parked noses in—and standing between them, wearing a jumpsuit unzipped low enough to show a red and white polka dot top, was Dinah. She wore red high-top Chucks, her nails were painted deep red to match her lipstick, and her hair was styled just like a model from the 1940s.

Inspiration indeed.

I carried the magazine reverently over to my easel and swung the arm at the top to the side so I could clip the magazine there.

An hour later, I had a rough sketch of the photo going when my phone buzzed.

My friends' band is playing tonight at the Bistro on B Street. Mostly '90s stuff but they play a few of the older tunes if I ask nicely. Want to meet up?

I'd been typing her an affirmative response when Dinah's subsequent texts came through.

Some friends from the shelter and Goth Dog will be there too.

We're having our board meeting right before.

It seemed she was doing her best to not overtly ask me out, but the fact that she felt the need to explain herself made me a little giddy.

Dinah had obviously been thinking of me.

Sounds cool. What time?

Totally nonchalant here. I looked from my phone to my easel and laughed. Yeah, I'd been thinking of her, too.

Eight?

I texted her that I'd be there and stood up to stretch my back. It was three o'clock. I had five hours. I thought about staying and painting more but my focus was interrupted. Now I had a million thoughts running through my mind that seemed of crucial importance:

What should I wear?
What were the other folks like?
Was this a date?
Was it just friends hanging out?
What should I wear?

I was so fidgety at dinner that night, Nell kept looking at me funny.

"What?" I finally asked her.

"What yourself? You're the one shaking the table."

"I thought that was Milo scratching," Matt said, looking under the table to find the dogs were not even in their usual spots waiting for scraps.

"Nothing." The more I protested, the redder my cheeks became. "Just antsy. I was going to run the trail today, but it was raining too hard. Missed my workout, that's all."

I hid behind my hair and shoveled in a bite of brown rice. It was too quiet. I looked up to find three pairs of eyes watching me curiously.

"What?"

Zack cleared his throat and Matt covered his mouth. Nell was the only one brave enough to speak because she knew she was my favorite.

"You just seem a little anxious, Aunty Em. We may have a bet going."

"Excuse me," Matt said as he picked up his dish and practically sprinted for the kitchen.

"Get back here, traitor."

Matt backed his way into his seat and placed his plate down on the table carefully, refusing to let go, as though he could protect himself from harm with it.

"Good. Now, what's this bet about?"

"Well, I simply think you're antsy being stuck in the house," Zack said, exaggerating his innocence. "But my dear husband and your beloved niece think you have a date."

I paused with my fork pointed at Matt. I tried to play it cool, realizing my own actions had betrayed me. "What makes you think that?"

"You had clothes laid out on your bed when I came down to get you for dinner," Nell offered.

"You were playing Spandau Ballet when you pulled up, rather than that death metal you listen to now."

"It isn't death metal. Ghost is really quite melodic. I mean, sure, they're Satanic and all, but they sound like the old tunes. You should listen—"

"You're not denying it's a date, Aunty Em."

I chewed on a cucumber long enough to come up with a good retort.

"She's not denying it," Matt said, finally letting go of his plate. "Who is it? Someone from the airport? Someone from the grocery store?"

Zack shouted, "I call the airport!"

"The grocery store?" I laughed. "Why would you think that?"

"Because that's the only place you go lately besides the hangar. I've never seen someone buy so little at the store. Who the hell goes to the grocery store and only comes out with bean sprouts and a bottle of Windex?"

"I was making stir fry and cleaning the kitchen, what of it?"

I couldn't hide my smile, though.

"Who is it?"

I got up from the table with my plate, figuring I'd keep them in suspense as long as possible. "Wait—who thought it was a date?"

They all looked at each other.

"Nell and Matt," Zack offered.

I rinsed my plate and turned to find the three of them in the doorway. "Well, it's not a date, I don't think, so you lost. Pay up."

Zack did a very '80s victory dance. "Pay up, sucka!"

"But I did get invited out to join a lady I met and some of her friends for a night of music."

A chorus of *ooooo*s was heard from the doorway.

"Okay, but was it at the grocery store or the airport?" Matt asked before handing over his cash to his husband.

I thought about it. "Technically, it was through Pawsitive Flight, but I guess the airport is right, too."

Matt whooped and did his own little shimmy that didn't look like anything any sane person would call dancing. My brother was a nut, and I loved him dearly, weirdness notwithstanding. He was the best friend I'd ever had, the one I'd confided in throughout my military career, and the one who'd seen me through the clusterfuck that had ended it.

I'd allow him his weird gyrations.

"Hey, Mattie? I don't suppose you'd want to go a little old school on me, would ya?"

He rubbed his hands together excitedly. "Just what do you have in mind, little sister?"

Chapter Five

At approximately 8:15 p.m., I pulled into the municipal parking lot off Main Street and sat for a moment to center myself. I was sporting a fresh black dye job to cover my natural chestnut brown, and I'd even put on a little makeup, something I hadn't bothered with in years. Matt had tried to encourage me to go full Siouxsie Sioux with the eyeliner, but I figured I'd ease my way back into the scene. I'd been contemplating getting my ears re-pierced, as well as my nose, and possibly even adding some visible tattoos. I may not have wanted to retire, but I figured I might as well take advantage of some of the freedoms civilian life offered.

I hadn't explored downtown Hayward much. The area appeared to be trying really hard to take back some of its character. The old buildings, for the most part, were in good shape, their brick fronts well maintained. Lots of people strolled along the sidewalks and every parking spot was filled. There were many empty storefronts, however. I passed a bustling brew pub, a movie theater, a candy store and a vintage clothing shop. Farther down, I found a bookstore with a cool Black History Month display, and the music store had jazz instruments and vinyl albums of all the jazz and blues greats throughout the 20th century.

Hayward was a diverse town, and there was a little bit of every-thing on display here, even the promise of revitalization. Matt told me the farmers' market on Saturdays was busy, and there were several themed street fairs in the spring and summer with Aztec dancers, mariachi, and even a blues festival. There was also a small historical society museum downtown that would make for an interesting outing.

I hadn't ventured out a whole lot, probably because I was still deciding whether or not to stay, but I knew enough to know that this was the kind of community I'd like to settle in. Checking out the area would help me make a decision, I knew that, so perhaps *not* going out had been my way of avoiding that decision.

Great, just what I needed, a little self-actualization on my way to meet a gorgeous lady I found intriguing. My timing was impeccable.

The Bistro was a small bar with about twenty tables inside and a few more out on the sidewalk, surrounded by a low iron fence. Space heaters were strategically placed. Thankfully the rain had let up two hours before, and the forecast looked promising for the next couple of days at least. I wanted to be able to get the crate back to Billie in Fresno…and maybe sign up for another transport. The more I did, the more of an informed decision I could make.

And if Dinah was involved…

I spotted a group of women sitting at a cluster of tables inside the bar near the window. Dinah was crouched on a seat, waving her arms as she spoke and acting out some sort of interaction. I stopped to watch her for a moment. She had the women in stitches and her energy sucked me in, making me want to move closer.

I tried hard not to be intimidated by the prospect of meeting these people. I didn't mind groups of people, usually, but thinking I'd likely have to explain why I'd retired had me nervous. I planned to say, "it was time for something new," because regardless of my feelings, those words were true. Anything else would lead to questions I wasn't willing to answer with a group of strangers.

Dinah noticed me then and waved enthusiastically. I tried on a smile, but it felt super awkward. Dinah gestured to her friends that she'd be a moment, and then all nine sets of eyes turned to look out the window and see what had Dinah trotting outside. *No pressure.*

"Hey! You made it." Dinah stopped in front of me and bounced on her toes.

I didn't know whether to stick out a hand for her to shake or—

Dinah moved first, giving me a light hug and kissing my cheek. "I'm so glad you came."

I knew I was red down to the plunging V-neck of my heather-gray t-shirt.

"Thanks for inviting me out."

When I didn't move forward, Dinah raised an eyebrow. "Did I tear you away from anything important?"

I barked out a laugh and ran my hand through my long bangs. "Only my family pestering me."

"Oh! You have family here?" She seemed surprised.

"Yeah. My brother and his husband and their daughter. I bought a house with them as an investment, so it seemed like the right place to come after I retired." I cleared my throat. "You said you live on a farm? With your sisters?"

"Yeah," she said, tucking a stray piece of red hair behind her ear. "My uncle sold us his place. My younger sister Cecily left the health care field for goats, I waited tables and worked for a vet's office for years, and our older sister Trudy sells real estate. She only lives there 'to supervise' she says, but truthfully, after her divorce, she was pretty miserable. We're all really close."

"Wow," I said. "I didn't know there was still any farmland around here."

"Oh, there are a few of us. Back in the hills. Our place is off Norris Canyon just past Castro Valley. You know where that is?"

I shook my head. "I'm still getting my bearings. I know Hayward and Oakland, where my brother's gallery is, but that's about it."

A group of teens approached us, and we moved closer to the wall to get out of their way, bringing us closer together. God, she smelled good, and the way she was smiling, I thought just maybe she was as nervous as I was.

"Sounds like you need a tour guide."

Feeling cocky, I asked, "Are you offering?"

She shrugged and tried to sound casual. "Maybe. I bet it looks cool up in your plane, though, yeah?"

"It does," I said. "I've only been up in her a few times, but yeah. It's nice to get away from the traffic and the noise. It's much prettier up there."

"I bet," she said, and then she shivered. She only had on a thin sweater over a halter top, and it was a bit chilly outside. I was about to ask her if she wanted to go inside when she spoke.

"It's freezing out here. Want to come inside? I promise, they won't bite."

"Well, that's disappointing."

Dinah barked out a surprised laugh at my joke.

"At least not at first. My friend Martha and her bandmates, Flor, Kat and Stella, will be playing in a little bit. Then there are my friends Tammy—who knows your niece from the shelter, actually—Abra and Stevie, who I met through Martha, and my business partner at the rescue, Carla, and her wife Marnie. Martha, Carla, Tammy, Stevie and I make up the board for Goth Dog. They're some of the best people I know."

"They won't be offended if it takes me all night to remember their names, will they?"

Dinah shook her head and reached for my hand. "Nah. They're all excited to meet you. They kind of think you're a rock star."

Her hand in mine fit just right. It might seem strange, but I always had a good feeling when the person I was with had hands that fit in mine. It was a weird quirk, sure, but it made me feel a little more at ease. Until I thought about what she'd said—and frowned.

"Then they'll be disappointed, I'm afraid." Expectations could make or break a good time. I hoped it was the former and not the latter tonight.

Dinah led me inside, where I paid the cover charge, and over to the table where four of the women were now standing.

"Ladies, this is Marianne." She named all of them again, and I nodded at each one, trying my best to remember who they all were.

They smiled at me like they were waiting for me to perform or something, as if I was the night's entertainment.

"Hi," I said like a dork, and took the chair at the head of the table next to Dinah.

"Thanks again for flying Prudence and her puppies up here. Your niece is a treasure, by the way."

"She is that." It was nice to hear someone else speak highly of Nell. She'd had a lot of attitude in school, which meant several trips for Matt and Zack to the office for meetings. They'd adopted her when she was thirteen, deciding that offering a home to an older child was even more important than having a baby. They still thought about adopting more, but so far Nell had taken all of their parenting energy, which they were thrilled to give. It had just taken Nell a really long time to realize that they were even more grateful to be given the chance to be parents than perhaps she was to have found them.

"How is Prudence?" I asked Dinah.

She glanced at the woman named Carla, and then back to me. "Carla has her and the puppies right now. Her stepdaughters are watching them tonight. But they're going away for the weekend, so I'll be taking them to my place."

I wanted to ask her more, like if Prudence was happy, if the puppies were developing well, whether they'd been seen by a vet yet, but before I could speak, Martha stood and squeezed Dinah's shoulder.

"We're off to get set up."

Dinah reached up and squeezed her hand, and Martha kissed her on the cheek, then turned to smile at me. "Great to meet you, Marianne. Have fun tonight." The four women in the band all said goodbye and left through a doorway at the back of the bar.

Dinah leaned over. "They play mostly nineties stuff. They're really good."

"I can't wait." I winked at her before I thought about it and wondered if I should be so forward.

Dinah sucked in a breath and seemed to be speechless for a minute. I could relate. I wanted to keep talking to her, but every time we tried, it seemed we'd both get nervous, or excited, or—

"Can I get you a drink?"

I wondered what the right answer was here. Were these gals big drinkers? I glanced around the table to see a couple of empty pitchers and several glasses with varying levels of amber liquid. "What are you drinking?"

Dinah frowned at her glass. "Some IPA, I think. They serve a bunch of local brews here."

"I'd love a Guinness or Kilkenny if they've got it."

Dinah pursed her lips. "She likes it heavy. Okay. Coming right up."

I watched her sashay over to the bar. She'd taken off her sweater, and under it was a white halter top that showed off a tattooed midriff. She wore black baggy pants held up with a thick belt and a pair of funky green lace-up boots. Her hair was pulled up in a messy bun, showing off more tattoos on her back. Damn, she had some beautiful artwork.

"How long were you in the Air Force?"

Carla sat with her elbows on the table, waiting for me to respond. She was probably in her early fifties and wore her salt-and-pepper hair in a short style that accentuated her high cheekbones and strong jaw. Her bright red button-down shirt contrasted nicely with her brown skin, and the thick black frames of her glasses gave her an edgy look.

And if I wasn't mistaken, she was about to interrogate me.

"Twenty-four years. Retired two months ago."

"What did you fly?" she asked.

"KC-135s and C-17s. Tankers and transports."

"Big planes," Marnie, the wife, said. "I had an uncle who flew those." In contrast, Marnie wore a short-sleeved navy-blue dress with small white polka dots. She looked like maybe she'd come from some sort of administrative assistant job straight to the bar.

I smiled, waiting for more questions.

"Dinah says you aren't sure what you're going to do now."

Carla's statement sounded judgy, but her words made me wonder if there was something else behind them. Dinah said they were business partners...but was there more to the story?

"I'm weighing my options. Don't want to jump into anything right away."

"Bet you had to deal with a bunch of assholes in the service," Tammy said with a laugh.

I shrugged. "There are rotten apples everywhere, right? No more than you, probably. I was pretty lucky for the most part."

"Thankfully the cops we deal with at the shelter are all pretty cool, but when I worked for another local department before coming to Hayward? *Maaaaan,* I tell you. I've never been mansplained so much in my life!"

The women all laughed, and I was content to sit back and listen to their stories. Dinah returned and handed me a pint of Guinness. We clinked glasses and I took a nice long sip. Matt and Zack didn't keep booze in the house, which I could appreciate, but I'd missed my Guinness.

"I like the black, by the way," Dinah said, just before the sounds of guitar tuning alerted us that the band was about to take the stage. "I wanted to tell you earlier. Very hot."

I thanked her with a goofy smile, that stupid shy business returning with a vengeance, and turned in my seat, leaning back against the window.

Dinah pulled her chair beside mine and our shoulders touched. When she leaned in, her breath tickled the side of my neck. I shivered and boldly moved a little closer, making our contact deliberate.

"Don't mind Carla," she said, making me look over to catch Carla staring at us. Carla let her gaze linger a moment, letting me know it had been intentional, and then she turned away. She carried herself as a woman who was used to commanding respect, like a cop, maybe.

Marnie seemed to notice the exchange and placed a possessive arm around Carla.

"She seems concerned about you." I leaned in and spoke close to her ear. The lavender scent tickled my nose and sent tingles through me. Not only did she smell good, but when I was with her, I could forget about decisions for a little while, and that went a long way toward helping me relax.

"Yeah," Dinah said, wrinkling her nose, her smile falling. She went back to watching the band, and I watched her, enjoying the feel of our shoulders together.

The band was actually really good. Martha was fantastic on vocals and really knew how to work the crowd. She seemed to flirt with the men and ladies equally, reminding me I was back in an area where people could be who they wanted and could want who they wanted without having to be too concerned about their surroundings. It was refreshing after years spent in parts of the country where that wasn't the case.

A space had been cleared in front of the band so the crowd could dance along to their favorite tunes from No Doubt, The Donnas, and The Breeders, all female-fronted bands from the '90s. I couldn't remember the last time I'd gone dancing. Matt and I would often go when I was home on leave, but that stopped around the time he and Zack adopted Nell. Now seemed like a good time to start doing some of the things I'd been missing.

I was about to ask Dinah if she wanted to dance when the music stopped.

"We're going to do a little older song for one of our best friends tonight. Dinah, come on up here and say hello!"

Dinah squeezed my arm before skipping up to the front. She waved at the now crowded bar and clasped her hands behind her back. Her youthful presence was all kinds of catnip for me. She seemed like the kind of woman I could have some let-down-your-hair, loosen-your-collar kind of fun with.

"Dinah, as you may know, is the director of Goth Dog Rescue here in Hayward, and this week, with the help of pilot Marianne Cross—everyone wave to Marianne!"

I sat up straighter in my chair and gave a lame wave. Was this planned?

"This week," Martha continued, "Dinah rescued dogs numbers nine hundred ninety-eight, nine hundred ninety-nine, and one thousand! It's a huge milestone for Goth Dog, so we wanted to celebrate with a song just for her."

Martha handed the mic to Dinah. "Hi everyone. Many of you here have donated your time and money in the past, and I sincerely want to say thank you. The Bistro has agreed to place a donation bin on the bar, so please, tip your servers and bartenders, and with your extra cash, give a little for the pups!"

She handed the mic back to Martha and did a little curtsy before skipping back to my side. As the band kicked into a familiar tune, Dinah reached for my hand.

"Is it presumptuous of me to ask you to dance?"

I took her hand and stood close. "Not when I was sitting here thinking about asking you first."

She raised an eyebrow at me, and her smile was nothing short of delectable. Dinah led me onto the dance floor with about fifteen other people who were trying not to fall onto the patrons sitting at the tables. Martha was doing her best Siouxsie Sioux and nailing it. The music caressed my senses and soon my hips were moving in the dip and sway motion that was a hallmark of '80s alternative dancing. My arms swung back and forth past my hips, and I let myself go.

Dinah moved like a temptress. She shimmied and swung her head back and forth, her hair falling from her messy bun in wisps around her face. She was obviously not wearing a bra beneath her halter top, and I caught glimpses of the curves of her breasts every time she raised her arms over her head. She danced with abandon, and it reminded me of scenes from movies with witches dancing in the moonlight deep in the woods, communing with nature. Not that I thought she was a witch, but she certainly had me spellbound.

The song changed to Garbage's "No. 1 Crush." Dinah made lingering eye contact with me and moved closer, into my dance space. She began to circle her hips and dip her shoulders in a seductive show of her sultry side, and I nearly lost the beat.

Martha came out into the crowd and started to dance close to Dinah, resting her hand on Dinah's hip and pressing her forehead against Dinah's as she sang the lyrics. Dinah sang with her, and their voices made a lovely sound together. Dinah rested her forearm on Martha's shoulder, and the two of them turned to look at me as they sang, "I'd sail ships for you, to be close to you…"

Martha pulled away as she sang the last line in a lower register, and Dinah gifted me with a sexy smile that had my libido standing at attention.

Oh yeah, to get her alone…

"Thank you! We're Mud and Honey, and we're going to take a little break, but we'll be back with more of your favorites."

Dinah took my hand, led me over to the bar for two glasses of water, and then to the seating area outside.

"I haven't danced in years, that was so fun," I said, downing half my glass.

"I wouldn't have guessed. You were great."

"Your *friends* are great. Damn. I haven't heard good live music like that in a long time."

I rested my hips against the low iron fence and Dinah sat on a table facing me, her elbows resting on her thighs.

"Did you go to bars a lot when you were in the service? Didn't you get to see some bar bands?"

I snorted and moved a little closer, feeling brave. I played with her fingers, linking them with mine. I was delighted she didn't pull away.

"A bunch of hairy, sweaty guys playing country rock. Let's see, um, a bunch of DJs spinning EDM while sweaty, drugged-out kids bounced in place and waited for the bass to explode, and when it did, they acted like it had never happened before ever. A lot of drunk karaoke. I did get to see Ozzfest in Japan a few years ago."

"Oh, you like the hard stuff, too?"

I shrugged. "It's great to work out to, great for running. But this… this was awesome. Perfect to dance to. Perfect company to dance with." *Too much, too soon?*

"We'll have to do it again." Dinah gave me a wicked sexy smile, and then she looked past me toward the bar.

"Hey, we're just taking off."

Marnie and Carla came out together. Carla glanced between the two of us with a raised eyebrow. *Why so judgy?*

"I'll be over tomorrow to go over the tax stuff with you," Carla said to Dinah, and she waved.

"Thank you, see you then."

Dinah cleared her throat and offered a nervous smile. "So…it appears we've reached the part of the evening when I ask if you want to come back to my place, or the part where you say, 'this was great, see you around.' Either of which is fine. I'd just like to know." She didn't sound as confident as her words led me to believe.

"I guess this *is* that part of the evening."

And I froze. I wanted her. I wanted to go home with her. I also knew that I would fall hard for this woman, and that might not be the best idea, since I wasn't sure what the hell I was doing.

My good mood deflated.

Once again, my inability to make a decision was mucking things up.

"Hey, I don't want to pressure you or anything." Dinah sounded hurt, and I realized I was probably sending her *all* the mixed signals and keeping her waiting for a response.

"It's not that," I said. But how was I supposed to explain? "You're not pressuring me. I'm just…I'm kind of in a holding pattern, which is really foreign to me, and while I want what you're offering—"

"—you're just here on leave."

"Well, not exactly. I mean, I'm out, but I just don't know how long I'm here—"

"And I'm not the girl in port who waits for her soldier to come back to town for a brief fling. I've been that girl before."

Her breasts brushed against my biceps as she turned to walk past me.

"Hold on. Dinah?"

She turned around and her smile was gone.

"Look, I had a great time. I'll see you around. Oh, and I'll let you know about Prudence."

"Dinah—"

"Goodnight, Marianne."

Chapter Six

I replayed my epic fail with Dinah during downtime the next couple of days. I helped Zack and Matt at the gallery as they readied for a showing of Matt's latest photography and another local artist's sculptures. The physical work was good to keep my mind off of Dinah.

I would have been pissed off except for two reasons.

One, it was true. I'd told Dinah when we'd first met that I wasn't sure what I was doing or whether I was even going to stay in the area. It was obvious we had chemistry, and I really wanted to pursue her, but then what?

And two, it wasn't fair for me to drag someone else into my world of indecision. I needed to get my shit together before I even considered dating anyone, much less a goddess like Dinah. That thought was motivation enough.

"Earth to Marianne!"

Zack's voice startled me, and I dropped the box of nails I was holding for him. I crouched down with a grunt, and I started scooping up the nails. Zack climbed down from the ladder to help me.

"Where did you go?"

I laughed and plopped down on my butt. "I don't know. My dateish non-date the other night did not end well. It seems as though my inability to decide what the hell I'm doing with my life means I can't even—"

"Get laid?" Matt said as he walked over. "Close the deal? What else are you gals calling it these days?"

I socked him in the arm as he sat down next to me.

"Well, you totally nailed this scenario."

"Enough, asshole brother!" But I couldn't help laughing at his cheesiness.

"Seriously, though, Marianne. If you could do anything at this point in your life, what would you do?"

I rolled my eyes and leaned back on my hands. "I can tell you what I *won't* do. I won't work for assholes or people I can't trust."

"I guess I'm out then," Matt said.

"You already have a manager, remember?"

He raised an eyebrow at his husband and sighed. "Yeah. My husband the slave driver."

Zack flicked his tongue at him. "You love every minute of it."

"Can I add 'not watch you two make obscene gestures at each other' to my list?"

"Sorry. We got off topic. So, no assholes or untrustworthy douchebags."

"Right. And I really don't want to fly people anymore. That leaves the FedEx job, which could be cool, I guess, but I might have to move if they need me elsewhere. I don't know. As much as I tell myself I like not having a schedule, I know that *not* having a schedule is making me crazy." I exhaled harshly and rolled my head around on my shoulders. Matt scooted behind me and massaged my shoulders.

"You have all day to stop that," I said on a moan.

"So we're clear on what you *don't* want to do. What do you like about your new normal?"

"Siouxsie. Being with you guys and Nell. Seeing Mom and Dad. Having time for my art." I dropped my head forward and sighed. "Dinah. Or at least the idea of Dinah, the idea of having a little romance, maybe?"

Zack leaned forward and squeezed my hand. "I can understand why that's a hard thing to want. After everything you went through…"

"Yeah. It's still hard. I guess I was pretty naïve to think Michael was going to let it go. I totally should have known that I couldn't speak out without repercussions."

Matt's arms wrapped me in a hug. He and Zack knew the whole story. Had been there for me when I came home; sent Nell to our parents so they could sit with me on the couch as I drowned my sorrows in whisky. Matt held my heavy bag as I beat the shit out of it, each punch angrier than the last. Zack took long runs with me through the hills, my feet pounding the ground in time to the angry music on my iPod. So much anger. Helplessness. Something I hadn't felt before. It sucked.

"Babe, you can take all the time you need to decide—"

"But that's just it! The longer I don't know what I'm doing, the longer until I can have a fucking life!"

Zack reached over and grabbed my ankle, giving it a squeeze.

"You know we love having you here, but I don't want us to be one more thing you feel obligated to do. All I know is, if you know what you *don't* want to do, that narrows it down."

"So I should tell Dad no consulting or airline connections, huh?"

I laughed. We all knew Dad would huff and puff, but in the end would acquiesce to whatever I wanted to do. He'd been furious over my treatment by my superiors and felt helpless that he couldn't do anything for me. If it weren't for him, though, I likely would have been court-martialed and not allowed to retire instead.

"I wasn't kidding when I told you I'd love to do a show with your paintings. What if I officially commissioned your work? How long would you need?"

I shrugged. "I don't know. I haven't done a show since high school. How many pieces you thinking?"

Matt grinned. "Usual six-to-eight at the minimum. I'd love that or whatever you can come up with. I know they'll be phenomenal. You've got plenty of money to get you by, you don't have to work."

By the time we got home and ate dinner, they had me talked into doing a show in four months. That bought me some time. I had a task, a purpose, and I could set my own schedule.

That left me in the position to pursue other things I wanted…

Chapter Seven

Everyone and their brother were out on this Saturday morning. The rain had let up, the sun was out, I'd already taken my run for the day, and now it was time for…pursuit.

I pulled into the parking garage off of Mission and after twenty minutes of waiting for people to park, to back in and out five times to get it right, for drivers to stop blocking the aisles, or for families of ten to stop walking down of the middle of the aisle, I parked my truck on the third floor. It was a dangerous walk trying to get out of there, as well. The same people who were in my way as I'd attempted to park were now determined to run me over as I walked out.

By the time I reached the street, my blood pressure had to have been up ten points.

The Downtown Hayward Farmers' Market had more stands than I would have thought for February, but then the winters were usually mild enough here that produce grew plentifully.

I passed by tables of strawberry baskets, mounds of grapes and citrus, along with different varieties of green leafy things. I stopped and picked up some salad fixings so I'd look like a legitimate shopper. It didn't matter, really. I intended to be clear with Dinah that I was there to see her.

Down about halfway, I noticed a booth that looked a little different than the produce tables under canopies. This one had wooden crates on top displaying jars of local honey, decorative soaps in wild colors, all kinds of body care products, eggs, and goat cheese. I recognized Martha from the band standing with a blonde woman, but I didn't see Dinah. I almost turned around to leave but Martha spotted me.

"Hey, Marianne! Come to check out our wares?"

I chuckled nervously, feeling the fight-or-flight instinct revving up.

"Absolutely. I was told you have some great stuff. Is, uh, Dinah around?"

Martha's eyes flared. "She is. She went to grab us some food. You're welcome to wait."

I came this far. I intended to continue my mission.

"Cool. Seems like quite the bustling marketplace here. You have good sales today?"

Making small talk was foreign to me, but I'd do it if it meant getting to talk to Dinah.

"Yeah. We sold out of our most popular soaps and lotions, I sold about half of my honey inventory…Cecily, how did we do on eggs?"

The blonde woman turned to face me and smiled. "I've only got two dozen left, actually."

"I'll take them," I said, reaching for my wallet. "I'm sure they'll get eaten at our house."

Cecily gave Martha a knowing smile and pulled out two cartons. She flipped them open to show me there were no cracked ones. "They're from our cage-free, organically fed chickens. If you bring the cartons back next time, we give a ten-percent discount."

"That's a great idea. Yeah, sure, I'll bring them back. Cuts down on waste."

"That's so cool that you flew Prudence up here," Martha said. "She's adorable. I'm trying to talk myself out of scooping up one of her puppies when they're ready."

"Why would you not? They're so cute," Cecily said.

"I can't have a dog until I move out of my parents' place. I've got the money saved up, just looking for a roommate."

"You should come out and join us at the farm! We've got room."

Martha wrinkled her nose. "Would I be on goat duty? Those things freak me out. They eat everything!"

Cecily rolled her eyes. "Goats are life. They make everything better!"

Dinah walked up behind her friends, looking into a bag. "Alright, who has the egg salad and who wanted the— Oh."

Dinah stopped short with wide eyes when she saw me, and then she gave a shy smile, tinged with discomfort. She wore understated clothes today and no makeup, and she was just as beautiful in her natural state. The thing that concerned me was, she wasn't as bubbly as she'd been previously.

Cecily grabbed the bag from her, and she and Martha moved to the back of the booth, where they stood giggling over their lunch options.

"Hey." I smiled, hoping she might relax.

"Hi." She looked at my bag. "Get what you needed?"

I shook my head. "Can we take a walk?"

Cecily and Martha both nodded with their mouths full of sandwich. Dinah started to say no, until Cecily stepped forward and elbowed her.

Dinah shook her head. "I see you've met my sister," she said, patting the blonde on the head.

Cecily grinned wide, keeping her lips closed.

"Nice to meet you."

Martha shooed us away. "We've got this. Market's nearly over. We don't have much to take back. I'll load up with your sister and you kids go have a good time."

Dinah started to protest, but Cecily gave her a little wave. She turned to look me over, and I smiled boldly. I intended to at least have her hear me out. The decision was ultimately up to her.

We walked back towards the parking garage. "Mind if I take this up to my truck?"

She shook her head, remaining quiet.

"I wanted to thank you," I said to her as we climbed the parking garage ramp.

"For what?"

"For reminding me that I had decisions to make—and that those decisions *are* mine to make now. I get to decide what I do, who I see, where I go."

Dinah smiled. "Guess that's a change of pace from the military."

We reached my truck and I turned to face her. "It is that." I unlocked the door and slid my bags carefully into the king cab. "I had some say, but not totally…not in the end." I sighed. "Will you come with me? I'd like to show you something."

She hesitated. "I don't know if this is such a good idea."

I resisted the temptation to touch her, hold her hand, show her how well we'd fit together if she gave me a chance.

"I just want to show you something, and then I can take you home. We're on your timeline. You can even send your girls my number, license plate, whatever, so you'll feel safe."

Dinah laughed and played with her ponytail, tugging on it and wrapping it around her finger. "That's not what I'm worried about. Alright. Let's go."

We climbed into my truck, and I turned on my iPod with the little Bluetooth speaker that fit into the cup holder.

"Hi-tech operation you've got here," she said.

"See, it's all about compromise. They don't make these trucks anymore, which is stupid because they were Ford's bestselling truck for a long time and they're perfect, especially if you live in a city with no parking. I refuse to give it up, so I make do. I used to have a cassette adapter for satellite radio, but it didn't work very well, and the contraption kept falling off the dash, so I went with option b."

Dinah looked at my setup with the charger cords neatly attached to the side of the console and plugged into the dash cigarette lighter. I'd even installed my own sub-dash compartment for extra storage.

"Are you the secret female twin of MacGyver? Looks to me like you could fix just about anything."

I shrugged. "I've had this baby for a long time."

"Does she have a name?"

Oh boy. "Yeah, um, Chrissie…as in Hynde, from The Pretenders."

Dinah laughed. "You sure had your share of musical crushes."

We took A Street and then turned left toward the airport's entrance, and I turned into the parking lot. Dinah sat up straighter. "Are you taking me to meet Siouxsie?"

I entered the code and the gate opened for us. "Secondly. But first, I have something else at my hangar to show you."

She folded her hands in her lap, but I could see she was vibrating with excitement. She whipped her head around as we navigated the airport tarmac, driving past the terminal to the rows of hangars beyond. I pulled up outside mine and turned off the engine.

"This is so cool! I've always loved the vintage planes. When I first discovered pinup girls in the calendars, I fell in love with the style, then I saw the military connection and fell in love with the girls on the planes."

"Well, then hopefully you're going to like this."

I unlocked the door and slid it open for us to walk in, closing it behind us. Dinah immediately walked over to Siouxsie and ran her hand lovingly along the wing.

"She's gorgeous! So tiny and cute!" She peeked in the window. "Where did you fit Prudence?"

I opened the door and showed her my little compartment behind the seat.

"It's not ideal. It would be better to have a bigger plane down the road. I figured I could eventually move up to a Cessna 182. The weight limit is closer to a thousand pounds and with a bigger tank, my range would be more like seven to eight hundred miles. I'd have plenty of room and ability to carry a couple of bigger dogs even."

Dinah turned to face me. "You're thinking about doing Pawsitive Flight on a regular basis?"

"Yeah. It combines the things I love, flying and dogs. And it introduces me to beautiful women."

Yeah, I was being a shameless flirt, but I'd brought her into my private sanctum to be honest with her, and I intended to be transparent.

Dinah smiled nervously, and then her gaze shifted past me to my art corner—and she gasped.

"Oh my God!" She hurried over to my easel and placed her hand on her chest. "Did you do this? It's…it's…"

"I found the program in my dad's stuff and, well, I was inspired."

"I'll say! I didn't know you were an artist, too."

"It's been a long time since I've done something like this, but yeah. I've loved drawing and painting since junior high. Matt—my brother —and I were major art geeks. He mostly does photography, but he paints a helluva lot better than I do."

Dinah placed a hand on my shoulder but couldn't seem to tear her eyes away from her likeness. "Marianne...I don't know what to say. It's so beautiful."

"Thank you. I'm going to do a gallery show with Matt in a few months. I feel pretty positive about finding the inspiration for more of these."

She finally turned to face me; her eyes wide. "Is that how you see me?"

I turned to look at the 11x14 canvas. I'd chosen to make her more prominent in the picture, big surprise. I'd taken a few liberties with the image; instead of the polka dot top underneath, the jumpsuit was open enough to see the curves of her breasts and one of her shoulders. I didn't attempt to put the tattoos on her, however, and she seemed to have more now than when the picture was taken about ten years ago.

"It barely comes close to how I see you."

I turned to look at her, my cheeks hot from the admission. My skin heated under her lingering touch, and I felt her warm breath on my cheek. I cradled her jaw and ran my thumb over her bottom lip, hoping she wanted the same thing I did, asking for permission.

She closed her eyes and brought a hand up to hold mine. Then she kissed my thumb.

Her eyes opened, and she smiled wickedly before nibbling the pad of my thumb.

I took that as an invitation.

Our bodies met in the middle as I took her face in my hands and pressed my hopeful lips to hers.

Dinah moaned and melted against me with her arms around my shoulders. She opened her stance a bit to lessen the height difference, and then opened her mouth to me. My tongue eagerly sought hers as my hands explored what I'd so lovingly used my brush to worship on canvas. As I'd painted her, I wondered what her skin would feel like, how warm she would feel if we were skin to skin. Would the height difference be weird? Would she care?

The answers were:

Soft.

Hot.

No.

And apparently not.

She pulled away to walk backward toward the couch, tugging my hand to follow her.

"I had no ulterior motives in bringing you here, I swear," I said as we lowered to the couch next to each other. "I merely planned to show you the painting."

She turned to face me and played with my fingers against my leg, exploring every crease, every angle of them, with her own fingertips. "Wednesday night...I let old hurts get to me and didn't give you a chance to explain."

She paused, and I waited to see if she would continue. As much as I wanted to keep kissing her, it seemed she had something to get off her chest.

"Dinah, you don't have to explain—"

"I know," she said, tilting her head to the side. She only made eye contact sporadically. "You might have guessed that Carla and I were together at one time?"

I nodded and she continued. "Well, she handles the business end of the rescue, which allows me time to do the outreach and placement work, as well as the fundraising, the parts I'm really good at."

"I get it."

"We're friends now, but I was kind of her Lesbian 101 relationship, and then she moved on. My two previous relationships were only here temporarily and moved on to other things, as well. Thinking you weren't going to be here long had me hesitant to go out with you, which sucks, because I really like you."

"Sounds to me like you've got good reason to be leery of a temporary thing." I gave her hands a squeeze. "I'm not interested in temporary, either."

She sighed and winced at me. "And here we've had one really awesome kiss and I'm spilling my bucket loads of issues on your couch."

I ran my hand over the arm of the couch. "Oh, this couch has seen plenty of issues. It was my brother's and it's survived knock-down drag-out brawls with his husband and their adopted daughter, as well as my grief over leaving the Air Force. A lot of tears have been shed on this couch, so don't worry. It might even have, like, psychic powers or something. It's eerie how much action this couch has seen."

"Like it's possessed with the drama poltergeists? Ha, that's rich," she said, dropping her head to my shoulder.

We both took a breather and listened to the rain outside.

"I thought it was done," I said. "It was so nice this morning."

"Changes quickly. Sometimes it even rains when the sun is shining brightly." She turned to lie back against the arm of the couch and slid her legs onto my lap. "I love the sound on the metal. It reminds me of our house growing up. We had one of those patio rooms with the metal roof? I loved to lay on the floor and listen to the rain pound on it."

She looked so inviting with her head resting on the pillow, her hair splayed out behind her, her right arm over her head. "I could do a whole series of paintings of just you. You are like an artist's wet dream."

She barked out a laugh. "Yeah, well, maybe you need a bit more hands-on figure studying before you get to the painting." She pulled on my hand until I hovered above her, my hand on her thigh and the other supporting my weight next to her shoulder. Her neck called to me. I brushed my lips under her jaw and felt her shiver. I nuzzled her, the fine hairs at the nape of her neck tickling me, the scent of lavender intoxicating up close. I had to taste.

"Oh," she gasped as I ran my tongue along her throat, loving the way she moved against me. She gripped my back and urged me closer, which I allowed, but I had a feeling she could get wound up quick. I wanted to draw this out, my exploration of this work of art.

I kissed her everywhere I could without removing her clothes. Earlobes, collarbones, the inside of her elbows and wrists, the hollow of her throat. She responded by writhing against me, my thigh snug against her core, as hers was to mine. I bit down on the tendon at the side of her neck, and she arched into me nicely.

"There's always finger painting," I said. "I'd love to get you nice and messy."

"Messy is good. I like messy." She laughed and cupped my ass, using her long fingers to grab nice big handfuls. "God, you're ripped! Your ass is fabulous. I could just touch you all night."

"Thanks, I think. I don't know, I like to run and lift weights."

"And thank God for that. You're so gorgeous, Marianne. Really. I'm so glad I met you."

"You're glad? Like really glad?" I teased, sliding my hand under her t-shirt. She sucked in a breath and arched into my hand as my fingertips found her nipple. She ground her pelvis against my leg in a steady motion now.

"Soooooo glad." She moaned and slid her hands down the back of my pants, doing some exploration of her own. I couldn't say I minded; however, I was quickly losing the ability to focus on drawing out her pleasure. I wanted to watch her come apart.

"So glad. You'll let me get you messy?"

"Messy, yes, please."

I had her out of her pants and spread out for me—and *lord* was she wet. I loved wet. So much fun to play with. It had been so long since I'd really had the luxury, the privacy, the opportunity.

Her hips bucked as I ran my fingers along the sides of her clit with just enough pressure to make her pant.

"Exquisite."

I was aroused as fuck, and my voice gave me away. It was low and hoarse, like a two-pack-a-day smoker after a night in a dive bar. I might have been shy when I first met her, but damn, that was gone now. I felt like a woman possessed, obsessed with the idea of pleasing her. I wanted to taste all of her, but this time, I wanted to watch her face.

"So good," she said, and I knew she was close.

I slid one finger inside her, and we both moaned at the contact. Her legs trembled as she neared release, her skin flushed a deep pink, and the sounds…

When she let go, it was a revelation. And loud. I couldn't help but smile. She was beautiful. And enthusiastic. I held her as she came down and—

"Marianne? You okay in there?"

Our eyes wide, we burst out laughing, and then shushed each other.

"Yeah, Vern. I'm fine. Thank you."

They heard his footsteps outside, and then he chuckled. "As you were, Lieutenant Colonel."

"Yes, sir," I called out.

And we lost it. We laughed so hard, I was reduced to wheezing and barking sounds.

"Well, I guess we know these are thin metal walls," I said. I didn't care that we'd been caught. I loved making her come, and I'd do it again just as soon as she'd let me.

"I'm mortified. Oh my God, I've never been so, um, so—"

"Vocal? I loved it."

She rolled her eyes at me, and I pulled her closer, her head tucked under my chin. "Yeah, well, now that I know what you're capable of, we may have to rethink our location."

She shivered, and I realized that it was getting colder as the afternoon went on and the rain continued.

"I should probably get you someplace warmer. This place is great, but it's not really climate controlled."

She tilted her head and smiled up at me. "Want to take me home and see Prudence?"

My heart flipped in my chest. I'd decided to stay here, at least for four months officially, but I knew in my heart I was here for good. I think I knew it after my conversation with Nell, or maybe even earlier than that, when I'd first lain eyes on Prudence and the pups. Twenty-four years on the move was long enough. It was time to start living my life the way I wanted to.

"Let's go see Prudence."

Chapter Eight

We hit some traffic on the city streets before we entered Crow Canyon, a two-lane road running through the East Bay hills between Castro Valley and San Ramon. Norris Canyon veered off to the right. It was a road I wouldn't have driven if the rain was coming down any harder. A very giggly Dinah gave me directions, and soon I was pulling up to an adorable farmhouse, complete with lace curtains in the windows and a tractor out front. An antique flatbed truck was parked in the middle of the lawn with flower beds on the back, full of tulips and daffodils. A few cats watched suspiciously from the covered porch as we made a break for it, dashing through the downpour to get to shelter.

"How is this place possible in the Bay Area?"

Dinah laughed as she unlocked the door for us. "It's kind of timeless. With the exception of paint, some modern conveniences like solar power and satellite TV, it's pretty much the same as when my grandparents and then my uncle lived here and worked the farm. They raised cattle, but Cecily opted for goats and chickens. The place is paid for and we're turning over a profit, so it's here to stay, hopefully, for at least another generation."

The living room was decorated in the cutest shabby chic, and the kitchen looked like it could have been in a 1950s Sears catalog.

"We've restored as much of the original fixtures and tile as we could. Our cousin has an appliance repair place and is an awesome handyman, so Chez Shaw is good to go. Can I get you something to drink? A towel maybe?"

"I'm good, but some water would be great."

She busied herself drying off and grabbing drinks while I looked around at the quirky place. There were elements of her personality, as well as evidence that a business was run out of this place. There were bunches of lavender hanging in front of the back windows, drying. The dining room had been turned into an office, and there were charts and boards hung on the walls that resembled the shit you'd see on Pinterest. Someone was a major planner.

"Oh, these are for the farm business over here, and this side is for the rescue. I try to keep our calendars pretty organized."

Dinah was a woman after my own heart with her attention to detail, but I never had it in me to make things pretty or decorated. My At-A-Glance planner was black and boring. There were no stickers or doodles on the pages, just my appointments and birthdays at this point. The pages were pretty empty for the first time in my life. I looked forward to filling them up with items of my choice.

"Let's go see our little mama." Dinah took my hand and led me up a set of stairs at the back of the house. "My uncle added on to the original structure, so we kind of have this Winchester Mystery House thing going on. There are three separate staircases leading to the three sections of the house up here. Six bedrooms in all for me and my two sisters and our menagerie. Come on in."

She led me into a room with a couch and a row of dog crates. I spotted Prudence and the babes immediately. I was thrilled to realize the pup was happy to see me, too.

"Hi baby," I said as I crouched down in front of the crate. Dinah opened the door and Prudence hopped into my lap, licking my face.

Maybe it was the day's events that led to my emotional release, or maybe it was Dinah's hopeful smile, but all of a sudden, I couldn't see through my tears. Or speak.

"Marianne?" Dinah sat next to me and rubbed my back as I blubbered like an idiot.

"Whatever it is, I'm here." She sat patiently, keeping just enough physical contact that it grounded me without smothering. I didn't need a tissue as Prudence took her clean-up duties seriously. All I could do was hold her squirmy little body and sob noiselessly.

When I finally got ahold of myself, Prudence stepped down from my leg and wandered back into the crate to check on her puppies. She was only gone briefly, and then returned to my lap as if she realized her job was not just to be a good mama, but to be my cuddle buddy.

I took a deep breath…and started from the beginning.

"I served much of my commission under 'Don't Ask, Don't Tell.' When it was over, I never felt the need to share my status. If I would have been seeing someone, maybe, but I wasn't, not seriously. I had this asshole of an officer working under me that couldn't shut his fucking mouth about how the gays were ruining the military, and how he wished the next president would just outlaw it altogether. He had problems. I made it very clear that I would not tolerate that shit and eventually I had to write him up for it."

Dinah moved behind me and began massaging my shoulders in a way that had my body feeling loose and less anxious.

"Sounds like you were in a difficult situation."

"It shouldn't have been, but he wouldn't let it go. Anyway, he and some of his buddies hung out at this apartment complex near the base where we were stationed, and I'd seen him a couple of times when I went over to see a friend. Her name was Carrie, and she was studying for her Promotion Fitness Exam and Specialty Knowledge Test. Carrie obviously had a crush on me, but I hadn't thought anything of it. I just wanted to help her get her promotion. She was a good officer and deserved it, she was just nervous about the exam. We'd only met a couple of times at her place, and always with other friends over. She wasn't under my command, so I wasn't breaking any rules of conduct. But then, Jacobsen was looking for a reason to fuck with me after I wrote him up.

"I should have known after our confrontation that he wasn't going to let it go." I sucked in a breath and exhaled, exhausted now. Talking about this shit really put me through the wringer. "The next thing I know, out of the blue, I was slapped with fraternization charges, and it was either retire or face a court-martial."

"Oh my God, Marianne! But…you said she wasn't under your command?"

I shook my head. "Apparently didn't matter. I was an officer, and she was beneath me. The Air Force tends to pick and choose their battles, and lucky me, they chose mine."

"All because of that guy? What an asshole! He would ruin your whole career over his stupidity?"

"Hatred is a powerful thing." I moaned when she found a particularly sensitive spot. "My father retired about five years ago as a general. I didn't want my father's name, nor mine, tarnished by someone's vengeance plot. I hate it that he won, but maybe…I don't know. It sucks I had to retire, but I have to look at the positives. It's been hard being away from my brother and his family and my parents for so long, and now? I don't know." I scratched Prudence's head and then turned to face Dinah. "Prospects are good. I think I'm finally ready to move on."

Dinah held eye contact with me for a long minute, and then she leaned in and kissed me slow and deep, letting me know she felt how much I'd been struggling with the circumstances around my retirement, and how much she wanted to be a part of my moving-on process.

Before things got too heated, though, Prudence barked at us. We broke apart, laughing, and Prudence pawed at me.

"It's okay, girl."

Her scruffy tail wagged back and forth as she looked between us as though asking permission to be a part of our little party. I scooped her up into my arms and snuggled her furry body.

"I think someone wants to move on *with* you," Dinah said, smiling expectantly. "She only gets that crazy over you, you know."

I held her up and pressed my nose to hers. "Is that true? You want to join forces with me against the world?"

She wiggled her butt even harder, and Dinah and I cracked up. She couldn't have weighed much more than twelve or thirteen pounds, but she didn't seem like a little dog because of her long legs.

"Well, she's got some work to do with these pups before she's ready to fly off into the sunset with you. We took them to the vet this week, and he thinks they're pretty young, like maybe only two or three weeks old."

"Wow, so she'd just had them when I picked her up, huh?"

"Seems like it. She'll need to be with them for at least another five or six weeks until they're ready to be adopted out."

I put Prudence down so she could go check on her puppies, who were starting to make little whimpering noises. She carefully walked around them and lay down so they could nurse. Dinah helped me up then closed the crate door.

"She gets distracted if we're in here," she said as she took my hand and led me out of the room. "Don't worry, Mama. We'll be back."

She closed the door behind us and led me across the hall to what I assumed was her bedroom. It was the girliest bedroom I'd ever seen in real life, and it totally fit her femininity. I loved being in her space, seeing the vanity with the large mirror where she likely spent her time creating the pinup looks I admired so much.

"So this is where the magic happens," I said as she closed the door behind me.

"Mmmm, that depends on you."

"On me?" I asked as she led me over to the bed and gently pushed me to sit down.

"Yes. It depends on you, and whether you have any place to be for the next—"

"Week? Nope."

She threw her head back with a laugh, and I tugged her closer, letting my hands wander her waist and hips.

"Besides, it's still pouring out there. I can't think of anyplace better to be."

Dinah smiled down at me and pulled off her shirt. "In that case, let's make a plan."

I wiggled my eyebrows. "A plan?" I unhooked her bra and groaned as she let it fall to the ground.

"Yes. I'm all about plans and schedules, you know. You saw my office downstairs."

"I did. A woman after my own heart."

"Mmmm," she said as I ran my hands up her back, captivated by the feel of her naked skin. "I propose we spend the next hour naked and under the covers, then you let me feed you, then we take Miss Prudence out, and then we get naked some more, and then—"

I took her nipple between my lips and ran my tongue over the tip, causing her to gasp and melt into me.

"That all sounds good, but I'm retired, you know, and that means I get to live in the moment and enjoy my current activity. And I intend to enjoy you for as long as possible."

Dinah laughed as I unfastened her pants and slid them down her slim hips. This time, the lacy panties needed to come off. I wanted my pinup girl bare for my viewing pleasure.

"Yes, ma'am," she said as she straddled my lap, yanked my shirt off and pushed me backwards on the bed. "Now, it's my turn to rock *your* world."

I laughed but it quickly turned into a moan. "Do I have to worry about who might hear?"

Dinah shook her head as she worked her way down my body. I pulled off my sports bra and sucked in a breath as she nibbled at my pelvic bone above the waistband of my cargo pants.

"Nah. Trudy spends most of her time at her boyfriend's house, and Cecily will be out in the barn for a while longer. She's trying to see if her latest breeding exploits took. She's up to her eyeballs in goat vulvas right now. Even if she comes inside, she won't mind one bit."

I cracked up at that visual, but then she had my pants off and did this thing with her tongue that rendered me boneless, helpless, and speechless.

Damn. This whole living-in-the-moment philosophy was quite attractive. I grabbed a pillow and propped up my head so I could watch the show.

"I love that smile." She smiled back at me and licked her lips. The sight of her pink tongue was my undoing.

"It's all yours, baby," I said before losing all of my faculties in mindless pursuit of an earth-shattering orgasm like I'd never known possible.

Hours later, while we lay on the floor in the sitting room with Prudence and her puppies, listening to Siouxsie and The Banshees and drinking some of Dinah's homebrewed organic tea, I couldn't help but think to myself how sometimes even the most emotionally eviscerating experiences can come with a silver lining, as long as you're open to the positives.

These girls didn't know it yet, but they were passengers on this new leg of my journey, and I intended to keep them close for safekeeping. It was time this flygirl settled down and started a family of her own; a family that included a retired Air Force pilot with a new mission, a gorgeous bombshell bent on saving all the furbabies possible, and a tough little mutt with precious cargo. Who could ask for anything more?

Acknowledgments

I want to thank Xio Axelrod for putting together the annual Love Is All anthologies and for giving me the opportunity to submit. I'm grateful to be in such talented company.

Special thanks to my bestie Christine for lending me her husband and sharing her love of flying with me throughout our long friendship.

Wendy, my long-time Roadie and Goddess, thank you for reading for me. Your support has been so important to me on my authory journey.

Thank you to all who work in animal rescue. It's such important work and requires love, compassion and patience. I'm grateful to Sunshine Animal Rescue (which is now part of the Hayward Animal Shelter), Hopalong Rescue in Oakland, CA, and San Francisco Animal Care and Control for helping us find our furry friends.

Joy Is A Phone Call Away

Joy Is A Phone Call Away

ACT ONE

Joy

December 2020

"Joy, you'll close up? You're sure? I just can't talk to another person. I'll literally donate a kidney through my nostril to avoid speaking, I'm that sick of humanity."

Karen was our director of the Atlanta call center for the committee to elect Democrat Warren Johnson, and yes, she was fully aware and encouraging of jokes invoking her name. Mr. Johnson found himself in a runoff election after the emotional November race, and it had been all hands on deck ever since with her leading the team.

"I happen to love humanity," I told Karen, "And I'd be happy to close up shop. I just want to finish three more calls tonight so I can reach my goal."

"Suit yourself. Just be careful leaving."

"Oh, don't worry. My brother's on standby to pick me up. He won't let the boogeymen get me."

She muttered something like "ain't the boogie men who worry me," then turned and waved as she went out the door. I was her second or third in command, it depended on the day, so I had the codes to the alarm and locks. And though I was tired, it was almost Christmas, and we'd be closing down until after the holiday. No stone could be left unturned in this important race, and that meant having dozens of conversations with potential voters about the issues that concerned them most.

Next on my list was Irma Santiago. I dialed her number, and it rang three times before a screaming woman answered the phone.

"¡Cállate! ¡El teléfono! ¿Bueno?"

I introduced myself in my barely adept Spanish and she laughed. "English is okay. Can I help you?"

"Yes, I'm calling—"

"Bernardo! Get the dog! El Diablo, that dog! Oy! The roast! He's on the counter!"

"I'm sorry, I seem to have caught you at a bad time—"

"It's always like this," she said with a sigh. "What can I do for you?"

"Well, you've probably heard by now about the runoff election—"

"Ay! Gilberto! You're spilling! Bernardo help him—"

"But you told me to get the dog."

"Bernardo! Oh, I'm sorry, what did you say your name was?"

"I'm Joy, and you sound really busy—"

"It's okay, really. I got five kids and two nephews staying with me and my husband. There's always chaos. Anyway, you were saying?"

I had no idea how parents did it. I thought kids sounded like fun, but then I'd witness a meltdown in a store, or a tragedy occur, and I'd question my own capacity. My parents had both worked insane hours in their professional jobs, leaving me and my brother to fend for ourselves or mooch off our grandparents, who lived in the same apartment complex. We were taken care of, but no one coddled us. I wasn't sure I would know what to do with a kid.

"I'll be quick. I just wanted to see if you had any questions about Warren Johnson, our Democratic candidate for the U.S. Senate? We're checking with voters—"

"He's not that one who was on the Twitter complaining about immigrants—"

"No, ma'am. That was his challenger, John Farmingham." Having one old white guy running against another old white guy, especially one with a similar name, was definitely a problem when working on a campaign. Folks were looking for change, and while it seemed like they weren't getting it with either of these candidates, Warren Johnson had recruited a diverse team to help him win. With control of the senate in the balance, we couldn't disappoint.

"Oh, dios mio, that man boils my blood. I will definitely be voting for whoever is not him."

I chuckled. I'd heard a lot of that while phone banking for the presidential election.

"That's wonderful. May I ask whether you plan to vote in person or by mail?"

"In person. I want to look those people in the eye when I deliver my vote."

"Those people?" I asked her. *The poll workers?*

"Those militia people. I saw them there last time with their guns, like they're gonna scare me away from voting. I've worked hard and no one is going to tell me I don't belong here."

"Yes, ma'am. I'm glad to hear it. Do you have any questions for me?"

"What? Jose! Put that down right now! No, you may not eat that candy bar while dinner is cooking!"

Oh, this woman was my hero. She managed to handle a conversation with me while dealing with chaos.

"I'm so sorry, Mrs. Santiago. I'm happy to let you go for the evening."

"It's okay. These kids make me crazy, but they're good boys. Did you need anything else?"

"No, ma'am. Thank you for taking the time to speak with me."

"Thank you for calling. I can't volunteer, but you sure have my vote."

"Thank you so much. Have a good evening."

We hung up and I made a note on the spreadsheet and then threw my hands up in the air and spun in my chair.

"Winning!"

I loved a good call where I could connect with like-minded people. It gave me faith in humanity. I would often tell Karen she needed to make calls so she could hear from the good ones. I was on such a high from the last call I was dancing in my seat as I dialed the next number.

"This is Dylan."

I was ripped from my moment of glory.

"Uh, I'm sorry, is this Dylan Whitley?"

"Yes, it is, may I ask who's calling?"

I wasn't prepared for the soft, sleepy voice on the other end of the line. I was expecting a dude because of the name, which was a lame assumption on my part. I did a double take and saw the Ms. before her name.

"Hi, um, hi. Sorry. I'm Joy and I'm calling with the party. The Democrats. The runoff. Oh my god, can I start over?"

The line was dead silent. I thought for sure she'd hung up on me.

Then she chuckled.

"Give it a shot."

"Great. Thank you. I'm not usually this bad."

"Okay."

I'm not sure what I was expecting, but more quiet distracted me again. I found myself trying to picture what Dylan Whitley looked like. What would the face to match that incredible voice be like?

"Are you there?"

Her voice startled me, and I jumped, knocking over a cup with push pins, which went all over the floor. I jumped up and smacked my shin on the corner of the desk drawer, which I always did, and I specifically reminded myself to watch out for every time I got up. I made a face to keep from shouting and then let out a long breath.

"I'm so sorry. I just... Hi. Let me start over." *Pull it together, Joy.* "I'm Joy and I'm calling from the Georgia Democratic Party, and I wanted to—"

"The runoff election."

I exhaled for probably the first time since she'd answered.

"Yes. I wanted to ask you if you were planning to vote?"

The line went quiet.

"I'd planned to, but uh...I've had a change of status."

"Oh." I wasn't prepared for that answer, but I was a professional. I could handle it. "Is there something I can help with?"

"Not unless you are a miracle worker."

"Well," I said and then barked out a laugh. "I bring Joy with every call, so miracles aren't too far out of my purview." She'd laugh at my stupid joke, or she'd hang up. Either way, I likely wasn't making a good impression. The dead air on the other end of the line was killing me.

"Do you always work this hard for a laugh?"

"I'll do anything to protect our democracy, so I guess slipping on a banana peel or a bad pun aren't too high a price to pay."

"Duly noted." And she laughed. It felt like a victory.

"I'm serious, is there something I can help with?" I wasn't ready to give up yet.

"We're past the deadline for requesting mail-in ballots, aren't we?"

"We are. Does that mean you're out of the area?"

She cleared her throat, and I could have sworn I heard a grunt of pain.

"I am now. I won't be on Election Day, but I likely won't be able to get to the polling place."

"Oh, well, I think I can help with that. I've got charts, graphs, schedules, lists, you name it, all methods of transportation necessary to get you from point A to point Ballot." My fingers twitched over the keyboard as I prepared to wow her with my resourcefulness since my humor hadn't done the trick.

"I'm afraid it's more than a matter of transportation. I'm, uh, disabled."

She said the word as though it were new and unfamiliar.

"That's all right," I said, rushing ahead. "There are paratransits and heck, we can even set up a private ride if you're okay with that."

She sighed.

That wasn't a good sign.

"Well, Joy, I'm *newly disabled*," she said, drawing it out to make a point. "So when I get out of the rehab hospital I'm currently in, I won't be real mobile."

My heart flipped around in my chest. "I'm so sorry. I'm sure that's a big adjustment."

"It is," she said. She said it matter-of-factly, but I heard pain in her voice. I pictured her in a hospital bed, the room dark as it was nearing nine o'clock. Maybe she was staring out the window at a lone light in the parking lot wondering what the future had in store for her. More pain? Hard work? Frustration. And yet she was strong enough to talk to a stranger on the phone.

I wasn't sure if she would want to talk to me or feel comfortable sharing her tale with a stranger, but since she hadn't hung up on me yet, I thought perhaps there was a reason fate placed her number on my list for calls tonight.

"I'm guessing you'll have to relearn how to do a lot, huh?"

"Yeah. Walking could happen someday, possibly. Maybe I'll be able to drive eventually, but it's gonna be a while."

"That's a blow."

"Sure is," she said, grunting once more. "Especially when you're used to being on your own. Gotta have my whole place retrofitted."

"For a wheelchair? I bet there are organizations that can help with that."

I was a fixer by nature, and a people pleaser and easer. This woman seemed as though she could definitely use some of the latter.

"There are. I'm waiting for calls back. Guess I'm not that great at waiting."

"Patience is definitely a virtue I struggle with. Mind if I ask what kind of support you've got when you get home?"

Yeah, I was being pushy, but again, she could hang up anytime. I wouldn't consider this call a success unless I'd turned over every stone and helped her in some way.

"Some guys from my unit. My uncle. That's about it."

"You at Ft. Benning?"

She cleared her throat. "I was. Airborne and Ranger Training. Instructor for the Mountain Phase at Camp Merrill."

"Oh...I see. Airborne is tough."

She laughed. "You'd think that, but I didn't break my back jumping out of a plane."

"No? Care to tell me how you *did* you break your back?"

"Training accident. Humvee. I spend a large part of my life arguing with people that planes are safer than cars, and now I'm living proof."

I loved that she was opening up and telling me her story. It was one of my favorite parts of making these calls. You never knew who was on the other end of the line, and occasionally you heard a story that would change your life.

"You're living proof that Army women are badass."

"I guess. You serve?"

"Nah. Doctor found a heart murmur when I went for my physical. Atrial Septal Defect. Army wouldn't take me. I was devastated, but also determined. Decided if I can't fight wars, I'd try to keep us out of them instead. Grad student at Georgia State, Andrew Young School of Policy Studies."

"Good for you," Dylan said. "That's tough. They fix your heart?"

"I'm living with it," I said. "Had to get used to a new normal. Sound familiar?"

She laughed. "Touché."

"Yeah, we keep on keepin' on, right? Anything I can do to help you keep on? I mean, I know we started out talking about voting, but I get it, you have more stuff going on."

"It's not that I don't want to vote. I voted early for the presidential election. Then this happened."

"I'm glad you were able to vote then. That was a big election."

"Yeah, fuck that guy," she said, and we both burst out laughing. It always made me want to do a victory dance whenever someone I called was obviously not a fan of our now-lame duck president. "Sorry, I—"

"No, no. No need to apologize."

"And I know this runoff election is important, too. I just don't see any way to get there. I think they're releasing me from here in a week. But I've got a long way to go. I can't even put my own pants on yet."

"But you will, though. And you will be home in time for the holidays, that is if you celebrate."

"Yeah, my uncle is coming to stay with me for a bit. Not sure what, if anything, we'll do for the holiday. We've got a lot of shit to take care of."

She was overwhelmed, with all the reasons in the world.

"So, you buy some pizzas, a case of beer, and you invite some of your Ranger buddies over and boom! You've got a ramp. Right? Maybe?"

She laughed. "You met my team? These guys are great with knots and weapons, but a nail gun and a table saw, watch out."

And somehow, we fell into easy conversation about men and power tools and the dangers of mixing them. It was great to hear her relaxing a bit and I lost track of the time. Her voice lulled me into a cozy state, and I wished I was curled up in my bed with my warm fuzzy blanket and my cat. And her.

And that hadn't happened for a long time, that feeling of real connection.

"Oh, hang on. My night nurse is here." She put a hand over the phone, and I heard muffled voices. I yawned and looked up at the wall clock.

It was ten fifteen. We'd been on the phone for close to an hour. Time had flown by and for a little while I'd forgotten that our world was on fire, that we were in a fight for our lives against a virus that killed indiscriminately, against attempts to revoke our reproductive rights, and against hatred of our queer community. I spent so much of my time being angry, but tonight I'd actually laughed. I'd wanted to ease Dylan, and I was the one smiling.

Damn.

"Hey, Joy? I'm sorry, they gotta do some stuff. I—"

"Of course. And hey, it was great to talk to you."

"You too. Really."

And at this point I crossed a line.

"Hey, I'm going to text you a number where you can reach me, you know, in case you need a little Joy in your life." Oh my God I was such an idiot. "I mean, in case you have any more questions—"

"I'd like that. Thank you."

She hung up before I could make it worse.

But wait. She said she'd like that.

I grabbed my cell phone and texted her my number before I lost my nerve. My phone started buzzing and I squeaked and nearly dropped it, played hot potato with it a few times before I got a hold of it and answered the call.

"Where the hell you at?"

"Oh shit, Colson, you scared the shit out of me. I was just going to call you."

"I'm outside, loser. You're late."

"I know, I know, I'm sorry."

Sorry, not sorry. And the smile on my face would not quit.

Please let her need some Joy.

ACT TWO

Dylan

"That's the first smile I've seen from you in a while. You cheatin' on me?"

My night nurse Tre was hilarious. He was gay, I was gay, and yet somehow, we'd become an old married couple in the nearly six weeks I'd been at this rehab facility.

"Not on your life. I ain't givin' you up. You'll still be wipin' my ass when we're old."

"Not according to your latest exam. Looks like Doc has you going home end of the week."

I knew it was coming and yet I had to focus on keeping the panic at bay.

"Really. Wow. You're ready to get rid of me, huh?"

"Uh uh. You're my most cooperative patient. Plus, you're like a buck thirty. My back's gonna be complaining about the heavy lifting after you're gone."

Tre hadn't had to lift me much lately. I'd gotten fairly good at getting myself from bed to chair, chair to head, head to chair and chair to bed. I wanted to sleep for five days after, but I could do it. Was grateful I could do it. It'd been a mystery just how bad off I was going to be when I first arrived at the hospital, but two surgeries and six weeks of PT and they were ready to let me loose on the world. Wild.

"Who was that on the phone?"

"Nosy much? It was someone calling about voting." My lips twitched to smile, and I did some weird thing to stop it from happening. Which Tre picked up on.

"Mm hmm."

Tre gave me some applesauce to make the pills go down easier. Anti-inflammatories, Gabapentin, muscle relaxers...I'd gone from someone who never took pills to having a whole regimen of medications, some of which I'd likely be on for life.

"You want some help getting to the bathroom? Looks like you had a particularly tough day of PT."

"I'll manage. I've got a little pep in my step tonight. Well, pep in my roll."

"Get on with it. You better tell me more."

Tre stood by to assist if I needed him, but I managed to get to my chair with less pain tonight.

"Let's just say she added a little joy to my night."

"Mmm hmmm, that's what I'm talking about."

I was used to the nurses hanging around outside the bathroom while I took care of business. In a way, it helped that I'd been in the military because I had no qualms about the lack of privacy. Tre kept asking questions and I finally had to tell him to leave me be while I brushed my teeth.

"But did you get them digits?"

I smiled. "She texted her number to me. I get the feeling that's against regulations, but then she said she could help me with resources, you know, for when I get out."

"She's resourceful, huh? Sounds like you're all set."

"A-ffirm. Now, help me get my ass back in bed. Brushing my damn teeth should not be this hard."

I'd had plenty of conversations with Tre about how grateful I was that my hands and arms were spared. They shook like those quaking aspen trees and they felt weak a lot of the time, but they hadn't let me down yet.

"All right, into bed with you, Staff Sergeant. May you dream of jumping out of airplanes into pillowy soft pools of cotton candy and marshmallows."

"Aw, man, now I'm hungry."

"Sleep tight, D."

"Thanks, man."

He ruffled my hair before turning the light out and shutting the door.

For the first night since my accident, my mind was full of happy thoughts, not flashes of the accident, not bitterness over being a casualty of 2020. I had a little Joy in my life, and a smile on my face.

"Home, Sweet Home."

Uncle Red pulled his truck to a halt in front of my place and patted me on the knee.

"Let's get you inside."

Red had been a hero of mine since the first time he took me fishing and taught me how to clean a fish. My mother's younger brother, he'd stood by my side through all of my big moments: when I came out, when I decided to join the Army, all of my promotions and achievements...and now he was here to help me through what was likely to be my hardest transition. With Mom gone, he was all the family I had, and he made up for it whenever he could.

"Thanks for doing all this," I said, feeling braver than I thought I would.

"It ain't much of a sacrifice. Your place is closer to work, and you got better internet."

I snorted. "I knew you had ulterior motives."

He cackled as he got out and came around to my side. He pulled my wheelchair out of the bed of his ancient F-150 and set it up, adjusting his mask before helping me out and into my chair. His work truck had several masks on the dashboard wrapped in plastic and he had a jug of hand sanitizer in the cupholder. I appreciated that he was trying to be safe. He'd been COVID tested a couple days before he brought me home and I was given a rapid test before I left the hospital. As soon as he had his results, we could get rid of the damn masks.

"Probably be easier to use your car when we go places, but I wasn't sure if your chair would fit in the trunk."

I'd opted for a manual chair that folded and was light enough that I'd be able to lift it when I was healed a bit more. I hoped once my ankle was better and I was stronger, I'd be able to walk. Some. Doctors said I likely could get back most of my mobility, but not all.

Red took a few minutes to figure the chair out. I let him fuss with it, grateful he was here to help me. It hadn't been too hard to encourage him to move out of his buddy's place and in with me. He was ten years older than my twenty-eight and more like an older brother, really. His Army service had also been cut short by an injury, and he'd struggled to assimilate back into civilian life. We got along great, and I thought perhaps we could be there for each other now. Helping me gave him a purpose. A mission. And he did great with a purpose.

He pushed me up the walk and then had to turn the chair backwards to get me up the four front steps.

"I wanted to talk to you about the ramp before I just went ahead and built it. There are a couple ways we could go with it."

"Let's make a plan. I've got willing participants to come over when you're ready."

And this was where my stupid smile wouldn't go away.

"Do you now? Well, alright. Hot damn, we'll make us a plan."

My phone buzzed as Red was pulling me in the door.

"You keep smiling down at that phone and I'm gonna have to ask questions."

"It's Joy. Remember I told you about that chick from the campaign?"

He grunted. "The liberal?"

"Yes, Red. The left-leaning, progressive Democrat from the great state of Nevada, now living in Atlanta, who is trying to save our republic one vote at a time."

"Yeah, well, don't matter who's in office, we still get screwed."

He wasn't too far off. Veterans like him weren't always given the best care. Veterans like me, too, now I supposed. I knew I'd have to get real good at advocating for myself.

Sure. Once I learned how to get around in my own house.

"I went ahead and widened the doorway to your bathroom. It still needs finishing and I'm gonna paint in there once we figure out about your shower."

Ugh. The ins and outs of retrofitting the house were overwhelming. The whole situation made me want to get in bed and stay there.

My phone buzzed again.

One thing at a time, darlin,' just like we talked about.

Joy. My own personal light. She'd called me in the hospital, actually made me laugh, and then broke the rules by giving me her number. I'd waited all of twelve hours to text her and was delighted when she answered right away. We'd traded texts off and on each day since, and if I was being honest, I was a little smitten with her. I had questions, though.

Was she just being nice?

Was she into me?

Did she pity me?

Could she handle hanging out with a disabled person and all that it entailed?

I'd always been a keen observer of human behavior and I knew there were folks in my life that were uncomfortable. That was putting it mildly.

My best friend Maury hadn't come to the rehab place for a few weeks and when he finally showed up with his girlfriend, he was drunk. He tearfully told me he was afraid he couldn't handle it. He knew he was being stupid, and I did my best not to confirm that with him.

He more than made it up to me, however. He organized our friends from the base to come out New Year's Day to build me a ramp. Uncle Red and I had come up with a plan. Maury and the gang were going to execute that plan.

And Joy was coming to help supervise.

I was terrified. And elated.

What would it be like to see her in person? I'd never been one for internet dating so the idea of getting to know someone intimately like Joy and I were doing, sight unseen, was odd. But I couldn't help myself. I kept my damn phone near me all the time waiting for messages like this:

I bet jumping out of a plane feels like having an orgasm.

I think survival skills are sexy.

I know you're good with your hands, Soldier, 'cause you've already got me tied in knots.

She even sent me pictures. She made me grateful for our democracy. I know that's a stretch, but if we didn't live in a country where people called each other to ask them to vote, I never would have connected with this woman who made me want to get out of bed in the morning and better myself.

And I was about to meet her in person.

New Year's Day arrived and with it a herd of Neanderthals...and a little Joy.

She was little, too. Petite, I guess you would call it. I wasn't huge, pre-injury I stood five-seven and about 130 pounds, but Joy was maybe five feet tall including her thick-soled shoes. She showed up in pants that were floods, platform Converse high-tops, and an oversized top that was cut to show her midriff. Her long black hair was twisted up in buns on either side of her head and her smile was infectious. She'd told me she'd been tested for COVID and quarantined so she could be with us today, and I was damn grateful to finally meet her in the flesh.

"Hey," she said as she hopped out of a truck and came running. She slowed to a stop in front of my chair and bent over to kiss me on the cheek. "Wait, you are Dylan, right? Oh my god."

I took her hand and gave it a squeeze. "I'm glad you came."

She shrugged and looked around at my gathered troops. "Hi! I'm Joy!"

"I'm happiness," Maury said, and Trent socked him in the arm.

"Don't be a dick. Remember? Good behavior."

"Oh, it's totally okay. I love a good play on words."

She looked down at me and gave me an exaggerated wink. I laughed louder than was called for.

"Now, I make you laugh. Good thing, I forgot my banana peel."

"Nice to meet you," Uncle Red said, approaching cautiously as though Joy and her liberal energy were going to bite him.

"Joy, this is Uncle Red."

Joy shook his hand a little harder than he was expecting. She pulled it up and down in an exaggerated fashion. Either she really was this enthusiastic or she was nervous. Didn't matter to me, which was true, just that she was here.

"Dylan told me so much about you. She said you were stationed at Fort Wainwright in Alaska? My father was there during his service."

Uncle Red cocked his head. "Yes, ma'am. About ten years ago."

"Is it true you were chased by a polar bear?"

Uncle Red rolled his eyes at me and shook his head. "It was a grizzly and yeah. Got too close to her cubs."

"Wow," Joy said. "I don't know what's scarier, that or jumping out of an airplane."

"Definitely the bear," he said with a nod.

"Okay! Where do we start?"

I for one was going to have to start by chilling out. I was way too pleased that she was trying with my uncle. I was starting to have feelings I wasn't sure I should be having. The therapist at the hospital told me I shouldn't make any major changes in my life right now, like getting involved with someone.

But when Joy smiled at me, I knew resistance was futile.

Three hours later, the guys had a good frame built for the ramp and I was sitting watching Joy paint the now-finished wall of my bathroom. She had more paint on her than on the wall, and wasn't that just adorable?

"These old houses were definitely built for small people," she was saying. "When my parents split and my mom remarried, we moved into a house like this. My stepbrothers were constantly running into the walls. But that may be a teenaged boy thing, you think?"

"Hmmm." I loved hearing her voice, but I'd had a big day already and was having a hard time staying awake.

"You okay? Want to lay down for a bit?"

"Yeah, I probably should. Can you grab my uncle?"

She paused and then said, "Sure. Be right back." She didn't seem to feel sorry for me, but it was definitely an awkward moment. I'd told her I tried to do things on my own as much as possible and that asking for help was weird. Now that she was here, though, it was a whole different situation and I hated to seem weak around her as much as I hated her thinking I couldn't do things on my own.

Red came in a few beats later.

"You need something?"

"Yeah, I need to rest I think."

I'd really pushed myself too hard. Everything was sore and my hands and arms were really shaking.

Red took one look at me and nodded.

"You mind giving us a minute?" he asked Joy.

Her eyes widened and I wanted to tell him it was okay, but I really didn't want her to see me have a meltdown or pass out, which I'd done a couple of times. Sometimes I didn't know when to quit, or didn't want to.

"I'll just go see if they need anything out front."

I hated to throw her to the wolves, but I was fading fast.

"You need the bathroom?"

I nodded and Red took over. He could tell I was wrecked, and he'd been so good about not giving me a hard time. The best part was that it wasn't awkward. He knew what I needed, and we made a good team. I was grateful for him, and I told him as much on a regular basis. When he got me to my bed, he made sure I had my phone next to me.

"Text me if you need anything. Take a nap."

"Be nice to her," I said before my eyelids refused to remain open one more second.

———

Joy

Dylan was even more gorgeous in person than her voice led me to believe.

Her skin was pale, likely from the weeks she'd spent in the hospital. She had short, dark blonde hair that was combed back almost in a pompadour and deep-set blue eyes that crinkled at the corners when she smiled just for me. She took off her sweatshirt when we got inside and underneath, she had on a t-shirt with the sleeves cut off. Her arms were so cut and strong... What would it be like to be held by her?

Dylan was so tired by the afternoon; it was tough to see her trying to be strong when she clearly needed a rest, but we'd discussed it before. I'd had the forethought to ask her how she wanted to handle when she needed help, like did she want me to ask, did she want to tell me, and she agreed she would tell me. I knew she was comfortable with her uncle, but it stung a bit that she asked for him when I was right there and more than willing.

I needed to get over myself. As much as I was a fixer and an easer, I had to let it be on her terms or this whatever we were doing would never work.

"What *are* you doing?" my brother had asked me the day before when I told him I was going.

"I don't know. I like her. We're getting to know each other. Why? What's wrong with that?"

"Nothing, I just don't know if you realize what you're getting yourself into."

"What? How can you say that? Because she's in a wheelchair?"

"No, dumbass, because she's just had the rug yanked out from under her and she's going to be struggling for a while. It's tough when your whole life changes in a second and there's nothing you can do about it."

My brother spoke from experience. He'd been in college, in the ROTC program and playing football when a knee injury sidelined both potential careers. He didn't take it well. Lost his girlfriend, nearly lost his license, and lost a whole year to drinking before he finally sought help. He had a great life now, but things had been dark.

"I'll be careful."

"I'm just saying, she may not be ready for any sort of relationship, and I know how you get. All-in Mulligan."

"Shut up." But I knew he was right. I often dove into relationships headfirst without measuring the depths, and I knew the landing would be unpredictable with Dylan.

But sitting here on her front porch with her uncle and three friends from Fort Benning, I thought just maybe I could fit into her life. Somehow.

"National Guard is at the ready for things to go sideways next week," the one called Deacon said. "Don't know why people can't just vote and be done with it. All these protests ain't gonna change anything."

Trent tried to shush him and looked between us to make his point.

"I hope there aren't any problems," I said, finishing my bottle of water. "They're hoping enough people voted by mail and voted early that the polls should be fairly calm. We don't know what the turnout is going to actually be."

"Yeah, well, it's not like it matters who wins anyway," Red said.

"Why do you say that?"

Whether I was curious or had a death wish, I probably should have kept my mouth shut.

The guys looked at each other as if to see who was going to answer the curious one.

"Cuz it's not like any of them really give a shit about anything other than staying in power. They make all these promises and then when it comes to delivering, they spend more time covering their asses than actually doing what their constituents need."

Normally I'd whip out my trusty data and tell them exactly what Warren Johnson had accomplished at the state level and what he planned to do if he was elected to represent Georgia in Congress, but these were Dylan's people, and they were important to her. I didn't want to cause any problems.

"And all they want to do is cut funding for the military and use it to fund abortions and government handouts instead of the defense of our country—"

"Deacon, come on, man," Maury said, nudging him with his beer. "Let's not—"

"It's okay," I said. "I get it, military funding is a big issue, especially when our current national leaders have been wavering back and forth on troop withdrawals and other issues that affect all of you. With such a big military presence here, it's important that whoever we elect has your best interests front and center."

"Right," Deacon said, but he frowned. He knew I hadn't agreed with him, but he couldn't exactly argue with what I'd said.

"Yeah, well, no one gives a shit about veterans neither," Uncle Red said as he took a deep pull on his beer bottle. "Once we're of no use anymore, they throw us away like trash."

"I'm hopeful that a stronger Veteran's Affairs department will mean more support for veterans on the national level, and here in Georgia—"

Red stood up and walked in the house without saying anything.

Oh, shit, Joy. Too much.

"I'm sorry," I said, wiping my mouth with a napkin. I'd ordered pizzas for everyone, and we were just finishing up. My stomach was sour now and I thought I should probably leave before my stupid mouth got me in more trouble.

"Don't mind him," Maury said, grabbing another slice. "He's worried about Dylan is all."

"I know," I said. *Me too.* "He's good to her. I'm glad she has him."

An hour later, Maury went inside to check on Dylan. When he came back, he shook his head. "She did too much. Red's in there helping her stretch out."

"Oh, poor thing. Is there anything I can do?"

Maury put a hand on my shoulder and walked me toward my truck. "Keep making her smile," he said. "Give her some space to figure things out. I'll let her know you said goodbye."

I hated leaving without seeing her, but I knew I'd make her uncomfortable and it seemed I'd outworn my welcome.

"Thank you. It was great to meet you guys."

Trent and Deacon waved, and Maury shook my hand.

"And keep on doing what you're doing. I know these assholes are pretty crusty when it comes to politics, but we need change in this damn country. I'm tired of being worried about my younger brothers out there driving while Black, you know? And these motherfuckers really tryna keep us from voting. Ain't that a bitch."

I elbowed him gently. "We're not going to let them. I will keep fighting to make sure everyone in Georgia, and our country for that matter, who wants to vote *can* vote. It's the only way to make the changes we need happen."

He winked at me. "You're just a little bit, but you got fire. I like it. I'm glad you came. We could all use a little Joy I guess."

"At your service." I clicked my heels together and saluted, then felt like a moron.

"At ease," he said. "Drive safe. I'll have Dylan check in with you later."

"Thank you," I said. I climbed in my truck and drove the half hour back to my house on the other side of Atlanta feeling a few degrees above despondent and several below hopeful.

How did I navigate this situation when Dylan had so much going on? Maybe my brother was right. Maybe hoping for some kind of relationship with someone whose life was in chaos was selfish and unrealistic. Only time would tell.

ACT THREE

Election Day.

The runoff today would determine if we continued to have a Republican-controlled Senate, or if perhaps we could finally break the logjam in Congress and start getting some relief to the people.

We'd done everything humanly possible to get the largest amount of votes in to decide. All eyes in the country were focused on our little state and the monumental decision about to be made.

All we could do was wait.

I had another two weeks off of school, but my internship on the campaign kept me extra busy in the days leading up to this momentous day. I staffed the phones to support the poll workers in case they needed anything and watched the news while obsessively checking my Twitter feed.

And my texts.

Looking for any contact from Dylan.

She'd never texted me after I left her house. I messaged her when I got home and told her how happy I was that I got to meet her and that I hoped she got some rest. The next day I messaged her again and all I got was a "thanks for your help. I'll talk to you soon."

That was it.

The radio silence was deafening.

Luckily, I had enough work to do to keep ten interns busy, but I couldn't stop thinking of her. Finally, this morning I sent her one last message:

I'm hoping you're feeling okay and enjoying your new ramp. The guys did a beautiful job. I know you said you would tell me what you needed, but since I haven't heard from you, I'm going to assume what you need is space. Maybe that makes an ass of me, I don't know. All that matters is you are okay and have what you need. If you decide you need a little Joy, I'm a phone call away.

Things went smoothly the rest of the day and with nothing else to do but wait, I went over two blocks to the Hard Rock Cafe with the rest of the staff to watch the returns and eat all of the food—socially distanced in a private room Karen had reserved for us. We debated whether to have dinner or dessert and opted for both, stress eating at its finest.

I was finishing my fries and about to start in on my chocolate shake, which was big enough for three people, when my phone buzzed.

How's it going so far?

I had to look twice before believing the screen said "Dylan."

I ate all my fries, a burger as big as my head, a side salad, and some other appetizer that I can't even remember and now I'm about to down a massive chocolate shake. It may not be enough.

I held my breath for her response. I had no idea what to say to her. Anything that came out of my fingers would likely convince her I was truly a mess, or I'd make a fool of myself groveling.

Red brought me to the poll to vote. We're still in town.

My heart pounded so hard I thought I might lose my burger.

I'm so glad you were feeling up to it. Are you okay?

"What the hell is going on with you?" Karen asked. "You look like you've got brain freeze and indigestion and you just lost a contact."
    I realized I was blinking my eyes like crazy to keep from crying.
    "She made it."
    "She made it? She got to vote? Hallelujah!"
    Of course, I'd told her everything and the staff had been on the edge of their seats waiting to hear what happened with my Ranger.
    "Where is she? You've got to go to her."

No I'm not okay.

"Wait! Shh! I can't think and text."
    "There's a surprise," Karen said.

What's wrong? Are you okay?

I gripped my phone so hard in both hands I got a cramp, and when I went to shake it out, I knocked my mostly empty milkshake tin over and drenched Karen's fries in chocolate.
    "Mmm, I haven't had shake and fries together since I was a kid," she said sarcastically, and proceeded to eat them as the staff squealed "ew!"

I need a little Joy in my life.

"Oh my god." I stood up from the table so fast I knocked my chair over backwards, feeling the need to go...somewhere. I had no idea where.

Suddenly the restaurant erupted in song as a large group began singing and dancing to "Celebration" by Kool and the Gang. It was so loud I couldn't hear my phone, only feel the vibration in my hand as it started to ring. I ran outside, dodging dancing servers and hearing my friends shout after me. I kept going until I was out of the chaos and then I hit answer.

"Hey! Are you there?"

"You sound out of breath. Are you okay? Is there trouble?"

"No," I said and then I really had to stop and breathe. I bent at the waist and made a mental note to start doing my cardio now that the election was nearly over. "I ran out of the restaurant. Are you okay?"

"Yeah," she said with a laugh. "I was going to try to find you, or see if you wanted to meet, but they've got streets blocked off around downtown."

"Oh, you're right, they do."

Police cars had some of the streets closed, but there weren't many folks out and about, no more than usual.

"It's so good to hear your voice," I said. I wanted to tell her I missed her, but I held back. I wanted to give her space.

"You too, and I'm sorry I didn't call. I was...New Year's Day wasn't a good look for me, and I hated that I didn't pace myself. I just didn't want to miss any time with you, and then when I woke up and you were gone..."

"I'm afraid I didn't make too good an impression on your friends."

"Not true. Red loves you and Maury thinks the Army was stupid to not take you. They just don't have manners."

"No, they were perfect gentlemen," I said in a fit of giggles.

"Hardly. Those guys wouldn't know how to be gentlemen if they were hit over the head with an etiquette manual."

My obnoxiously loud laugh caught the attention of one of the police officers. I waved and he frowned. I needed to get off the street.

"Where are you? I want to see you...I mean, if you feel up to it."

"You better believe it. We're near Centennial Park."

"I'll be right there."

I took off at a fast walk up Baker Street, pulling my coat tighter around myself to ward off the cold, but I was soon out of breath. Stupid heart. Stupid out of shape body! It took me longer than I'd hoped, and my feet were numb by the time I crossed Park Avenue. I saw the truck that had been parked at Dylan's house pulled over to the side of the road. As I approached, Dylan's smiling face appeared in the passenger window. She rolled it down and rested her left hand on the window sill. I quickly used some hand sanitizer then grabbed it and squeezed, hopefully not too hard for my level of excitement.

"I found you!" I sounded like I'd just run a marathon after smoking three packs of cigarettes.

"You did find me." Her smile was shy, which threw me because she was so strong, so incredible.

"I'm so happy you're here," I said, letting go of her hand. I used it to tuck my hair behind my ear and adjust my mask, playing off how badly I was crushing on her. I thought I'd never see her again, and here she was. And she'd sought me out.

"We can't stay parked here," Uncle Red said.

Dylan turned and said something in a frustrated tone that I couldn't quite make out.

"I'm sorry, geez," Red protested. "It's not like I got a pair of tits to flash, Dylan. I don't want to get a ticket."

"Hey, Red," I said, leaning down so I could see him. I waved and he waved back while continuing to grumble.

"You've gotta be tired. I don't want to keep you, although my tits have gotten me out of tickets before."

Red snorted and Dylan cracked up.

It was so good to hear her laugh.

"Are you still working?"

I nodded. "In a loose definition of work. I get paid in pizza and cold coffee and 'valuable experience.' But I should go back to the office and help close up. We've gotta pack up starting tomorrow and get ready for whatever comes next."

"Any idea what that will be?"

I shrugged. "For me? Finishing school in June and finding a job working for the Man."

I'd told her previously that I hoped to be in DC eventually, but there was plenty of experience I could get at the state level first.

"The Man sucks," Red said, then spit tobacco into an empty can. "Glad I don't work for him anymore."

"He kicked your ass then kicked you out, old man." Dylan laughed at her own joke.

"That's right."

"And that, Red, is exactly why I want to keep fighting."

"I respect that about you," Dylan said loud enough for Red to get the point.

He grunted. "Guess someone has to."

It was a small victory, but I'd take it.

"Well, I thought maybe if you had time in between elections and political battles, you might want to, like, hang out."

I looked down at my Apple Watch and saw that I had a gazillion texts from my co-workers.

"Hang on," I said. I knew it was a shitty thing to say in that moment, but I wanted to be sure these were "atta girl" messages and not "get your ass back to the office" texts. They let me know they'd send the results as soon as they had them, but it would likely be a couple of days.

"Looks like I've got some time in between battles."

"Great. That's good, right?"

I was so glad I wasn't the only awkward one. We grinned like loonies at each other until Red cleared his throat.

"Oh, um, so—"

"Is this a good time?" I asked as I peeked in the window. "Got room for one more?"

"Yeah. Yes. Sure, uh—"

"Let me move your chair to the bed." Red groaned as he climbed out of the truck. He mumbled under his breath as he reached into the king cab and struggled with Dylan's chair. Self-preservation told me not to ask if he needed help.

"Look, I'm sorry—"

"You needed space. You'll need it again. I'm a big girl. I'll have to learn not to try to fix everything with my endless resources and ideas."

"And I gotta take naps."

"I like naps. I think our country would be a better place if nap time was a common practice. It'll be part of my platform in case I ever run for office."

"You'd be great." She reached for my hand again and pulled me closer. "You *are* great."

"*You're* great," I said back to her.

"This is me wanting to kiss you, which I intend to do when it's safe. Remember this face because there's gonna be times when I will be nervous and not ask. And since I can't exactly dip you in my arms like the movies, I need you to recognize this face." She made a circle with her finger while pointing at herself and she could not have been braver if she was standing on the ledge of a plane ready to jump into battle.

I stepped back and pulled my mask down. "Well, this is my face wanting to kiss your face," I said making the same circle.

"Would you get in the car already? The damn cops just made a U-turn up ahead. They're probably coming back here so get on with it and then anyone riding in this truck better buckle up." He put the car in gear and looked around for the cops.

"I—it's okay? You sure?"

"If you don't mind sitting on the other end of the couch at my place."

"And I can grab a shower when we get there if you've got something I can change into." *Stupid virus. This was not how I hoped to spend our first alone time together.* I was so going to get tested again and quarantine so I could be closer to her. And with masks off. Because I wanted to kiss her.

"Perfect," she said. "Hop in."

I climbed in behind her and put on my seatbelt as Red made the truck lurch away from the curb. Dylan smacked him and reached for the oh shit handle.

"Slow and easy, sergeant," she said in that cool and collected voice of hers.

"Yeah yeah yeah."

I texted Karen to say I'd met up with Dylan and her uncle. She let me know she was rooting for me. Especially because the campaign staff made a wager when I ran out that I wouldn't be back.

I'll see you at the office tomorrow.

Her response was super quick.

You have more important work to do right now. Take the day off. I've got other grunts who can pack.

Her text ended with a winky face emoji.

I reached up and squeezed Dylan's shoulder and she covered my hand with hers.

I did have more important work tonight and there was no place I'd rather be.

Even if it meant listening to Red's country music on the way back. And his singing. And his constant digs at liberals, which I knew were for my benefit as he'd always glance back at me and smirk.

Oh, this was going to be fun.

My phone buzzed again, and I thought it was Karen with more emojis, but Dylan's name popped up.

Thanks for bringing a little Joy into my life.

I laughed, which caused Red to turn around. "Something funny?"

"No, sorry. Please, keep singing."

"Damn right, I'll keep singing."

Told you, Joy is just a phone call away. And in your backseat. And wherever you need Joy to be.

"Are you seriously texting her in the same damn car?" Red grumbled.

"Keep your eyes on the road."

Thanks, Joy. I'm so glad you're here.

And I was full to the brim with my namesake emotion. I checked the early returns and our numbers on my phone and things looked great. I was about to spend some quality time with an incredible woman who wanted to spend time with me, and wasn't that a perfect way to celebrate?

My little catchphrase was true. Sometimes joy *was* just a phone call away, and Dylan was my joy in an unreal time.

The End...

Acknowledgments

This short story is my way of saying thank you to all of my friends and family who wrote letters and made calls to help support voters all over the country. To Stacy Finz and Alice Gaines, thank you for sharing your experiences with me. Thank you to the Romancing the Runoff folks for raising $470,000 to help with the Georgia run-off election support. And to the creator of this anthology, Adrienne Bell, thank you so much for sparking the idea. I'm grateful to have such brilliant friends who were willing to get on board to support our democracy and right to vote.

I also want to say a heartfelt thank you to those who must overcome huge obstacles to make it to the polling place. Let's remember it's not a matter of hopping in a car and driving down the street to the polling place for some. Many folks have to take busses, paratransit, taxis, etc. and need assistance to walk or roll in and cast their ballot. The stories of folks being wheeled out of nursing homes so they could sign their ballots inspired me to do my part. It's exhausting and it's stressful under normal conditions, but this year especially, differently abled folks have had extra challenges.

Lastly, to the members of our military. Thank you for your service and sacrifice. Thank you for going above and beyond to protect the rights we share, most importantly, the right to make our voices heard and to make our mark at the polling place.

Let Me Stand Next To Your Fire

$$\textit{Let Me Stand Next To}$$
$$\textit{Your Fire}$$

ACT ONE

She sits on a lounge chair in front of the bright orange glow. Watching the reflection of the flames in her eyes is like viewing an old twenty-millimeter film as it flickers and dances. I've often said that she could never be more picturesque than at this very moment and been proven wrong time and again. She's swimming in an old wool sweater with a giant cowl neck, and as I watch the soft material brush against her neck as she talks, I swear I'm going to combust.

Lena is my best friend.

She is the most beautiful woman I've ever seen.

And I'm hopelessly in love with her, and she doesn't have a clue.

I slide my chair a little closer to take advantage of the hand she has dangling, palm up, extended from the armrest. She might be trying to make a point in our conversation, but I can't draw my eyes away from her, nor cease my internal debate over whether or not her hand's position is a potential invitation.

"All I'm saying is maybe we should just go." She smooths her satiny black hair with her other hand and then stretches her pink sweatpants-clad legs out, her bare feet illuminated by the fire. Her outfit doesn't match in any sort of way, but then she doesn't care. Lena wears what's comfortable. Period. She had a pedicure today and hasn't chipped it yet, which she'll consider a win. I've never seen anything as touchable as her toes.

"Things are so crazy at my company. You hate your job," she continues. "We could be like that one movie where the women run away together."

"*Thelma and Louise?* You haven't killed anyone lately, have you?" I always distract her with humor when she talks like this.

Doing a geographic sounds nice, but we've always been realists. We make plans and stick to them. We've always been the room moms and the sports team volunteers for the kids. We were dutiful wives and mothers, and now it's just us. Although, I have to admit what she's describing sounds like a dream come true.

"What are you talking about?" She turns, and the curve of her bottom lip glistens in the firelight. Maybe she's just taken a sip of her water. Maybe she ran her lovely pink tongue over it.

Here, in the darkness, I can stare a bit more freely than I normally would. I fantasize about those lips. I've watched them move for years, but how would they feel? What would she say if I pressed my own against them?

"Remember? They went on the run because one of them killed her mans."

And then she laughs.

It slays me.

She inhales, and as she forces sound from her lovely chest, it creates the spark that sets off the wildfire inside of me. The flames catch every flammable substance in their path until they are consumed and the fire, like me, is desperate for more oxygen.

"That's right. I haven't killed anyone, sorry. Can we still go?"

She rests her chin on her right shoulder and looks up at me with those soulful brown eyes as dark as this March night. It's the Spring Equinox, the start of a new season, and I can't help but wonder if maybe…

Could there be a start of something new for us, too?

I want to give her everything she asks for. I can't maintain this charade any longer. I can't breathe.

The fingers on her inviting hand twitch again, and I'm helpless.

I know her hands are warm and soft, so soft. She's touched me with those fingers many times before. Braided my hair when it was longer, applied my makeup with a steadier hand than I ever could, and zipped up a stubborn dress while protecting my delicate skin with her hand on my back. Those actions, so innocent, and yet they've fueled my wonderings for all this time. Does she know how my ridiculous heart has held onto those moments? How those brushes with intimacy fed my soul for so many years?

How do I tell her I've longed for her for what feels like a lifetime? Since we had drama together in seventh grade? Since we got drunk on the elementary school playground in the dead of night as teenagers and avoided getting caught? Spent hours fighting over unworthy boys? Since we cried over the phone while thousands of miles away in college? And after moving back to our hometown with our husbands, we raised our children as neighbors…

All of this adds up to the realization that I've been in love with Lena since we were thirteen years old. Back then, I thought the intensity of my love for her was because she was my best friend. She'd stood by my side when everyone else laughed at my latest clumsy move, lack of social graces, and absent fashion sense. I was a hopeless mess facing a world of unforgiving peers while struggling with my mother's mental illness, but Lena never cared about trivial shit. She cared about me. In return for her loyal friendship, I listened to hours of tearful protests over her issues with her parents. They weren't happy with her "life choices." At thirteen. Who makes life choices at thirteen? We made "the next five minutes" choices at that age. When we became parents and our own kids hit that age, we totally laughed at how ridiculous we'd been back then and how unrealistic our parents were.

Lena has been my "ride or die" since then. But somewhere along the way, I realized that the hours we spent lightly scratching each other's backs in bed on countless sleepovers was more than just soothing each other. For me, at least. I'd memorized the topography of her body; the cut of her shoulder blades, the slight curve of her spine from scoliosis, and the scars from the acne she tried so hard to hide that made her self-conscious but were perfect in my eyes. Every bit of her was beautiful to me and, I touched her with as much reverence now as I did then.

She'd figured out that she was queer before I even had a clue about myself. *Always the late bloomer, Dani.* After her cheating husband left her, she opened herself to all possibilities and dated frequently. Watching her live her life out loud and seeing her kids root her on pushed me toward my own realization.

I loved my husband Tucker desperately and still mourned his death from cancer two years ago when we were both forty-five. It was so unfair. Our kids had just finished high school. We should have had more time together. We had plans.

Lena loved him, too. They were football buddies, shouting at the TV in tandem while I chased the kids around them. They ogled women together when the three of us went out for dinner and fought over which one of them would have the best chance at scoring. When he died, Lena held me through my tears and helped me take care of the business of being a widow. Along the way, I had an epiphany.

I'd absolutely loved Tucker with my whole being. I was sexually attracted to him. He was my best friend.

And I felt the same way about Lena, even though we'd never crossed that line of intimacy.

Oh, how I want to cross it.

Now that we're fading into middle age, our bodies have begun withering subtly with each passing day. Lena had a breast cancer scare last year and is under a doctor's care for brutal arthritis. I'm looking at a medically necessary hysterectomy soon. We watch our children live their lives to extremes, usually making good decisions like we taught them. Life choices. My Casey married his sweetheart right out of college, and my Beth shares a house with Lena's Andre and Arabella while the three of them navigate graduate school and big, important careers. Lena and I talk all the time about how proud we are of what they've accomplished and pat each other on the back for being great moms.

But what now? I work for the corporate offices of a grocery chain and write cozy mysteries on the side. Lena's a CPA and dreams of running a bustling tax business out of her home that will keep her comfortable throughout the year. Do we keep doing these things until we can't anymore and then die? In separate households mere doors away from each other? Or could we actually run away? Live a different kind of life in a different sort of relationship?

I wish for the rest of our days to be spent wrapped around each other like a warm sweater, protecting us from the harsh realities of aging. I want all of our nights to be like this one. The two of us gazing at the sparks from the fire traveling from the flames in the metal pit up toward the sky to dance with the stars.

I finally take the bait and slide my fingers against her palm, lacing them with hers. It's not that unusual for us to hold hands. It's the safest way for me to pretend we're more than lifelong friends.

"We *could* run away," I say, afraid to sound too hopeful. "Or we could just stay right here by the fire."

My heart throbs as the minutes pass, and she doesn't move her hand. She merely breathes in and out, her chest rising and falling, a thoughtful smile playing on those lips.

"It *is* a beautiful night. And I love the fire."

I love you.

I wish I could say the words and she would understand.

"Yeah. I'm digging this fire pit," I say instead. "All we need is marshmallows and some sticks."

"I don't need anything else," she says. And then she squeezes my hand.

*I don't need any*one *else.*

I wonder how much longer I can keep holding her hand before she pulls it away. What is the appropriate amount of time for a friendly clasp of hands? Is it just until the other acknowledges their affection with a slight squeeze? Then do you count to three and let go?

Or is it go on three?

A chuckle slips out as I think of the ridiculous scene from *Lethal Weapon,* and I use the distraction to let go, but as our fingers slide apart, she fumbles. She grasps for mine in a firmer hold. Then adds a second hand, which means she's now facing me.

"Can I say something?"

"You can say anything."

She hates it when I answer like that. It's usually followed by the juvenile *"it's a free country."*

But this time I don't respond like a brat. I've been feeling a sense of urgency lately, and it makes me bold, so when she rolls her eyes, I answer, "I'm listening."

She exhales as though she's about to make a confession. I know this as I've been on the receiving end so many times. Her deepest darkest secrets, fears, loves, joys… And I've rewarded her by keeping a big secret from her. How's that for a shitty best friend? I often wonder if she would view my omission as a betrayal. Keeping my true feelings from her could be a mistake. But the consequences would be too much for me to take if she doesn't reciprocate.

"Okay, I don't really want to run away, but I want…that. Like, the two of us, together, taking on the world, having adventures. It's always been you and me. I want it that way."

She groans as the words leave her mouth, and I start dancing in my chair and singing, doing my best Backstreet Boys impression.

"I'm sorry," I say, trying to get myself together. The giggles have taken over in a desperate plea to ease the tension in this conversation.

A loud pop from the fire scares us both, and then she's laughing with me. As the hiccups set in, we lay back and gaze at the stars until our breathing is normal again.

And she reaches for my hand, which I'd left palm up, dangling from the armrest.

I think I'm feverish. Did she mean it? Was she saying what I've so desperately wanted to say to *her* for many moonlit starry nights over the decades?

She squeezes gently.

"We could go on quoting silly songs and making movie references all night, or I could quote your stupid favorite line from that stupid testosterone-laden fighter pilot movie."

My mouth runs dry… "Maverick, you big stud?"

She nods slowly. "Take me to bed—"

"Or lose you forever?"

Those lips slide into that smile of hers that always results in her getting her way. The one that she used several hours ago to get me to agree to cook tonight, and to pick up the Ben & Jerry's, and to make her a fire in the backyard.

"Yes. No. I mean the middle part."

"Are you tired?"

She drops my hand and sighs.

I fear I've snuffed the fire out, sucked the necessary oxygen from it in my desperate attempt to protect my heart.

"Dani, are you really going to keep up these evasive maneuvers?"

"I...evasive?"

"You'll joke to get out of dealing with anything. Don't joke with me. Be honest with me."

"What are you asking me?" I turn to face her and fight back the panic threatening to suffocate me.

"Have you ever thought about us?"

I open my mouth fully intending to continue playing dumb. She deserves better than that.

"You mean being intimate?"

She smiles at me and blinks several times. I notice she took off her makeup before coming over. She looks so much like the Lena from high school. Maybe her face is slimmer, more angular, but she's my Lena. I know I can tell her anything, and she'll take it and keep it. She'll protect it. She'll respect it.

"I know you haven't been with a woman," she says, "but you told me once that you thought about it."

I *had* told her that. One night after she'd been on a date she'd come over and we sat outside just like this, minus the fire pit. She told me everything. How different it was having a woman pleasure her, how weird it felt to be the one playing with boobs, and we'd laughed for hours. I can't believe she remembers my confession.

I want to experience that someday.

What I'd left out was that I wanted it to be *her*.

"Are you serious, Lena? Don't play with me."

She rests her elbow on the arm of her chair and grins wickedly.

My heart goes from zero to eighty-five in less than a second.

"Yeah. I want to play with you, but I'm not playing. Come on. Tell me you never thought about us, and I won't bring it up again."

I don't answer her right away. I can't even look at her. I'm terrified. Will she understand how I feel? My hesitation is only because… what if? What if I'm a bad kisser? What if she doesn't find me attractive like that? What if I lose the most important person in my life?

I can't look at her. "I've thought about it. For a long time."

My admission is out there. I can never take it back. It will hang between us no matter what happens next.

"Da-ni." She gives my name the singsong treatment, trying to get me to look at her, and I laugh. I can't ignore her. Ever. She'll pester me, poke me in the arm, pull my hair, whatever it takes to get me to look at her.

Her smile is full of mischief and promise. And yet…

"What about the last part of that line? That's my biggest fear."

She shakes her head. "You're never getting rid of me."

She stands from the lounge chair and pulls me to my feet. Nearly the same height, roughly the same build, definitely both nervous, our hands tremble as we embrace.

This is different from hugging her.

Our hugs have always been full-bodied, bordering on wrestling moves meant to subdue an opponent. One of us would lift the other off our feet, we'd rock back and forth, and the world would always be right.

Tonight, we are drawn to each other, and I make a point to pay attention to every point of contact. Our arms brush first, and then our chests meet next. The rest of our torsos press together—her's fit, mine soft—and our thighs connect. But it's her face, so close to mine, that is my undoing. I rest my forehead on her shoulder, and I shudder, letting the air out of my lungs so I can feel her even closer to me.

"I've waited forever for you." My eyes burn. "I would have continued waiting forever."

Her lips graze my ear. "I was afraid you would *take* forever."

She forces me to look at her, and the excitement flickers in her eyes like the flames dancing beside us.

"I want forever. With you. I want so much."

I brush her hair back from her face, to be certain, to stare into her familiar eyes and see the truth there. My thumbs caress her cheeks, and I let one drift toward those beckoning lips I'm longing for.

"What do you want?" I ask, though I'm getting the hint. She's already slid her hands inside the waistband of my yoga pants and up my back to unfasten my bra.

"Let me stand next to your fire," she whispers, and she takes my thumb into her mouth, biting down just enough to weaken my knees.

My nerves never cease to bring out the songstress in me, and I whisper-sing the Hendrix lyrics.

She silences me with her kiss and my world burns.

Flames consume us both as I finally kiss her, and I'm surprised that it's not awkward. There's no unease. It's just like kissing Tucker, but not. I feel the same warmth fueled by trust, familiarity, and love. I'm vulnerable before her, but she kisses me, and I'm not afraid. It's her but it's *not* her. I'm kissing Lena, but it's a *new* Lena that I have yet to experience, and she's scorching.

"You taste good, like warm honey," she says. "Let's go inside."

"*Inside* inside? Like the bedroom? Lena—"

"I promise we'll only do what you're comfortable with."

A laugh escapes. "I'm not *comfortable* with anything."

She pulls back but I hold her in place.

"Dani?"

"No, wait. This isn't comfortable," I say and my voice lowers.

Now that she's in my arms, it's like the volcano has erupted, and lava flows freely down the mountainside, scorching everything in its path, clearing away the doubts that had cropped up like tiny seedlings since the last eruption.

"This is what it feels like to watch pyrotechnics. It's terrifying and thrilling at the same time, but not comfortable." I slide my hands down her sides and grip her hips tightly. "Front row at Metallica, remember? The fire nearly scorched your fake eyelashes off, and my face was red for days afterward. It was a rush. That's what I mean."

Lena runs her hands up my ribcage and her thumbs graze my breasts. I want more than a graze. I want her to really touch me.

"If you want a rush, take me to bed."

Instead of finishing the quote, I kiss her once more. For luck. For bravery. For reassurance.

She's my Lena and she loves me. Whatever happens when we go inside, she'll always be mine.

"What about the fire?" I ask, always the responsible one. I don't want to be responsible for the neighborhood burning down.

She pulls away and shovels sand over the embers, and then places the cover over it.

It's so dark outside I can't see her face as she approaches me.

"Get your ass inside before we explode," she says as she passes me, and I am done making jokes. I come after her and she squeals as I chase her through my dark house. I'm a fireball hurtling through space and she's, my target. She stops at my bedside and places her hands on my cheeks. "You're so hot, Dani. Come keep me warm."

"Burn, baby, burn."

ACT TWO

I wake up to banging noises and a suffocating feeling I can't ignore.

I suck in a big breath of air and realize my mistake. I'm drowning.

"Are you okay?"

It's Lena.

Well, it's Lena's hair. In my face. Over my face, actually, and probably in my lungs now.

She flicks her mane back and pushes up onto her knees. I cough a few times and she looks worried. Then I grin.

"Good morning."

Her smile is brighter than the sun coming through my bedroom window since I left the drapes open. We'd been in a bit of a hurry last night.

My smile is goofier than, I don't even know. I'm plumb out of descriptive language this morning.

"Hi."

Wow. Apparently, I'm out of most words in the English language.

Lena laughs and straddles my waist.

"Hi."

She's fucking gorgeous and she's all mine. Finally.

The fact that she kisses me again, pre-toothbrushing, leads me to think she enjoyed last night as much as I did.

The fact that she's still naked and kissing her way down my neck, to my breasts, to below that—

"Oh. God. *Lena.*"

Just as I'm able to relax—I'd had the same problem last night—and I'm losing myself in the rhythm of her tongue, I hear banging again.

"What the—"

I hear laughter. Familiar laughter. Feminine familiar laughter.

Oh God.

"Lena."

"Mom?"

Lena stops her, um, activity.

I pull the sheet over her.

Beth knocks on the door twice and comes in without waiting for an answer.

I smile innocently.

"Did I wake you?" Beth asks, confusion on her face.

Lena snorts.

Beth stops just as she's about to plop onto the bed.

We stare at each other.

"Hi," I say, which makes Lena laugh again.

"Mom?"

"Yes?"

Oh. Good. I apparently know another word.

"Did you...is that...am I?"

Lena pulls the sheet off her head, her hair wild, and tucks it around herself as she curls up next to me.

"Yes, we forgot you guys were coming over," she says. "Yes, it's me. And yes, you're interrupting."

I still have the same innocent smile on my face. It's kind of frozen there now, and my cheeks are starting to hurt. If I try to speak, my face will probably crack.

"Hi." I say again, and this time Lena loses it.

"What's going—Mom?"

Andre and Arabella come in behind Beth and now there are three pairs of puzzled eyes peering down at us, astounded.

"Hi." Lena gives her kids a little finger wave and they look at each other.

"Mom, did you forget we were coming for breakfast?" Beth appears to be most preoccupied with the lack of food prepared rather than the fact that she just walked in on her mother having sex with the woman she's considered an aunt her entire life. *That's my girl. Food first.*

"I... maybe? We, um—"

"We were up late last night, so we decided to sleep in." Lena replies matter-of-factly.

"When she says last night, she really means this morning," I say, taking Lena's hand and lacing our fingers together on top of the sheets. "What was it, four? When we finally went to sleep?"

"Mmm hmmm, yep. Four sounds about right. Anyhoo, all the fixins are in the fridge because Dani went to the store yesterday and she cooked me dinner—"

"And I bought you Ben & Jerry's, which was delicious. Good call by the way."

"It *was* a good call. You're welcome."

Lena leans over and kisses me and I'm just so damn happy I could care less that our kids might be about to stroke out over what they just walked in on.

Lena turns with eyebrows raised and looks at Arabella. "You guys can get started on the food and we'll be out in a jiffy. Kay?"

The three kids nod, look at each other with their heads tilted to the side, brows furrowed, and they file out of the room, closing the door behind them.

And we burst out laughing.

"I really did forget," I say, surprised at myself.

"I didn't," Lena said. "We always do brunch with them on the first Saturday of the month."

I snap my fingers. "That's right! Wow. I never forget."

Lena squeezes my hand. "See how easy that was?"

One of the conversations we'd had late into the night had been about how the hell we were going to tell the kids about our change in status.

"For all they know, this could have been going on for a long time," Lena had said with a shrug. The sheet had been draped around her waist, and I'd been a little mesmerized by her swaying breasts, not gonna lie. I'd spent so many years trying not to gaze fondly upon them and now that they were mine to ogle, I quickly lost all focus.

"I guess it could have been."

Lena had scolded me for not talking to her sooner. "I always thought maybe," she'd said. "But I never wanted to push you. I know how much you love Tucker."

"Somehow I think Tucker would be quite pleased with how things turned out," I said to her, shaking my head. "He suggested once that we invite you to move in with us, after what's-his-name left."

"What's-his-name," she said, rolling her eyes. "That might have been fun, but I don't think, as much as Tucker liked to goof off with me, that he would have shared you with anyone."

That was when I'd cried. And just like all the other times I'd needed her, Lena had held me through it all.

"I kept waiting for you to date someone, anyone," she'd said. "Then I would know you were ready. But you're so…"

"Clueless? Stubborn? Lame?"

She'd shushed me and kissed my tears away. "No, silly. You needed time. I wanted to give it to you, but it's been hard."

"Thank you," I'd whispered, snuggling up against her. Our legs were entwined, and she kept tickling me with her toes, laughing when I'd jump. "Thank you for waiting for me."

"You are so worth the wait."

ACT THREE

"So now what?"

We'd taken a leisurely shower and dressed after being so rudely—and terrifyingly? Embarrassingly?—interrupted by our progeny. I'm still not sure how I feel about the events of this morning, but Lena takes it all as if it were perfectly natural. It's one of her qualities I've always admired the most, her unshakeable confidence, her steady calm. It's hypnotic watching her go through life as though everything is just as it should be. Even when she had her cancer scare, she'd faced it like, "Okay, what happens next?"; whereas I was freaking out and doing my best not to show fear. I should know by now that she will always be strong enough for the both of us.

Apparently, we'd taken just the right amount of time. Arabella and Beth had fixed all the breakfast treats and were still grumbling about having to cook when they'd come expecting to freeload.

"Andre's doing his laundry at home," Arabella says as we join them. "He said he'd be here in time to do the pancakes."

"Excellent," I say, popping a piece of bacon into my mouth. "Mmmm almost as good as mine."

"Hmph," Beth grunts. "Would have been better if it was waiting for me when I got here."

I grab her in a hug and squeeze her tight.

She squeezes me back tighter.

"Thanks, babe," I whisper in her ear.

"Are you happy, Mom?" She whispers back.

"Ridiculously."

We separate and she starts whisking the eggs.

The door opens and Andre waltzes in followed by the fourth and final member of the peanut gallery.

"Surprise!" Casey scoops me up and gives me a big hug, a shit-eating grin on his face. Since he was definitely my not-so-mini-me, I imagine he looks much like I looked a short time ago when his sister and best friends caught me in bed naked with *my* best friend.

"I didn't think you were coming," I say, but I'm thrilled.

"Georgia's spending the day with her mom, and once I got Andre's text, there was no way I was missing breakfast."

Ah. Conspiracy.

"Now that we're all here," Arabella says, hopping her butt up onto my counter. "We have some questions."

"You haven't made detective yet," Andre says, teasing his sister, our rookie police officer.

"It's okay," I say. "You're all entitled to some answers."

Lena chuckles as she pours herself some coffee. "Entitled is right."

Andre hip bumps her and she nearly spills her coffee.

"Guys! This is serious," Arabella says.

"Go ahead." I cross my arms over my chest, preparing for the onslaught. For a moment, my heart sinks and I wonder, what if they're really upset? What if they can't get behind this? What if Andre and Arabella don't want—

"Which one of you is moving?" Arabella finally asks.

"Yeah, and if it's Mom," Andre says, "Is she taking the TV? Cause if not—"

"All you care about is the TV? What about our childhood home?" Arabella asks. "What about—"

Lena and I crack up. We should have known our kids would react this way.

"Guys," Lena interrupts. "This..." She gestures between us as she takes her place next to me. I like it. I like being able to just slip my hand around her waist and hold her close to me. It's weird, but I like it. "This is only about ten hours old. Nobody's talking about selling houses yet."

"Yet," I echo. "I'm thinking we might want to keep that TV. It'll be great out on the deck with the hot tub."

"You're right! I can watch football and relax in style."

"We can put the extra fridge out there too, right next to the hot tub so we don't even have to get out for beer."

We high five and the kids stare at us like we've lost our minds.

I definitely like it.

Andre starts pouring pancake mix on the griddle while Lena does more brainstorming about how to combine our households. Casey votes for Lena's couch to sit on the deck so he can watch the game too. We pile all of the goodies on our plates and make our way to the dining room table, which has always been set up to seat eight. Our families have always been close, and will continue to be, no matter what Lena and I choose to do.

I sit at the head of the table and Lena sits to my right. She takes my hand in hers and I pull her over to kiss her, thrilled that this is my life. Everything else is details we can work out later. Or, there's always running away. She wiggles her eyebrows at me, and I figure she'd agree to anything as long as we're together.

She's the most beautiful woman I've ever seen.

She's my best friend.

And I'm hopelessly in love with her.

Good thing she feels the same.

The End…

Love and Pride: Bolder Breed Studios Vol. 2

Love and Pride: Bolder Breed Studios Book Two

Popstar Unice Love is thrilled to be recording a high-profile holiday tune for charity, and super-producer Lydia Pride knows she can do something special with Love's exceptional vocal instrument. Sparks fly between the spirited ingenue and the seasoned musician, but Unice will need to get past the obstacles that have held her back and learn to speak up for what she wants, and Lydia will have to let her in if they're going to make beautiful music together.

Chapter One

Feedback Magazine
December 2019

**Holidays with Love and Pride: The Magic of Bolder Breed Studios
Krishnan Guruvayoor**

What do you get when you cross a multitalented pop ingenue whose star is on the rise, and a veteran producer who walks the edge of mainstream with one foot in the game and the other in a puddle of opaque brilliance? This year, you get a phenomenally refreshing holiday gift. Incognito Records has put together a heartwarming collection of traditional holiday songs recorded by artists who are part of the LGBTQ community. Their goal is to raise money for the #LoveIsLove Foundation, which was started by Reese Matheson and Toby Griffiths when their musical *Boy* came out two years ago. With artists like Just Like Love, Hush, Unice Love, and Backdrop Silhouette on board, the album will be a mix of genres from metal to pop punk to soulful pop, a collaboration unheard of previously in the music industry.

I'll be chatting with all of the artists involved as they share their reasons for participating in this special project and what it was like stepping onto the hallowed grounds of Bolder Breed Studios outside Portland, Oregon.

Unice Love and Lydia Pride have created a masterpiece collaboration for this project comparable to David Bowie and Bing Crosby doing "Little Drummer Boy," or the smash hit from Mariah Carey and Walter Afanasieff, "All I Want for Christmas is You." I've come to the Bolder Breed Studios compound outside of Portland, Oregon, to meet with the pop star and producer. They are currently working on Love's fourth album, which promises to be yet another smash. The unlikely pair—who share they have recently become a pair in work *and* life—took some time to chat with me and explain how they hope their Christmas song will bring solace to those who struggle with the holidays and help change negative attitudes toward the LGBTQ community, which those of you who followed my former blog as The Guru will recognize as a cause near and dear to my heart.

We meet in a dark leather booth in the bar area of the main lodge Lydia Pride calls home. Pride and business partner producer Morrison Jones set up the studio here outside of Portland a few years ago, and not only have they turned it into a thriving community for musicians and artists, but they've built a three-thousand-seat outdoor amphitheater that boasts excellent sound and comfort for guests. Pride and Love have just come from a swim break after working in the studio and the elder stateswoman is making the ingenue squeal by flinging her wet curls at her.

Krish: *Thank you both for agreeing to chat. I hope I'm not interrupting the creative flow.*

Unice: *No, you're good. Lydia is packing to run off and meet up with Alicia Keys anyway.*

She elbows her and Lydia rolls her eyes but leans in so Unice can kiss her on the cheek. Immediately you can see how they move together, in sync, like a well-oiled machine. Makes me wonder how that translates sonically.

Lydia: *I'm only going to be gone for a week, and then we'll finish recording this album before you leave to go on tour for four months.*

Krish: *I can imagine it would be tough to be apart after you've just found each other. It certainly was for my partner and I.*

Unice: *It is weird, but then I don't think either of us expected this to be anything other than a quick recording session. My label approached me with the idea of covering "Let It Snow" as part of this album to raise funds for the #LoveIsLove Foundation. After everything that happened to me last year, I jumped at the chance to be a part of the project.*

Unice is referring to the attempted shooting at her Miami concert last year. Thankfully, no one was hurt. The resulting trial revealed the depths of the conspiracy behind the attack, which resulted in Unice canceling tour dates and tightening her personal security. It was a scary reminder that there is still hatred toward those who are part of the LGBTQ music community as well as their allies. My partner, metal singer Silas Franklin, and I have experienced this firsthand, but we are blown away by the support we've had as our story has been shared on social media. Unice has emerged from the incident more determined than ever to be a part of positive change and we at Feedback magazine are pleased to support her. It's good to see her strong, confident, and excited about her latest endeavor.

Unice: *When I came up here, I thought that was it. I'd sing the song and be onto the next thing. Instead, I ended up—*

Lydia: *You ended up finding your true voice.*

Unice: *I did, didn't I?*

Lydia: *Look, Unice needs a support team, don't get me wrong, and once we all agreed to play nice, I was able to show Unice that she needed to trust herself in order to shine. She does that just fine on her own.*

Unice: *Mmm-hmm.*

Lydia: *What?*

Unice: *You left out one very important piece. I needed this place—and you—to show me what I was capable of, so don't discount that.*

Krish: *So, what was it about working with Lydia that turned out to be a game changer for you, Unice? In life and in your career?*

Unice couldn't believe she and Lydia were about to spill the beans to the world the story of how their relationship came to be, but she trusted Lydia, and Lydia had said she trusted Krish, otherwise, she never would have let him into her inner sanctum. Their home.

That was the first lesson Unice learned when she'd arrived at Bolder Breed Studios back in October. Lydia was all about trust, and she definitely had her rules.

October 2019

Unice worried the address her manager Velma had been given was wrong when they'd turned off a highway outside of Portland, Oregon, and pulled up to a brick hotel-looking building. The country road seemed to be leading them straight into the plot of a horror movie, and her nerves weren't eased when they got out of the car and heard only...nature. Unice had never been somewhere so quiet in her entire life. No cars flying by or honking, no helicopters or sirens. Just a blissful breeze blowing through the trees, the crunch of gravel under her shoes, and the occasional call of a bird.

She'd been further convinced they were in the wrong place when they walked into what appeared to be the main building and saw a typical check-in desk, but then a woman dressed in a band tee with a scene hairdo and ripped jeans popped up from behind the counter and hurried over to welcome them.

"Oh hey! Glad you made it."

"Is this Bolder Breed Studios?" Unice asked as Gladys stepped up next to her.

"She's supposed to meet with Lydia Pride," Gladys said with a little more force than necessary. "Is she here?"

"I'm Rose. You must be Unice?"

Unice accepted the hand the woman offered and was eased by her cheerful smile. "I am. And this is my manager Velma and my assistant Gladys."

Rose shook hands with the two women, who were eyeing her suspiciously.

"*This* isn't the studio, but yeah, you're in the right place. Let me show you to your rooms so you can drop off your things, and then I'll take you to Lydia."

Gladys and Velma whispered to each other, but Unice focused on the back of Rose's head as she walked in front of her down the hall. It seemed like the only time Unice wasn't following someone—or someone's agenda, these days—was when she was onstage. The rest of her time was scheduled to the millisecond and guided by someone else.

"I hope your drive down from Seattle wasn't too bad. Traffic can suck." Rose turned and smiled—and slowed down to walk beside Unice.

"It was fine."

"You're a lot farther out of town than I thought you'd be," Velma said. "I was expecting Portland to be…" She gestured around with her two-inch-long, pearl-white acrylic nails as though they might claw the description right out of the air.

"In the twenty-first century, at least," Gladys said, wrinkling her nose at their surroundings. "I feel like we just stepped back in time. This is some *Grapes of Wrath* kinda place here." The Hoyt sisters had grown up in Los Angeles, as had Unice, and were most comfortable in the city. Portland wasn't quite *city* enough for them, Unice could tell.

"This place used to be a poor home, a place for the unemployed, unhoused, unwanted. The folks we bought it from turned it into a winery, and now we've made it a home for us wayward musicians and artists. We're still updating some of the place, but the rooms have all been modernized. You'll have everything you need to be comfortable for your stay." Rose's smile was confident. Unice got the sense Rose was used to the place being underestimated.

Rose made it a point to answer Gladys's and Velma's questions, but she'd spoken directly to Unice.

This is nice.

Somewhere along the way, Unice had allowed others to speak for her, plan for her, *do* for her. She'd let it happen. After the incident, well, it had just been easier to let everyone take over. It drove her nuts, but she was too conciliatory to speak up. For now.

"Thanks. I love it already. I'm sure it will be great."

Rose pulled out a pile of actual metal keys, antique fancy-looking ones, and sorted them in her hands. "You're staying 'til Sunday? Working with Lydia today and tomorrow, spa treatments Sunday before you take off Monday, that sound right?"

Unice opened her mouth to answer and—

"We'll see how things go," Gladys said. "If Unice isn't comfortable, we may head back to Seattle early."

"I'm sure everything will be great." Unice mustered up a brave, professional smile. "I'm looking forward to being in one place for three nights. I haven't had that in a while."

Rose gave a little pout. "That's gotta be rough. I live here most of the time, but I've traveled a bit with our business partner before, and when he goes, he's *gone.* Whirlwind trips where you can barely remember what day it is, much less where you rested your head the night before."

Unice laughed, and it sounded a little like clearing cobwebs to her. *Did anyone else notice?*

"Baby, we were in Seattle for a week this time." Velma patted Unice's shoulder.

"Yeah, but two different hotels and then a night with my aunt, and—"

"Who knew the first hotel would be so nasty?" Gladys shuddered.

"I swear I got bedbugs just stepping in the lobby. You don't have bedbugs here, do you?"

Rose shook her head and handed them each a skeleton key with a heart keychain that had the number on it.

"These rooms each have one bed, so I gave you three right together. I know you requested a suite, but our two suites have been rented long-term, and our two bedrooms were set aside for folks from the wildfires."

"Oh, that's so nice of you," Unice said. "The fires have been awful. My parents—"

"Unice, maybe we shouldn't stay here," Velma said. "I know you prefer to room with one of us—"

"It'll be fine," Unice said, a little too forcefully, and Velma's expertly arched eyebrows disappeared under her bangs.

At one time, Unice had been intimidated by the older woman, but once she got to know Velma Hoyt, she understood that her sternness was about protecting her clients' interests, and she appreciated that. She was a tall, curvy Black woman who ran Unice's career like a tight ship, happy to make Unice her sole focus. She and her older sister Gladys left lucrative agency jobs after fifteen years in the music business to work for Unice full time, and Unice was grateful for them both.

"Oh, shoot," Rose said, looking down at her phone. "I forgot to tell Lydia you were here. Let's put your things away and then I can take you to the studio."

"Go ahead, babe," Velma said. "I'll get your stuff settled. You and Gladys can go."

"Lydia is only expecting Unice. She's very particular about who she lets into the studio. And no cell phones." Rose's smile never wavered, but her voice was firm.

Unice felt bad for her if she was going to challenge Velma and Gladys. She was lucky to have the best manager and assistant in the business, even if they were a little—okay, a lot—overbearing.

Velma and Gladys exchanged looks and then turned and faced Rose, shoulder to shoulder. "Thank you. We'll just take a minute with Unice and then we'll be ready to go to the studio." Velma put a hand on Unice's shoulder and guided her into the middle room of the three they'd been given the keys to.

Unice glanced over her shoulder with an apologetic smile for Rose.

Rose didn't seem ruffled at all. "No prob. I'll be up at the front desk. Come on over when you're ready."

"Thank you," Unice called out.

Gladys closed the door and turned to face her. "Unice, are you okay with this? I'm not sure how I feel about sending you in alone. Are you okay without your cell phone?"

Unice turned around in the center of the simple but clean room. The walls were covered with a tan wallpaper and green wainscoting. Large windows let in ample sunlight across the white duvet and dark wood floor covered with a bright multi-colored rug. The en suite bathroom was neat and tidy with a large walk-in shower. She smiled at her handlers. She appreciated their protectiveness, but she felt positive about this place. It wasn't fussy or too modern. It felt like staying at a relative's house. "I'm fine. I like it. It's peaceful here. Fewer distractions."

Gladys crossed her arms over her chest. "It's the boonies out here. I don't like that we're not in the same room. I'm sure it's safe enough, but with things the way they are, I'm just concerned."

Unice sighed. She hated being reminded.

She released her first solo album after three years on the teenage-friendly hit show *Advantageous* and from the beginning she decided that she was going to be very open about her sexual orientation. She didn't want any coming-out scandals, and so she'd deliberately let people know through her actions and her interviews and conversations that she was gay, although she'd been discreet with her few dating experiences.

She'd received death threats on her last tour from a hate group, so she'd hired a private security firm. The group members had taken offense to her videos that prominently featured members of the LGBTQ community, and they posted that she should stay out of things like civil rights and the Black Lives Matter movement and focus on being an entertainer. Then an FBI investigation uncovered a plot for gunmen to take over her show in Miami. They caught the suspects coming into the arena and neutralized the threat before anyone was hurt, but it was too close for comfort. They arrested three men on-site and two for the online threats, and she'd had to testify at the trial. It had been a harrowing experience, and since then, she never went anywhere alone. This was the first trip she and the Hoyt sisters had taken without her personal bodyguard in a long time. The label assured them that Bolder Breed's compound was a secure, safe place. Stephenee was on call just in case. Unice hoped they didn't have to bother her.

"We'll put you between us at least," Velma said. "I'm a light sleeper. I'll hear if anything happens."

"I'm sure it will be fine," Unice said. She really wanted life to get back to some semblance of normal, and this trip was a first step. Velma and Gladys both had advanced belts in Kajukenbo. The three of them trained together with her fitness coach, Randy Ramos, in LA. So she felt safe-ish.

She walked over to the window and looked outside. There was a large fountain in the middle of the driveway, and the sound of the water was soothing. If it weren't so chilly outside, she'd have loved to open her window and listen all night. Open windows overnight, however, were a no-no.

"I'll put your stuff down here, okay, honey?"

"Thank you. I just...I need...a minute."

Her two gatekeepers stared for a moment, looked at each other, and then left the room, closing the door behind them.

Velma and Gladys had this way of staring at her as if she might break. She *had* broken. But she'd been doing so much better. And this trip was one she'd actually been excited about. She'd wanted to work with Lydia Pride ever since she'd heard her collaboration with Dolly Parton on the music for a recent YA film on Netflix. Then she looked up some of the other artists Lydia produced: Courtney Love, Lady Gaga, Alicia Keys...she had a wide reach when it came to pop music, and her songs were identifiable in that they tended to be departures from those artists' main collections of songs.

Unice wanted departure.

She wanted to go deeper, wanted to do more than be the airheaded, sheltered, performing puppet her critics thought she was. She wanted to write her own songs, wanted to stop relying on stage shows, skimpy outfits, and shaking her ass to sell records. Wanted to prove she was more than just a teen television star, more than a pretty face with a decent voice.

But there were roadblocks and complications in the way of her plans. She owed the label another album soon, and they'd expect a certain sound. They were lining up producers without her input, and she had more tour dates scheduled after the first of the year. And now she had this charity album to contribute to.

Okay, she *was* excited about singing a holiday song.

She was a huge geek for Christmas. Ever since she was a kid, her family had some serious holiday traditions. Her mom had freaked out when she'd told her she would be contributing to this charity project without even knowing what song Unice would be singing. Her grandparents were totally thrilled. She got a little warm, fuzzy feeling when she thought about it being a part of her story, her legacy; that she would someday be able to share the song with her children and grandchildren.

She'd been staring out the window long enough. It was time to meet Lydia Pride.

Unice was determined to play this right. She wanted to learn from this woman; she wanted to create the best song she could.

She needed to prove that she was a grown-ass woman, and she was going to take charge and—

"Unice! Come on, honey. You don't want to keep her waiting." Gladys and Velma stood in her doorway, looking around at her room, probably noticing that she hadn't moved.

"Sorry. Give me one second."

Velma raised her eyebrows and closed the door again.

Unice took a quick second to use the restroom and then she hurried out to the hallway. She'd wanted to change out of her traveling clothes —black and white floral palazzo pants and a matching black long-sleeved, fitted top with cutouts on her side and shoulder—and fix her long rose-gold ponytail, but she'd wasted her few precious moments to herself staring out the window. Her light-brown skin could use some sun, her large brown eyes, probably her best feature, were a tad puffy, but she'd left the makeup off hoping it would go away.

No more stalling. It was time to take that first step toward being her own boss.

"Here, let me fix your hair," Gladys said, whipping out her brush and pulling Unice to a stop by her ponytail. "You've got wispies."

"You sure you don't want to change?" Velma pulled out her phone and checked her itemized list for the day. "Did you take your supplements this morning? I forgot to ask you at breakfast. We'll have to let Lydia know that you have to take a break at eleven forty-five to stretch and then eat lunch. We don't want that back spasm coming back."

Unice sighed as tears stung her eyes. Of course, those could have been from the force Gladys used to yank her curly hair into submission. She knew better than to pull away. Her baby fine hair was tough to manage and despite having a tender head, she sat for braids, extensions, up dos, whatever her stylist suggested and tried her best to keep from crying. She'd gotten the hairbrush plenty of times growing up from her aunties and mom, and even though she was twenty-five years old, you never forget that feeling.

"There. Oh, I should have brought my makeup kit. Well, you look fabulous, and from what I've seen of this lady," she said out the side of her mouth, "she's not about fashion."

Okay, maybe she would be her own boss…later.

Chapter Two

"Lydia is just finishing up some mixing, but you can go ahead inside. Just have a seat in the chair by the desk, and she'll be with you shortly. Gladys and Velma? If you would like access to the indoor pool or spa, or if you'd like some coffee, I can walk you over to the dining room."

Rose smiled and gestured for Unice's support team to leave her, and Unice was ready for there to be a fight.

"Unice? Are you fine with this?"

"The dining room is just over there," Rose said, pointing to a large building across the walkway. "There's WIFI inside, and you can make yourself comfortable. I did look over your list of requests for your stay, and our chef will be preparing food that meets your requirements for your meals. We've also reserved the yoga studio for you later this afternoon."

There was a moment where looks were comically exchanged, where no one knew quite how to proceed.

It was Unice's chance to assert herself.

"I'll be fine. Thank you, Rose. Just go on in?"

Rose winked at her and guided Gladys and Velma away from the studio door.

Leaving Unice alone in the brisk fall morning.

She turned and faced the doors and took a moment to admire the lettering that spelled out *Bolder Breed Studios, Pride and Jones.*

She wondered how Lydia and Morrison Jones had connected. They seemed like they were from different worlds, but they'd both had huge success producing a variety of artists, a who's-who of rock, pop, EDM, alternative…they both had clout in the music industry and were doing well enough that they owned this huge complex out here. To be honest, she was surprised she wasn't working with Jones. Her label had almost exclusively set her up with male producers to this point. That fact added to her nerves about opening the door to this experience.

Will she hate me?

Will she be like the others who think I'm just barely passable?

Will she take me seriously?

Unice shivered and placed her hand on the cold handle. She pressed down with her thumb, nearly ripping her acrylic nail off, and she pushed on the heavy wood door. She stepped inside, and her cheeks burned as if she were standing in front of a fire. The studio was much warmer than the chilly fall day outside. Music was playing loudly from behind a set of French doors to her left. The building was a converted two-story home and had dark wood on the walls, similar to what she'd seen in the lodge. In front of her was a staircase with deep red carpeting that led to the second floor. She wondered if someone lived here, too.

Unice was drawn to the sound, and she paused in front of the sliding French doors; wondering if she should tap? Or knock? She knew how involved she could get listening to music, and she didn't want to scare the person sitting behind the massive soundboard. But then, Rose said Lydia was expecting her…

She carefully slid the French door to the side, grateful it didn't squeak or scrape, and she slipped into the studio. She sat in the chair at the desk just like Rose told her, and she gawked at all of the equipment surrounding her. Shelves contained drums of every size, shape, and brand she'd ever heard of. A collection of microphones hung from a gleaming silver rack, and there were a variety of amplifiers stacked against the far wall. The soundboard took up a huge space—and sitting in the driver's seat with her back to Unice was none other than Lydia Pride. She leaned forward over the board with her hands slid out to her sides, her fingers tapping the ledge in time to the bluesy rock music playing.

The figure sitting in front of the board was slender, with narrow shoulders bunched up around the ears. Lydia was dressed in a black and gray oversized sweater with the ends of a plum-colored scarf hanging down her back. Her dark hair was streaked with silver, and it fell in loose curls around her shoulders. She wore a beanie pulled down over her head and fingerless gloves. Her nails were natural and unpainted, and her outfit was rounded out by dark leggings and clunky black boots.

Unice watched the genius as she operated the table's switches and knobs like Willy Wonka in the chocolate factory. Her skilled fingers were nimble and…tiny. Her size surprised Unice. She'd imagined the woman with the louder-than-life pipes would be more substantial.

Unice was used to folks being smaller than her. At 5'9", she wasn't petite. Her curvy shape had been honed and toned by hours with her trainer, Randy, and Julissa Estrada, her choreographer. Her father was a six-foot-six-inch Nordic giant former NBA star, and her mother was a biracial Black woman who'd been a hip-hop dancer in the early days of the genre. She performed and toured with some of the biggest names in the game before she decided to hang up her Reebok hi-tops and become a mom. It was in Unice's genes to be big and beautiful, and since she'd emerged on the far side of puberty, she'd been comfortable in her own skin.

"Come over here," Lydia said, interrupting Unice's thoughts about how weird it would be to not have a full workout today. Still, she was way more interested in what Lydia was doing.

"Sit over here. I want you to listen to this."

Lydia flicked her fingers impatiently at the chair next to her, not making eye contact. Unice moved next to her and sat down. Lydia still didn't look at her.

The music Lydia had been playing stopped, and she flipped a few switches. The sweet and gentle sounds of an acoustic guitar filled the room, light and breezy, and Unice found herself leaning closer. She listened carefully as if she could make out each note. Then the piano came in, and goosebumps raised on Unice's arms. She shivered as the sounds caressed down the back of her neck and spine.

When the track ended, Lydia switched off the sound and turned in her chair to face Unice. "So, we're making a Christmas song."

Unice lost every bit of cool she'd fooled herself into thinking she had.

"Yes, Miss Pride. 'Let It Snow' is my mom's favorite. It's going to be a surprise for her."

"Uh-huh."

Lydia looked her up and down, and the corner of her mouth quirked up. Not quite a smirk, not a smile. Definitely not impressed. "Why not write your own song?"

Unice's heart seized. "I, well…the label—"

"Right, I know," she said. "But do you ever write your own stuff?"

Unice slid her hands between her knees, and her shoulders tightened in a shrug. "I don't play any instruments."

Lydia took a cigarette out of a metal box, and Unice tried to hide her shock. *Is she really going to smoke in here?* She was a singer…didn't she know how bad it was?

"You play an instrument. Your voice is your instrument." She tapped the cigarette on the table for emphasis. "Don't ever forget that."

"Okay," Unice said. "Well, I mean, I write. But, like, no one's ever looked at my stuff. It's not anything."

Lydia looked her over again and nodded. Unice wrapped her arms around herself and braced for unpleasantness.

"Well, let's show you around and talk about the sound and feel."

"I was thinking traditional, like with the bells and piano and—"

"Did you like what I was playing when you came in?"

"I loved it," she replied with no hesitation. She'd done her homework on the 39-year-old Lydia Pride, and though she managed to make artists' voices reflect them and their sound, there was always something unique, something different about the tracks, so listeners would be like "it sounds like so and so but it's different, but I love it, but is it really so and so?"

Lydia's eyes flared, and she leaned in as if to conspire. "Screw traditional. Let's do something special, something that will…I don't know, give people a moment that's more than cheap gimmickry."

Unice dropped her arms. "Isn't a traditional cover of a traditional holiday song what this is supposed to be about? Why I'm here?"

Lydia smirked. "You're here because your label thought we'd make a good pair," she said, her eyebrow quirking up. "I'm not saying I can't handle traditional, Miss Love." She pointed at Unice and swirled her finger. "I'm just wondering if you're ready to break out of that little package they've wrapped you in and do something fresh. Doesn't matter to me," she said on an exhale and tugged her beanie as she turned back to face the board. "I've got your backing tracks ready to go. You have your lyrics?"

"I know them by heart." Unice swallowed hard and slumped a little in her chair. This was not going as she'd hoped. "I'm sorry. I don't mean to sound ungrateful. I just don't want to get in trouble with the label. They're expecting 'Let it Snow,' aren't they?"

Lydia waved a hand in her direction. "Doesn't matter. Forget I said anything. Let me play your track for you."

She poked at the keyboard sitting in the middle of the board and then sat back as the familiar-yet-different tune started.

It was the right song, but she'd changed the arrangement, slowed it down.

There was a haunting quality to the song this way. Instead of bouncy and cheery, it was…sleek, sensual. Emotional.

"Wow," she breathed as the music finished.

"Wow?" Lydia chuckled.

"Yeah. Wow. That's not the version I'm used to."

"It's not your grandmother's 'Let It Snow.' If we're going to do it, I thought we should make it…yours."

Unice wondered what exactly she meant by that. Did Lydia see her like all that? She hadn't really explored her sensual side, but after hearing Lydia's backing track? That's exactly what she wanted to do. She was about to ask more questions, but then Lydia stood from the chair and stretched her back.

"Let's get some vocals down, shall we? Have you warmed up yet?"

Unice stood and shook her head. "Not yet."

"Alright. You got it? Or did you want me to start you off?"

Unice had worked with vocal coaches before, and of course she'd had singing lessons, but she always liked adding some new exercises to her repertoire. And if Lydia wanted her to sing like what she'd just played her? Yeah, she was going to need all the help she could get.

"I'd love to warm up with you."

Lydia grinned and led them to the middle of the studio. They did some breathing techniques that seemed to go on for a long time. Unice wasn't used to this much detail when it came to her breathing, but she wanted to trust in the process.

"Okay, now follow my lead."

And Lydia unleashed that big voice of hers that stretched an impressive four-octave range. It was fierce in the lower registers and then so, *so* beautiful when she reached her peak.

Unice watched her in awe. Their voices were very different. Lydia's was a low, raspy, husky contralto compared to Unice's usually light and breathy soprano. When Lydia finished, Unice was still staring.

"Okay. Your turn."

Unice cleared her throat, and she started to follow Lydia's lead, but Lydia cut her off.

"Miss Love, do you know you're really not using your diaphragm here? Don't play around. Your voice will go out."

Unice was startled when Lydia stepped behind her, her head just below Unice's chin. She placed a hand on Unice's belly and spread her fingers. Her hand was warm through the thin material of Unice's stretchy shirt. She shivered as Lydia's curls brushed against her arm.

"Do that run again."

Unice took in a breath but what came out of her mouth sounded like a pubescent boy going through a voice change. She burst out laughing, and even Lydia chuckled.

"Let's give that another try."

Lydia moved closer, and Unice's skin burned under the light pressure of her hand.

Unice closed her eyes and tried to let go of the nerves. She opened her mouth and tried to dig a little deeper...

"That's better. Feel that?" She pressed her hand against Unice's upper abdomen. Oh yeah, she felt that. She'd never had a hands-on vocal lesson before. She wasn't sorry one bit. "Now do it again."

By the time they finished the warm-ups, Unice had broken a sweat. She'd worked out harder than she had on some of her cardio days. She was even a little out of breath.

"Now you're ready. Pick a mic. What kind do you prefer? I've set out a selection for you."

Unice touched the retro hanging mic and smiled. She loved the old-fashioned feel of it.

"Nice choice. I would have figured you for the Shure performance style since you're primarily a performer."

Coming from Lydia, that felt like a dig.

"I think this kind sounds better. Plus, it kind of makes me feel glamorous. Is that weird? It's got that throwback vibe."

Lydia smiled at her, genuinely, for the first time.

"Glamorous, huh. I can see that. I can see that for you."

Lydia hooked up the mic she'd chosen and connected the cable to the soundboard.

"You need a stool? A music stand?"

Unice shook her head and tossed her long ponytail over her shoulder. "No, I'm okay."

Lydia looked around as if she'd forgotten something. "Okay, well, let me get you some water, and we'll give it a go. Yay, Christmas."

She turned to leave the room...but not before Unice noticed her making a face.

This was not off to a good start.

Unice worried that she'd irritated the super-producer by questioning her. And while the arrangement she'd put together for Unice was soulful and warm, it seemed as though Lydia didn't want to be there.

Well, Unice would show her passion, would show her she wasn't wasting her time.

Lydia closed the door, and entered the studio and Unice once again was floored by how quiet it was. The room was soundproofed, and when the diminutive Lydia sat down, Unice could barely see her. It seemed as if she was all alone in this magical place in the middle of nowhere.

Which could be a good thing. How many times had she wished for solitude with her music? She loved working out songs by herself, really experimenting with her voice, but she was alone so rarely now…

"Okay, Miss Love, I'm going to play it from the top. Let's sing it through once and see how the arrangement fits for you. Don't worry about going balls out this first time."

Unice giggled and felt her cheeks flush.

Lydia smiled and rolled her eyes. "I'm sorry, I forget you're probably not used to my potty mouth. I understand things are pretty wholesome in your camp."

Unice shrugged. "I guess. Once you perform as a child star, people tend to have expectations. Either they think you're going to start pole dancing and hooking up with celebrity boyfriends, having media meltdowns, or they think you'll end up in a barbershop shaving your hair off. There's not really a middle ground. I think it's important for me to try to break that cycle." *Even if I do sometimes feel like I'm losing myself trying to please everyone else.*

Lydia held up her hands. "Hey, that's cool, man. I wasn't trying to say anything negative. I simply don't have a filter, but I'll try for you."

Unice cocked her head to the side. She hadn't ever had a producer or anyone try to do anything to respect her wishes. They never curbed their language or cut out inappropriate comments. Especially some of the men she'd worked with. The fact that Lydia knew enough about her to even be concerned touched Unice. As if she needed more reasons to admire the woman.

"You ready?"

Unice nodded, and she took a deep breath.

She let Lydia's arrangement roll over her, and she sang the lyrics from the heart. She sang of playing in the snow like she had as a child or sitting around the fire with her parents watching Christmas movies while they ate popcorn. Her cheeks hurt from smiling as she let the words flow from her as they'd done for so many years.

When the song finished, she stepped back from the mic and closed her eyes. In this moment, everything was good. With her eyes closed, here in the quiet, she was safe.

Chapter Three

Unice sat in the dining hall after the morning recording session with Lydia. Gladys and Velma scolded her to eat and stop pushing her salad around with a fork.

"All I'm saying is that if you're not feeling it, we will force the issue. You need to be happy with the recording."

"I know." She took a long sip of iced tea. It wasn't that she didn't love the song. The arrangement was new and exciting. She just kept thinking of what Lydia had said.

"I'm just wondering if you're ready to break out of that little package they've wrapped you in and do something fresh."

Is that what she was? Is that what people in the industry thought of her? She'd heard enough about her riding the coattails of her popular television show into a bubblegum-pop career, but she knew better. Yes, some of her songs were on the fluffier side, but she'd worked so hard to be taken seriously.

It reminded her of that saying, "not to work harder but smarter", and working with Lydia, taking some risks, felt smarter. More of the same wouldn't help her grow, so even if it was a little uncomfortable, she needed to trust the process. She was just about to share her thoughts with Gladys and Velma when Lydia appeared.

"Hey, can I join you? I'm Lydia," she said, introducing herself to Velma and Gladys. She shook their hands and then lowered herself into the empty seat at their table.

"It's great to meet you," Velma said. "How did things go this morning?"

Lydia glanced at Unice and then turned her attention to Velma. "It's a good start. We recorded a couple of solid tracks. I'd like to clean it up a little more this afternoon." She turned to face Unice. "I've also got something else in mind, if you're game."

Her dark eyes twinkled, and Unice was sold. Anything that made this tough lady twinkle had to be exciting, and definitely worth her time.

"Absolut—"

"She needs to work out this afternoon, and she has to eat at—"

"I wrote a song for you." Her gaze hadn't left Unice's, and Unice felt a thrill at being caught in the woman's tractor beam. That twinkle in her eye said, *Trust me. I promise it'll be sensational.*

"A song? For me?"

Lydia nodded and smiled. "After you left. Are you done eating? You want to come—"

"Yes."

"Unice! You haven't finished eating, and you really should go for a walk before—"

Lydia held out a life preserver in the form of her small hand as she stood, and it took Unice less than a second to take it and stand up, allowing the producer to take the lead.

"Unice!"

"I'll find you for dinner," she called out. "I swear."

Lydia pulled her out the door at a trot, and Unice laughed the whole way.

"I'm sorry," Lydia said as they jogged to the studio. "I wanted to let you eat, but I don't want them pulling you away until you've heard this."

They took the steps up to the studio two at a time. Lydia held her hand until she needed it to slide the French door open.

There was a man in the studio. Not a man, exactly. A star. A superstar. A very handsome superstar wearing…were those paisley satin pajama pants? And a matching pink chenille sweater?

"Miss Love? This is Morrison Jones. Morrison, this is Unice Love."

He stood and shook her hand, offering her a shy smile. Shy? His clothes were certainly loud enough.

"Nice to meet you."

Unice might have said the same back to him, but she was pretty sure she just smiled. He'd been in the hugely successful band Shady Grace, which was one of her father's favorite bands of all time, and now he was an accomplished producer, someone she'd hoped to work with at some point. Unice was definitely star-struck.

"I called in reinforcements. I want you to listen. Come here, come here."

They moved into the studio, and Unice followed.

Lydia sat at the piano and Morrison picked up an acoustic guitar. They took a minute to get set up, during which Unice stood in the middle of the room, not knowing whether to sit, stand, or turn cartwheels.

"Take a seat if you want," Lydia said, playing a series of warmup notes on the piano.

Unice looked around and saw a stool in the back corner, so she moved it a little closer and perched on it, unsure how to feel about the fact that Lydia had written a song—for her—in the time it took her to eat a salad.

Morrison nodded to Lydia as he began playing a melody.

Unice was often envious, watching musicians play off each other, noting their subtle shifts like dancers moving across a floor. They were so in tune with each other it was as if the rest of the world fell away and it was just them. Unice wondered what it would be like to have that kind of connection with someone.

When Lydia sang, it was Unice who experienced that falling away.

Pretty little package
    Is this all you ever wanted
    To stand up there alone
    While they take you for granted?

Blisters on your heels
    Bruises on your knee
    Think you've lost the feeling
    Is this who you wanted to be

What would it be like
    To set your heart free
    To unwrap that package
    For all the world to see

Step out of your shadow
    Take your place in the spotlight
    No more looking through windows
    To find the star so bright

Don't let them tell you
    Who you're meant to be
    Break out of that package
    And let them all see

When the lyrics wrapped, and Unice's tears had run down to her collar, Lydia watched her reaction as she played the last few bars of the song. Unice might as well have been sitting naked upon that stool with several spotlights illuminating every angle of her exposed body. She could hardly breathe.

Correction. She *couldn't* breathe.

"Excuse me." Unice promptly scurried from the room. That was really the only way to describe her movements. The doors seemed more cumbersome than they had been when she'd entered this morning feeling lighter and more excited than she had in months.

All it took to change her view was one song that hit a little too close to home to bring the weight back to her limbs. She finally burst out of the front door and ran down the steps. She hesitated, not knowing if she wanted the solitude of her room and a bed to finish crying on, or if she wanted to keep moving.

The fact that Gladys had her room key solved that dilemma.

Unice took off at a good clip toward the orchard that surrounded the compound. She stayed on the wide gravel path between two sections of different fruit trees in order to avoid twisting an ankle and worsening her situation.

She ran until her lungs burned. Then she paced.

She wanted to scream, but she had no clue where she was, and she didn't want to startle someone in the orchard.

She spun around at the sound of gravel crunching under tires.

Lydia came flying down the path toward her in a golf cart and skidded to a stop a little too close.

"You planning to run all the way back to Seattle? You move *fast*." She climbed out of the cart and walked up to Unice. "People normally clap when my songs are over. Or they clutch their chest and swoon. What is this all about?"

Unice opened her mouth and closed it. How was she supposed to explain her reaction? "I'm sorry—"

"No, I don't want to hear apologies, Miss Love. I get the sense you apologize for things a lot. I want to know what you're feeling."

"Exposed, okay? Naked! I wasn't expecting that."

Lydia stood right in front of her with her arms crossed over her chest, rocking back and forth on her feet while looking at the ground. "Does that mean you liked it?"

Unice barked out a laugh. "Liked it? I don't know *what* to think. I loved the music, but I hate that you see me that way. I hate that people have these expectations of me. I hate everything!"

Unice started pacing again, and Lydia watched her for several passes before speaking.

"Miss Love, I don't see you any kind of *way*. I see *you*."

Unice stopped in her tracks and thought, *yeah. You do.* "I hate it that you call me Miss Love."

Lydia smiled. "You started it. You called me Miss Pride."

"Did I?"

"And I *do* see you. At least I think I do. And I think you want to be seen."

"I do."

Lydia held out her hand. "Come on. Let's go for a ride. I have an idea."

"Should I be scared?"

Lydia grinned. "Depends."

Unice let Lydia lead her to the cart and tried to decide if she should be embarrassed…or flattered. They climbed in and Lydia turned on the quiet whirring motor.

"Unice. I love your name, by the way."

Unice's cheeks burned. "Thank you. I'm named for my grandmother. She was a singer, too. Gospel."

"That's nice. My grandmother went to jail for killing her husband."

Unice doubted she would ever *not* be shocked by the things that came out of Lydia's mouth. She deadpanned everything, and the more they talked, the more she realized that she wasn't joking.

"That's…Wow. Were you close with her?"

Lydia turned a sharp corner and reached out a hand across Unice's body to keep her from falling out? She guessed? Whatever the reason, it was nice.

"Yeah. When I was little. My mom and dad moved away from her because of the drama. They didn't want me and my siblings to see what was happening, so we weren't there when *it* happened. I'm glad, I guess, but I was mad for a long time because it just didn't seem fair, you know? Grandmas aren't supposed to go to jail."

"It does seem uncommon." Unice wasn't sure what to say, and she knew it was best to listen. She had so many questions, she didn't know where to start.

Lydia pulled out a cigarette as she took another sharp turn that caused Unice to lean against her.

"Sorry." Lydia licked her lips and grinned at Unice.

"You don't really smoke, do you?" Okay, that was probably rude.

"Sometimes. Depends how together I feel. Today I feel good." She leaned into Unice and bumped her shoulder. "Sometimes, I just need to hold something. Need to know it's there."

"Like a security blanket?"

"Yeah. Like a security blanket. That causes cancer. And wrecks your instrument."

Unice laughed. "I guess."

"Alright, so check this out. I know we're just supposed to do this Christmas song or whatever, and I can't believe I'm doing this, but when I first saw you, and you sang for me…I think you need me."

"You think I need you."

Lydia turned sharp again, and Unice leaned against her, maybe lingering longer than necessary.

"I think you need me. I think I can be your guide on a little musical adventure that you'll really dig and be proud of." She pointed out the edge of the property, and then they continued driving up and down the aisles of the orchard. "Your albums have done great for you so far, your sound has been fine, I have no problem with any of it, necessarily, but I think you're in a place in your career where you've established enough of a presence with your fans that they'll trust you to take them on a journey."

"A journey."

"Yeah," Lydia said, swerving a bit and nearly running them off the raised gravel path. "Oops. I always forget I can't go so fast through here."

"It does seem a bit risky."

"The music or the ride?"

Unice laughed. "The ride. The music…this is all happening really fast."

"Yeah, maybe slower is better." Lydia grinned again.

"Not necessarily." Unice crossed her legs and placed her hands daintily in her lap.

"Are you flirting with me?" Lydia faking surprise was hilarious.

"Am I allowed to flirt with you?"

Lydia shook her head and chewed on her lip. "I don't know. You just met me." She pressed a hand to her chest as though she were suddenly demure.

"And you seem to have me all figured out. Doesn't really seem fair."

"Maybe it's *you* who needs to figure you out. I'd like to offer you the conduit to do so."

Unice's breath caught at her words. "Tell me how."

Lydia parked the golf cart, and Unice stopped staring at her long enough to see a beautiful sight.

They were surrounded on all four sides by tall fruit trees where two main roads through the orchards met. Peaches and plums. Sweet and tart. It seemed fitting to be discussing this particular juncture in Unice's life while sitting at a crossroads with a person who seemed to be her polar opposite, but who could be instrumental in Unice's recreation.

Unice wasn't the bluesman looking for fame. She was the pop star looking for herself.

"I'm offering you my studio and my services. Stay here, with me. For a week. Let's explore that instrument of yours. Let's take a look at those 'whatevers' you've been writing. Let me help you find your voice."

Considering her offer had my mouth watering.

It was a tempting proposition, or it could be if I had the courage.

"What? The? Heck? Unice?"

After riding around in the golf cart for what seemed like hours, Lydia brought Unice back to the studio where they found an angry Gladys and Velma.

"Let me handle it," Lydia said to Unice as they climbed out.

"No. I've got it."

She'd wanted to open up to Lydia and share with her thoughts she'd never been brave enough to tell others. Maybe she'd do that. Over the week. The week her manager and assistant were going to lose their shit over.

"Where have you been?" Velma asked, her hands on her hips. "We thought something happened to you! I was going to call 9-1-1, but we checked with Rose, and she told me you guys were out in the orchard."

Gladys placed a hand on her shoulder. "You never take off like that, Unice; you scared the crap out of us."

"I'm sorry to have worried you. I've made a decision."

Gladys and Velma looked at each other, and then shot glares at Lydia.

"Can you excuse us?" Velma snapped at Lydia.

"You're excused."

Unice's eyes bugged out.

Lydia smiled at the women and seemed to be completely unaffected by their dismissal.

"Miss Pride—"

"Look, this is my place—"

"Gladys, Velma," Unice said, afraid the conversation was going to go south real quick. "I want to stay. In fact, Lydia has invited me to stay and work on some songs…" She somehow drew strength from Lydia's presence at her side, but the words were her own.

"Unice, honey, we have to catch a flight out of Seattle. You've got appointments in Los Angeles on Monday and Wednesday for your choreography sessions with Julissa."

Unice knew all of the people around her had schedules and weren't just at her beck and call, but she'd made up her mind. "Gladys, I'd like for you to cancel my appointments this week. I never do this, I know. I also know we have the tour coming up soon and I have to practice, but I need this."

She held her breath, hoping there wouldn't be a lot of pushback. What Lydia offered her on their orchard excursion was exactly what her heart told her she needed.

"Unice, you can't just—"

"Velma, I really want to do this."

Her tone must have been enough because Velma and Gladys both backed off a bit.

"I'll see what I can do," Gladys said, pulling out her cell phone.

Velma sighed. "Unice? Can we please talk about this? What's going on?"

"Give us a few?" Unice hoped Lydia recognized her need to smooth things over.

Lydia squeezed her forearm and then nodded to Velma before walking off toward the main lodge. "I'll be in the dining room after I check in with Rose and tell her to call off the search party."

Velma was not pleased. "That woman is a piece of work."

"Lydia wants to work on some songs with me, and after what I heard…I want to try."

"Unice, honey, I don't think this woman is the right person for you to be working with. You know she's got an attitude."

"And the men I've worked with don't? At least she listens to me."

"That's not fair. We're all looking out for you," Velma said, her expression full of worry.

"I'm sorry, I didn't mean that toward you. I meant the other producers I've worked with expect me to do whatever they say, no questions asked, and yeah, they've helped me make some great albums, but I want…I just want to try something different."

Velma crossed her arms over her chest. "The label didn't approve this."

Unice shrugged. "There's still time to give them their testosterone-laden, ass-shaking record if this doesn't work out. They haven't even finalized who I'm going to work with yet."

Velma snorted. "You ain't lying." She sighed. "Pride is pretty amazing. I don't doubt she can come up with something more imaginative than 'Can't Stop, Won't Stop'."

That song was their inside joke. The last album cycle, a Swedish producer had wanted to work with her on "a party anthem," and yeah, it had turned into another barely literate, repetitive-as-all-get-out, annoying club song.

Unice put her hands in the air and pumped them while making beats sounds, and the two danced around until they ended up in a hug.

"I love you, you crazy girl."

"I know you do, thank you. I love you, too," Unice said. "I'm just having a moment, you know? Lydia…"

"Uh-huh. I think I know what kind of moment you're having." Velma stepped back. "Just make sure you're not leaving out your business to get into some…*business*."

Unice pressed her lips together to hide her smile. "I swear," she said as she raised her right hand. "There will be nothing funny about this business."

"Unice, I'm serious. Lydia Pride has been known to break some hearts."

"Velma, it's about music. I think she can really help me find my voice."

"I didn't know it was lost."

Unice held the hands of her manager and smiled while her eyes filled with tears. "I think I've been lost, and I didn't know it. She played me the song she wrote and…she took one look at me, and she knew. I think she knows a lot about how I feel, and I don't even know her."

And that was the bottom line. Lydia had seen something in Unice, and maybe she'd find out just what it was about her that had inspired Lydia to write such a hauntingly beautiful song.

"Just be careful. What do you want us to do?"

Unice thought for a moment. Did she want them to stay? She knew they were bored when she was recording because it took forever, and they couldn't even be a part of it this time. Lydia was clear. Other than having Morrison maybe help with the instrumentals or a band, she worked solely one-on-one.

"Why don't the two of you go have some fun in Portland? There's gotta be trouble for you to get into. Stay here, stay somewhere fancier, whatever you want. Take a vacation. On my dime."

Velma raised her eyebrows, and Unice laughed. She knew that look meant Velma was questioning her sanity.

"You're giving us free rein with your credit card, is what you're saying? Are you for real?"

"Completely. Now, go have some fun while this lady here works me to the bone."

Velma didn't seem convinced that Unice hadn't lost her mind, but she apparently trusted her enough to leave. "I was going to call Stephenee. Maybe she can come stay—"

"Velma, go. Let Stephenee have her vacation. Take Gladys and have some fun. I bet Rose can give you some recommendations."

Unice's eyebrow wiggling did the trick. They walked back to the main lodge and went to Gladys's room to make a plan. She really did have the best team working for her. Maybe this week on her own with Lydia would give her the gumption she needed to take more leadership in the business that was Unice Love.

The ladies decided they were definitely coming back to sleep, but Rose let them know about a Brazilian BBQ place near downtown that had them salivating. They planned to get into some trouble, and Unice encouraged them.

She watched them drive away, waving at the rental car.

Whatever happened next, Unice was on a new course.

Lydia Pride had invited her on an adventure, and she was ready to get started. Maybe. Definitely.

Chapter Four

Unice found Lydia eating a big juicy burger and fries in the dining hall.

"You send them out into the wilds of Portland?"

Unice sat down with her whitefish, wild rice, and broccoli. "Yeah. With my credit card."

Lydia chuckled. "That's one way to get rid of them." She winced. "I'm sorry, I'm sure they're wonderful people, but in my experience, having an entourage in the studio is just a recipe for distraction. When I'm making music, I want my artists completely focused on what we're doing. I want the two of us—or if it's a band, the group of us—to connect on that level where only music happens. When you get managers and friends in the studio…undue stress can result and, it affects the outcome. So, I just don't allow it. If that causes grief, I apologize, but I've gotten to this point following my instincts, and they're usually right."

She looked pointedly at Unice with that loaded statement.

"I'm happy to try it out. I'm just not used to it, and neither are they. They've been really supportive of me during a rough time, so I tend to tolerate a lot of stuff."

Lydia took a sip of what turned out to be—*oh sweet goodness*—a chocolate milkshake. Unice couldn't remember the last time she'd had ice cream. She watched Lydia's lips purse around the straw and wondered if the shake tasted good. Wondered if Lydia tasted good.

Oh. Shoot. She'd promised Velma no funny business.

But she could have a crush, right? That wasn't out of line?

"Yeah, that was some crazy stuff, man. Thank goodness for The Man and his surveillance, huh? That could have been a disaster."

Strangely enough, Unice didn't experience the usual clammy hands and tight throat when Lydia brought up the single most terrifying incident in her life.

"I've never been so scared in my life." Her voice came out just over a whisper, and Lydia leaned closer to hear her. "I almost quit. Everything. I didn't think I could do this anymore."

"Wouldn't blame you. I'm friends with Jesse Hughes from Eagles of Death Metal, and I spent a lot of time with him after the Paris shooting. He went through some shit, I tell you."

Unice watched her take a bite out of a burger that was bigger than her head. It was easier to focus on how much she missed burgers than the topic of conversation. Then again, Lydia made it easy to talk about things she usually avoided. Which was strange.

Lydia lifted her chin. "That looks good. Not very exciting, but good."

Unice sighed. *Here we go.* "I have to be careful with my diet. It's not a weight thing—"

"Mmm-hmm. Something about Irritable Bowel—"

"Yes, and I don't like talking about it."

Especially not when she was eating.

Lydia grinned around a big bite. She chewed and swallowed before she spoke. "We all have our issues. I get it. I'm not trying to give you a hard time."

"Good. I mean, thank you." She added the last after Lydia's eyes bugged out.

"Now I see why my song hit so close to home."

Unice shrugged. "Food is just one of the many things about my life that folks tend to criticize. I guess I get edgy sometimes."

"People don't understand that being a performer requires you to take extra care of your voice, your metabolism and energy, your whole body. If anything breaks down, you put yourself and others out of work. It's like having a job that requires you to drive all the time. If you don't take care of your car, you can't do your job."

She really gets it.

"Do you miss it?" Unice asked her. "The touring?"

Lydia Pride had fronted an early 2000s all-female alternative band that'd had a few critically acclaimed hits before they crashed and burned in true Hollywood style. Unice had read that Lydia then moved to Nashville for a while and began writing songs for pop-country groups. Then she met Jack White, who introduced her around, and she took it from there.

"I was never a big fan of touring. I like having roots, you know? I like being in the same place for longer than twenty-four hours. And honestly, I was never very good at the whole band thing. I like what I like, I do what I want, and along the way I discovered that I'm good at helping other people create who they are."

"Well, let's see what you do with me." Unice dropped that challenge and then focused on eating her fish to keep from laughing.

"And she drops the gauntlet. Very well, milady. I accept your challenge. Hurry up and eat and let's get started."

They talked about musical influences—most of hers, Lydia found surprising, and most of Lydia's favorites were ones Unice wasn't really familiar with—and Lydia whipped out her phone to make Unice a playlist.

"The Kills you should definitely listen to, and Tegan and Sarah. Also, Bishop Briggs. Meg Myers. These are all chick singers with extra guts, I guess, I don't know how to explain it. Their sounds are exciting to me. Not that I hear these sounds specifically for you, but I want you to just hear how they're different, their passion, you know?"

Unice's head was spinning by the time they left the dining room. As they walked to the studio at dusk, Lydia seemed to be dragging her feet.

"Let's start by playing the Christmas song once more and see if you're happy with it before we dive into the good stuff. Let's just get that out of the way."

"You sound really excited about that."

Lydia turned to her. "Look at you. We share one meal together, and now you're busting my balls."

"I'm sorry," Unice said, laughing at Lydia's fake shock. "I'm just sensing your disdain for the most wonderful time of the year."

Lydia curled up her lip and growled. "Maybe I'm just tired of having Christmas shoved down my throat."

"What's so wrong with it?" Unice had heard there were people who didn't like Christmas, but she'd never met one in person. They were like an endangered species found only in the wild. Apparently, the wild was just outside Portland, Oregon. Unice was so curious about Lydia, and she had so many questions. So far, Lydia had been open. She hoped that continued because she intended to learn from her…and learn *about* her. It was refreshing to be treated like a grown-up, and with Lydia, she felt like she was being taken seriously as an artist…and as a woman. She wanted more.

"Come on," Lydia groaned as they reached the studio doors. "Let's work on the song first. Then I'll tell you all about Christmas in the Pride home."

Maybe Unice wasn't the only one who hadn't been taken seriously.

They sat at the soundboard and listened to the tracks they'd recorded that morning. Unice was grinning from ear to ear.

"I can't believe I sound like that," she said with a giggle, covering her mouth.

"What? Like a grown-ass woman who knows what she wants?"

Lydia quirked up her lips on one side and gazed at me pointedly, that twinkle back in her eye.

"Is that what you hear?"

"I'm starting to. Now, why don't you channel that vibe and go do it one more time, just for shits and giggles."

Unice ran her tongue over her teeth and made a clicking sound, gave a little head bob, and strolled into the studio with a little more swagger than she had before. She let Lydia's arrangement slide over her like velvet against naked skin. She pictured lipstick stains on a wine glass, staring into a lover's eyes over candlelight—

Staring into *Lydia's* eyes across a table, a romantic dinner.

Yeah. This was definitely turning into some business.

She let her voice flirt with the lower level of her range and added a breathy quality, a little rasp here and there. *Mmm mmm mmm* this felt good. It seemed a little naughty to sing a Christmas song like this, but she loved the power she felt. She didn't hold back.

When it was over, her body flooded with heat, and goosebumps rose on her skin.

That's how she knew she'd had a good take.

She walked back into the sound room and sat down in the chair she'd just vacated.

"That's a wrap, you think?" Unice asked after they listened to her third and fourth takes of the song. It sounded great, and even though it wasn't exactly what the label was expecting, Unice loved it.

"Are you happy with it?" Lydia asked.

Her eyes stayed on the soundboard, but she was smiling. She tapped her finger on her lips and smiled like she had a secret.

"I am. Thank you for pushing me."

"Good. You're welcome. Now we can get on to the fun stuff."

Unice cocked her head to the side. "Will you tell me why you don't love Christmas?"

Lydia flipped some switches on the soundboard and sighed. "The grandmother I told you about? Yeah, we used to spend Christmas with her when we were little. Santa came there, not to our house. We didn't even have decorations. My father wasn't Christian, so…"

"I see," Unice said. She could understand where Lydia was coming from.

"Anyway, after Grandma went to jail, that was it. I missed it for a long time, and then I just felt guilty and spoiled for being worried about a stupid holiday when she was in jail. I used to write her letters and give them to my mom to send, but I don't think she ever sent them." She shook herself and inhaled sharply. "Enough sad stuff. You ready to work on something else?"

"Was your grandmother abused? Is that what happened?"

Lydia nodded and sighed. "Her second husband. Yeah. Until she couldn't take it anymore. He was so controlling…I hate seeing that. Pushes my buttons. He wouldn't let her go places, see her family without his permission, that kind of thing. Really bothers me." She turned to look at Unice. "It's part of my 'no entourage' rule too. I see that kind of relationship all the time in the music business, and I won't ever be a party to that."

Unice thought about her own team, and she exhaled. "I think in my case it's been more that they all stepped up to take care of me so I wouldn't break. And when I *did* break, they stood by me. It's hard for them to step back now, like they think I'm still that fragile. It was easier to let them have control over everything…until it wasn't. I need to open my mouth more."

Lydia smiled. "Yeah, you do. You need to sing."

Sharing time was effectively over and they dove into the songwriting process. They moved into the studio and sat on a couch with a mic suspended in front of it and flanked by guitars on racks. Lydia noodled on an acoustic guitar.

"I want you to just sing—whatever comes to mind, stream-of-consciousness kind of thing—don't focus on the words, focus on the emotions."

Unice let out a breath and swayed to the music Lydia had settled into. Since they'd been talking about so many heavy things, the emotions were right there. Raw, heavy, exciting, and powerful. Unice let go and didn't care what words came out of her mouth, only that the sounds matched the music tickling her senses. It went on and on until she was out of breath and reached for a water bottle. Lydia smiled and put down her guitar.

"That's some shit right there, Unice. That's who you are. That's what's inside of you. Did you know it was there?"

Unice shrugged. She wiped at her eyes before a few tears escaped. "Maybe? I've done a good job tamping all that down. I can't function if I let it all float around all the time." She waved her hands around, wiggling her fingers like she was sprinkling pixie dust or something.

"I get it. But you were able to tap it when I asked, and that's great. Some people can't, they keep everything locked inside until they don't know which end is up. Flex it, take it out for walks. Work it out like you do that body of yours and you can do anything, babe."

Unice's chest swelled with the compliment. Damn, she was glad she'd taken this woman's hand.

Lydia then showed her how she'd written the song earlier, how she'd had a riff in her head, and then she thought about all the things she'd noticed about Unice when she came in.

"It doesn't always come together like that, but when it does. Boom."

"Boom," Unice repeated, and then Lydia made an explosion with her hands and they both started laughing.

And then it was midnight.

"I can't believe how late it is! The time flew by."

"When you're having fun, yeah."

Unice felt her cheeks warm. "You were having fun?"

Lydia turned to face her, and their knees brushed. She didn't remedy their proximity. "Yeah. Surprisingly."

Unice bumped Lydia's knee and clicked her tongue at her. "Surprisingly? I'm fun! I can *be* fun."

Lydia leaned forward and placed her hand on Unice's knee. "You *are* fun. I had fun."

For a moment, neither seemed to know how to proceed. Lydia blinked. Unice leaned close enough to smell some sort of ocean breeze fragrance. Lydia smiled, and the lids of her gray eyes lowered, her gaze focused on Unice's mouth. Unice reached for a lock of Lydia's silky hair and twirled it around her finger.

Was she out of line for wanting to kiss Lydia? She felt out of *control*, but not out of line.

Lydia seemed to be holding herself back, as if she were mentally cataloging all the reasons kissing shouldn't be part of their plan. But being here with Lydia had released the chokehold Unice had on her life, and she didn't want to rein anything in.

A car horn honked outside, and whatever was trying to happen in that moment shrank back out of sight as they giggled nervously. Unice found herself hoping that given a few more days, perhaps a moment like this would resurface...and she wouldn't be too shy or hesitant next time.

"I guess that's my cue to walk you back."

Unice smiled. "I'm not going to be able to sleep. I'm too wired."

"Well, you better get rest. I've got plans for you tomorrow."

Lydia having plans for her made her shiver in the very best way.

They walked over to the lodge and, once inside, they came across Gladys and Velma sitting at a booth in the bar with Rose. With their pants unfastened. Groaning.

"Girl, all there is to do in this town is eat! I'm so full!" Gladys reclined in the leather booth and rubbed her stomach.

"Thank you, Lydia, for dinner. It was delicious. I've never had so much meat in my life, and that's including that singles resort in Mexico," Gladys said while making lewd gestures that made Unice cringe.

Lydia put her hands together and gave a little bow.

"I thought you took my credit card?" Unice said, confused.

"Called in a favor, that's all," Lydia said. "You're welcome."

Unice couldn't get over the generosity of this woman. Unice had known her exactly a day, and she'd taught her more about songwriting than she'd ever learned before, that anyone had ever bothered teaching her...and now she treated Unice's team to an expensive dinner? Okay, that may have been self-serving, as she'd obviously wanted them out of the way, but Brazilian restaurants weren't cheap. She knew that.

"We got these, too, but didn't have any room after we had ice cream in that haunted house place." Velma pushed a pink box toward Unice.

"Rimsky? Love that place," Rose said while Unice read the lettering on the box.

"Voodoo Doughnut?"

"Ohhhh," Lydia said, shaking her head. "Soooo good. One of the reasons I rarely go into town is because I always bring those back. Morrison and I both. Did you get the...um..."

"The genitalia-shaped one?" Gladys clicked her fingernails together in a devious fashion. "You know we did!"

"Those are the best," Rose said as she poured another round of tequila shots for Velma, Gladys, and herself.

Unice lifted the lid of the box and saw so much sugary goodness inside, she wanted to weep with joy. She had a cheat meal coming up tomorrow… "You'll save one for me?" She batted her eyes at her beloved manager, who had her figured out.

Velma stared at her for a long time. "First come, first serve."

Gladys slowly dragged the box away from Unice. "Yeah, Unice. If you snooze, you lose."

"Early worm gets the bird," Velma said, and cracked up.

Velma and Gladys were a bit tipsy and quite hysterical over their clichés.

Lydia's gaze met Unice's over the table as she spoke quietly to Rose. "I'm headed to bed," she announced. "Unice? I'll see you in the morning?"

"You will," Unice said. "Thank you, Lydia."

Lydia waved as she climbed the stairs. She'd mentioned that she had an apartment on the second floor and that Morrison lived up top. Unice watched her climb the steps and sighed. She really did have a crush on the woman.

Unice watched her go with so many questions running through her head.

How can I give something back to someone like her?

How can I show her how much I appreciate her?

How can I sneak one of those donuts tonight and hide it without these loonies getting it from me?

"Unice, you're going to have to tuck us in," Gladys said as she stood and buttoned up her snug pants. "Velma, grab the donuts, would you? Guard them with your life. I want that Butterfinger one for breakfast."

Velma stood and wrapped an arm around Unice's waist. "You had a good night. I can tell. You haven't stopped smiling since you came inside. Mmm-mmm-mmm." She shook her head, mock scolding Unice.

"It *was* a good night. Thank you for bringing me here, Velma. I think this trip is going to be something great."

Chapter Five

The next day, however, Unice began to wonder if she'd make it through a day, much less the week, with Lydia.

Her first job was strategizing how to get her girls out of the compound so she could work. Rose mentioned a big market in Portland where they could go shopping and, uh, walk off the food they'd eaten the night before.

Speaking of the food…Unice fought a hard battle over the pink box of donuts and came away triumphant with a portion of the male genitalia, as weird as that was, and a rainbow sprinkle cake donut that was hands-down the best donut she'd ever had.

Then Rose showed her to the yoga studio, and Velma set up her laptop on Skype with Randy, who put her through an awful workout, made worse by the fact Unice hadn't slept much. Then she went for a run with Morrison at her side in the orchards. He'd shared he didn't like running much, but he needed it, and the two of them kept a good pace. She showered and was ready to just throw her hair up in a ponytail and go, but then Gladys insisted on doing her makeup, and her beloved assistant was moving slowly from her hangover.

By the time she ran them off in their rental car and got to the studio, it was nearly eleven and she'd kept Lydia waiting.

"I'm so sorry." Unice's stomach sank. "I didn't get in a workout yesterday, and Saturdays I always go for a longer run." She hated feeling like she had to justify her actions, but Lydia was quiet this morning. Different. A little closed off.

Lydia continued to flip switches. "It's not like we set a time."

Unice noticed the irritation in her voice and hated that she may have inadvertently upset her.

"I know. But maybe we should, you know, have a schedule so I won't leave you waiting when I have to do my workouts."

Lydia looked at her over her shoulder. "I get it. It's fine."

Unice had felt a connection between them last night, and this morning that connection was tenuous at best.

"Your time is valuable. I don't want you to think I don't appreciate you."

Lydia shrugged and whatever stiffness there was between them seemed to pass. "Let's get to work then."

That lasted all of an hour before Rose came in.

"I'm sorry to interrupt," she said to Lydia. "Unice, you have a phone call."

Unice felt a jolt run through her. Lydia wanted her focused, and this wasn't focused. She hated that her life kept creeping into what felt like the beginning of something really good for her. In a lot of ways.

"Excuse me," Unice said.

Lydia pulled out a cigarette and stood from the board. And then she lit it.

"I'll be right back," Unice said as she followed Rose out of the studio.

"This isn't really my place to say," Rose said as they got outside. "Well, it *is* because Lydia is my cousin and I work with her, but it's *not* because she would hate it if she knew I spoke to you."

"Please," Unice said, placing her hand on Rose's arm. "Lydia's important. I don't want to upset her. I get the sense that she's been let down before."

Rose looked around and then leaned closer. "She has. She's been burned plenty. That's why she has her rules. And distractions are her biggest pet peeve. It's a big part of why she moved up here. She's had several pop stars who, well, pop in and out of her life, and it irks her. If you're going to…work with her," she said that pointedly, "you really need to decide what's important to you. If you're going to work with her, you need to be all in."

Unice put her hands on her hips and sighed. "You're right. I'm going to fix this."

Rose smiled and gave her a one-armed hug. "Right on. I like you. I get what she sees in you."

Unice blushed. "Thanks. I don't want to be another person disappointing her."

"Good." Rose winked and opened the door. "The phone is on my desk behind the counter.

"Thanks!"

Unice trotted over and picked up. "Hello?"

"Hey, girl." It was Gladys. "Sorry to interrupt, but Julissa wants to know if we can reschedule for the following week, and if so, she needs to rearrange some things and wants to get started."

Unice winced. There was a part of her that really wished she didn't have anything looming on the horizon. She wanted to get to the point where she could take some time off and start fresh. Maybe that could happen. Eventually. But she had to fulfill commitments.

"That's fine," Unice said. "I just need this week."

"Okay. I rescheduled your appointments on Monday and Tuesday for three weeks out, no problem. And your mom called. I told her you don't have your cell phone and that you'll call her when you take a break for the day. And the label representative wants to make sure that Lydia sends the demo in as soon as possible, so they can get working on it. We're on a short timeline here."

"Got it," Unice said, mentally cataloging all the things she needed to do to make this week work. "Thanks, Gladys. I appreciate you working your magic."

"No problem. Go have some fun with your pro-du-cerrrrr." She cracked up at her own self, and Unice groaned.

"And who's the grown-up here?"

"I'm just sayin', you know, don't keep the lady waiting."

She laughed as she hung up and Unice shook her head.

"Everything okay?" Rose asked.

"Yeah. It could have waited. I'll talk to Gladys when she gets back. I think I'm going to send them back to Seattle, and then home to LA. That may be the only way for me to get rid of distractions."

"You're probably right. I talked to Velma for a long time, and she filled me in."

Unice took a deep breath. "It's been a really rough time."

Rose nodded. "I get why they're so protective of you, but Lydia and I will take care of everything. And Morrison is here, too."

"Thanks," Unice said, opening her arms for a hug, which Rose accepted enthusiastically.

"Of course, any time. Whatever we can do, okay?"

Unice found herself tearing up, but this time it wasn't from fear, or being uncomfortable; it was due to the kindness of strangers who were willing to be there for her on her journey to reclaim herself. That felt like a step in the right direction.

She returned to the studio to find a note from Lydia taped to the locked doors of the building.

Had to run to town to pick up instruments at the shop and get more tape.
Actually, I needed a break.
When you come back, think long and hard about what you're doing here.
I'm happy to invest my time if this is what you really want,
but it has to be what you want and what you're willing to work for.

Lydia

Ouch. Unice hated that her hectic life and schedule had negatively impacted Lydia, and she didn't want her to feel anything less than treasured.

There also seemed to be a double meaning to Lydia's words. She wanted to know where she stood with Unice, and Unice wanted to make it clear.

She needed to show her how she felt, what she wanted, and what was important.

So she went back to the lodge and wrote about it.

Lydia returned a couple of hours later and found Unice in the bar.

"Hey."

Unice had been so involved in what she was working on, Lydia's voice startled her. "Hi. Lydia, I'm s—"

Lydia held up a hand. "What did I say about apologizing?" She didn't seem mad. She seemed…embarrassed? "I'm the one who owes you an apology. I was frustrated, and I didn't want to say something I didn't mean. You can't change who you are and what your life is like overnight. I can't expect that. And I don't want you to resent me for making you choose."

"I would never—"

"And I have a confession," Lydia said. And she blushed as she shifted back and forth on her feet. "You flirted with me—"

"I did." Unice smiled and turned her body to face Lydia.

Then she noticed the unlit cigarette in her hand.

"And I liked it. But Unice…I don't know. I think part of my deal earlier was because I've been down that road and it didn't end well."

Unice's smile slipped. She dug through her memory of the stories she'd heard about Lydia—not that it was fair to take that as fact, but maybe there was something.

"I didn't tell you all the reasons I hate Christmas. Let's just say that there was a certain ingenue that I worked with when I first started producing that chose that wonderful time of the year to go back to her husband."

"That's awful," Unice said, reaching out a hand and taking Lydia's, the one with the cigarette in it. Lydia shifted it to her other hand and shoved it behind her ear. She'd left off the beanie today and her curls were wild around her face. She had more gray hairs than Unice had noticed before.

"See, I thought she would change for me, so I broke some of my rules. That was the last time. One of my rules since then has been not to get involved with artists I work with."

Unice went to let go of her hand, but Lydia held on.

"I'm sorry. I was out of line, then—"

"No, see, I specifically didn't tell you that was my rule, didn't I? I told you, I noticed something different about you when we met, and I told myself I wouldn't compare you to the others. And I didn't. And then I did. So that's my confession."

Unice smiled. *Oh.* Lydia was leaving herself open. She was taking just as big a chance as Unice was. Somehow the fact that the stakes were high for each of them put them on level ground in a way they hadn't been before. It made Unice feel brave.

"You asked me to give you my undivided attention in exchange for learning from you how to use my voice in a different and exciting way, and that's what I want to do. Need to do. So I gave it a shot, and this is what I came up with."

Lydia frowned down at the notebook Unice had been doodling in. "You just wrote this today?"

Unice grinned and patted the seat in the booth next to her. "I wrote it for you. It's an un-Christmas song."

Lydia laughed and then she started reading…

I wrote you a letter and left it today
    I'm sorry to tell you I'm going away
    It seems you've got other plans this year
    And if I'm not with you I can't just sit here

You've got your worries and obligations
    I've got my hang-ups and superstitions
    And all through the season I'm struggling to say
    The words that will keep you from going astray

Christmas songs are overrated
    They deck the halls with melancholy
    Arguments at the family table
    Instead of all the holly jolly
    There's just one thing I want to say before I leave
    Keep your songs and Christmas glee
    I'd rather have you and me

The holidays you talk about
    Are filled with joy and cheer
    But holidays are nothing more
    than sadness, pain and fear
    Every gift is wrong somehow
    And every smile's a broken vow
    And all through the season I've been trying to show
    That what we have will only grow

Unice held her breath as Lydia read the words she'd reached deep inside herself to find. She was amazed that once she'd started, they really began to flow.

Lydia glanced up at her a few times, and her olive cheeks seemed to darken. She blinked a lot. She pulled out a cigarette and tapped it on the table. But she didn't light it.

"This is… It's really good. I can already hear it."

The smile she gave Unice was dazzling. It was the smile of a confident frontwoman, a bold producer, and a woman to reckon with.

Unice was ready for that reckoning.

"You like it?"

Lydia searched her eyes for a moment and then reached for her hand. She kissed the back of it, her lips lingering. "Yeah. Come on."

Lydia dragged her giggling and stumbling from the booth, and they ran all the way to the studio.

Lydia dashed up the steps, and at the top, she opened the door and held it for Unice. "After you," she said, gesturing for her to go in first.

Unice paused inside the doorway as she gathered the courage to do what she was here to do…take what she wanted.

Lydia closed the door, and Unice moved closer. She bent down, her lips hovering inches from Lydia's.

Lydia's gray eyes searched hers. And then she closed the distance.

Unice pressed her lips to Lydia's in a confident statement of intent, and Lydia kissed her back with equal determination. Their bodies met in a smooth embrace. Unice ran her hands over Lydia's shoulders and down her narrow back. Lydia had on platform boots, so their height difference wasn't as pronounced.

Lydia moaned and pulled Unice's hips even closer. She ran a hand up Unice's spine and grasped the back of her neck, squeezing gently.

"Look at you," Lydia murmured, running her tongue over Unice's lips. "A grown-ass woman who takes what she wants."

Unice smiled. She wasn't typically so forward, but Lydia had inspired her in more ways than one.

"I do want." Unice's hand trembled as she tucked one of Lydia's curls behind her ear. She was in the throes of an adrenaline rush, the likes of snowboarding down a steep slope or flying over the lake on a jet ski. She loved feeling the power, and yet she knew that one false move and she'd crash and burn.

"Mmm. Want. I like want." Lydia dragged her fingertips up Unice's ribs and the side of her breast, causing Unice to shiver. She took her time tracing lines across Unice's shoulder and up her neck, along her jaw, and over her earlobe. She gave Unice's hip a little tug and pushed her back against the wall.

Unice's eyelids fluttered shut, and she sighed as Lydia explored her throat with her lips.

"What do *you* want?" Unice asked her, sliding down the wall a few inches. Lydia slid a thigh between hers and made contact with Unice's core.

Lydia may not have heard her as she'd slid the collar of Unice's stretchy long-sleeved top down over her shoulder and proceeded to kiss and nibble along her collarbone.

Unice let her head fall against the wall, and her eyes rolled back. She hadn't been intimate with anyone since she'd parted ways with her last girlfriend days after Miami. Cherish hadn't wanted the attention that the incident brought to Unice's life and Unice didn't blame her. Now, anyway. At the time, she'd considered Cherish's actions to be selfish, but she really couldn't blame her for putting herself first.

Unice wanted to be selfish now. She wanted Lydia.

"I want to take you upstairs," Lydia whispered against her throat. She'd slid a hand under Unice's top and gasped when she discovered Unice hadn't bothered with a bra today. "What do you think about that?"

"I…oh yes. I want to…Yes. What's upstairs?"

Lydia pulled back and gave Unice that smirk again, the twinkle in her eye flooding Unice's body with heat.

"More studio space. And a guestroom. My place is too far away for what I want to do right now."

"So," Unice smiled. "Will there be more singing up there?"

Lydia held out her hand. "Oh, I'll get you singing, all right."

Unice laughed as she let Lydia lead her up the stairs. She was ready to make some beautiful music with the woman who encouraged her to set her voice free.

Chapter Six

Later that night, Unice used the phone in the guestroom of the studio to let Gladys and Velma know that she'd see them in the morning for breakfast and that they should just go on to Seattle without her. Lydia said she'd take Unice to the airport when she was ready to head to Los Angeles. Surprisingly there hadn't been much arguing from Velma, only the mention of her "business," followed by laughter and the click of the phone disconnecting.

Unice and Lydia spent the whole night talking and laughing and exploring each other until they eventually fell asleep in each other's arms, unable to string coherent words together any longer.

The next morning, they dressed, grabbed breakfast from the dining room to go, and snuck up to Lydia's apartment to eat.

"I can't believe this place," Unice said, sitting in the window seat which overlooked the orchard. "It's so beautiful here."

Lydia sat across from her drinking coffee. "Best decision I ever made, moving out here. This building has some great vibes, and the grounds are stunning. You should see it when the trees are covered with blossoms in the spring. Incredible."

She nudged Unice with her toes, which were painted black with sparkles.

"Were you always a nature lover?"

Lydia wrinkled up her nose. "You kidding? I grew up in Vegas and San Francisco. I'm a city girl through and through. But I don't know, things change, people change, and my life definitely changed. Same with Morrison. We love it here."

"I can't believe I get to stay here for a whole week," Unice said with a laugh as she finished her bacon. "Even though we're going to be working, it feels like a vacation."

"I want that for you. We're going to work hard, but I want you to relax. I want this to feel like home for you."

"Home. That sounds nice." Unice thought of her apartment in Studio City. It felt more like an extended stay hotel than a home. Her parent's house was home-ish, but she was little Uni there. Daddy's girl. Mommy's baby. She'd grown so much since she left home five years ago that it was weird to be under their roof and their expectations.

"You live in LA, right? How much time do you actually get to spend there?"

Unice sighed. "I haven't been home for longer than two or three days for over a year."

Lydia whistled through her teeth. "Then I'm so glad you'll be here. I'll work you, but I'm going to make sure you relax, too."

And she *so* did.

Gladys and Velma left Sunday afternoon, and Lydia worked Unice until late in the evening. Monday they slept in, went to Multnomah Falls for a hike, then watched movies in the theater, stuffing themselves on popcorn. Tuesday through Friday Unice got up and ran with Morrison, then she and Lydia worked in the studio during the day and then spent their evenings talking, writing, and loving. By Friday night, they had written eight solid songs and had ideas for more.

Unice had moved her stuff to Lydia's apartment Sunday afternoon, at Lydia's invitation. It was just so easy. Everything between them was easy, even when Lydia pushed her to reach deeper into her emotions until she thought her tears should have dried up, they communicated effortlessly and the push and pull between them was natural, not forced at all. Lydia encouraged Unice to ask for what she needed, and in return she was upfront with Unice about how she was feeling.

But then Saturday came and it was time for Unice to pack and leave. She sat sprawled on Lydia's floor rearranging her suitcase for the seventh time, sighing in an exasperated manner that apparently was loud enough Lydia heard her from the other room.

"What's going on in here?" Lydia asked from the doorway.

Unice threw down the neat stack of pants she'd folded, rolled, and then folded again. She cursed and crossed her arms.

"I'm feeling some kinda way."

Lydia came over and sat beside her. They leaned against the bed with their legs outstretched, staring at the pile of stuff that somehow needed to fit in Unice's suitcase. It was amazing that it seemed to have grown from when she'd arrived despite the fact they hadn't gone shopping.

"Is that feeling something you want to share?"

Unice tilted her head and rested it against Lydia's. Lydia took one of Unice's hands in hers and gave it a squeeze.

"This has just been so…it's been great. I feel more relaxed than I have in forever, and I'm not ready for it to end."

Lydia massaged Unice's hand. She'd been trying to teach Unice some basic piano, but Unice tried so hard, like she did everything else in her life, that she'd managed to tweak her hand and it was sore.

"Who says anything has to end?"

Unice sighed again, this time in a huff, and Lydia chuckled.

"I have to leave. And I don't want to, but I've got appointments and rehearsals…"

"Nowhere in that list do I hear an ending. I'm still going to be here, you're going to keep working on your songwriting, and we've already got a call into your label about the album…"

That had been Lydia's brilliant idea earlier in the week. She'd called up Velma and told her to let the label know that she wanted her name on the shortlist of producers for Unice's next album, and she wanted to do the whole project. Velma agreed to work her magic and said she felt good about the label's response. The fact that they already had some demos to send made their case stronger.

"I just...I like this life, Lydia. Working with you, running in the orchards with Morrison, I feel settled. And it's good."

"It *is* good," Lydia said, turning to kiss her cheek. "And it's here for you when you're ready."

Unice turned to look at Lydia. "What do you mean?"

Lydia placed her palm on Unice's cheek and rubbed her thumb over Unice's cheekbone. "When you're ready to take that step, make that change, I'm here. This place is here." She smiled and raised her eyebrows, her gray eyes searching Unice's.

"You mean come back?"

Lydia nodded. "Come back. Stay with me. Live with me. Here. Continue to make beautiful music with me."

Tears stung Unice's eyes. Lydia had thrown her the life preserver she needed the moment she sang "Pretty Little Package" for her. Now she was offering her...more. And Unice wanted more.

"But you've gotta do something first." Lydia let go and turned to sit cross-legged next to her.

"What's that?"

Lydia linked her fingers together in her lap and fidgeted with her hands. "Being with you, Unice, has been such a wonderful surprise. I never in a million years thought I would ever want to settle down with someone again, much less a popstar fifteen years my junior. But you bring me joy, you brought back a spark in my life that I thought was gone for good, and I want it. I want more. But I don't want you to rush this. If the label approves us working together, you come back, we work, you go on with your merry little life. And then, when you've taken some time away to miss me, and you will," she said with a wink. "Then you come back to me when you're ready."

There was a softness to Lydia's mouth when she said this. Gone was that forceful, take-charge attitude she had when they worked together; gone was the playful arrogance...and left was a vulnerable smile. A smile that was hopeful, one that cried out, "I'm trusting you not to take my heart and mistreat it." And as much as Unice was ready to throw her clothes around the room and hop back into bed to stay, she knew the time away was as much for her as it was for Lydia.

"I will." She reached out and took Lydia's hands in hers. "I hear you, and I will do what you ask. And I will miss you."

"Good." Lydia hooked a hand around Unice's neck and kissed her hard as though she were making a statement this time. "Now get your ass packed before you miss your flight and I gotta hear it from Velma."

"Yes, Miss Pride." She batted her eyelashes at Lydia and Lydia rolled her eyes. She tossed a shirt over Unice's head and then climbed to her feet.

"Hurry up."

Unice made quick work of her suitcase, more determined now to do it right and move forward.

They were going to work things out, in music and life. Love and Pride. They would create something beautiful and see where it led them. No holding back. An equal partnership with compromise and care, and a little bit of magic in the form of some excitement and *whoa*—out-of-this-world chemistry.

And that kiss sealed the deal.

Epilogue

KRISH: *So how long was it until you came back?*

The women look at each other and laugh.

Lydia: *Well, I ended up going to LA a week later on business and that was when we met with the label.*

Unice: *Yeah, and they gave us, like, the three weeks until my tour started to finish the album because it was either that or put it off for another eight months, so we came back to Bolder Breed—*

Lydia: *And we finished the album in two weeks with a week off before her tour so we could go to Hawaii.*

Unice sighed loudly and they laughed.

Unice: *Hawaii was awesome. I came back totally relaxed and when the tour took off, I was in such a good place…It was my best tour yet. Annnd… we spent Christmas together.*

Lydia: *We did. And it wasn't terrible.*

Lydia gives her a smile full of gratitude and Unice winks at her. There's obviously more to this story, but they let me know this isn't a topic they want to discuss further. I absolutely respect their privacy. Christmas isn't for everyone, and that's okay.

Krish: *The album releases this spring and early buzz is that it's going to be a smash hit. What would you say this whole experience taught you? How has your collaboration with Lydia changed your career?*

Unice: *Lydia recognized that I was at a crossroads and showed me just what I was capable of. That's what it took to kickstart my reinvention.*

Lydia: *Look, the album still has that signature sound Unice's fans adore, but we threw in a little extra soul that titillated them as well.*

Unice: *I love it. I love the new sound. Lydia is truly a genius. And Morrison Jones will have co-producing credit on a few songs as well. He played several instruments and co-wrote a couple of the songs. He's a wizard.*

Lydia: *He really is. Morrison and I have worked on a few projects together, but this was the first time he was totally in the director's chair for a song I wrote. It was a great collaboration. I just might be tempted to make that comeback album with him.*

Krish: *You heard it here first,* Feedback *readers. Will the great Lydia Pride grace the stage once more?*

Lydia: *Maybe it will be a Christmas miracle.*

Unice groans at this and they laugh, pressing their foreheads together. The two brilliant artists gaze lovingly at each other and it's clear that they're conspiring. And what a conspiracy they've pulled off!

"Let It Snow" was a huge hit for Love and Pride and the album raised a considerable sum for the #LoveIsLove Foundation. I was able to hear early cuts from the new material they're working on for Love's next album, tentatively titled *Reinvention*. Love seems to be recovering from the terrifying events of the past two years. She also seems to be shaking off the last remnants of the teen dream girl image she's been saddled with since embarking on her solo career. Are her fans ready to let her grow up? Have she and Pride founded a partnership that will last in this business that tends to eat up new relationships and spit them out? That remains to be seen, but for now, I am thrilled to be among the tight-knit circle who has heard their new collaboration, and I am ready for more Love and Pride.

The End...

The Maiden and the Crone

The Maiden and the Crone

Grad student Elia has one last project to complete before earning her degree—a paper deconstructing the feminine archetypes. The perfect opportunity for an interview presents itself during a trip home for spring break. Rosalind Ford is new in town and "a woman of a certain age." She's purchased the outrageous mansion built by a country music superstar in Elia's small hometown, making her a mystery Elia can't wait to solve. She's nothing like Elia expected, and their conversations throw Elia's plans for her future into the air. Roz offers Elia an enticing opportunity, one that will give her a shot gaining valuable experience while working closely with the attractive older woman, or it could draw her into Roz's personal tragedy. What's the right move for a maiden who is smitten with a crone?

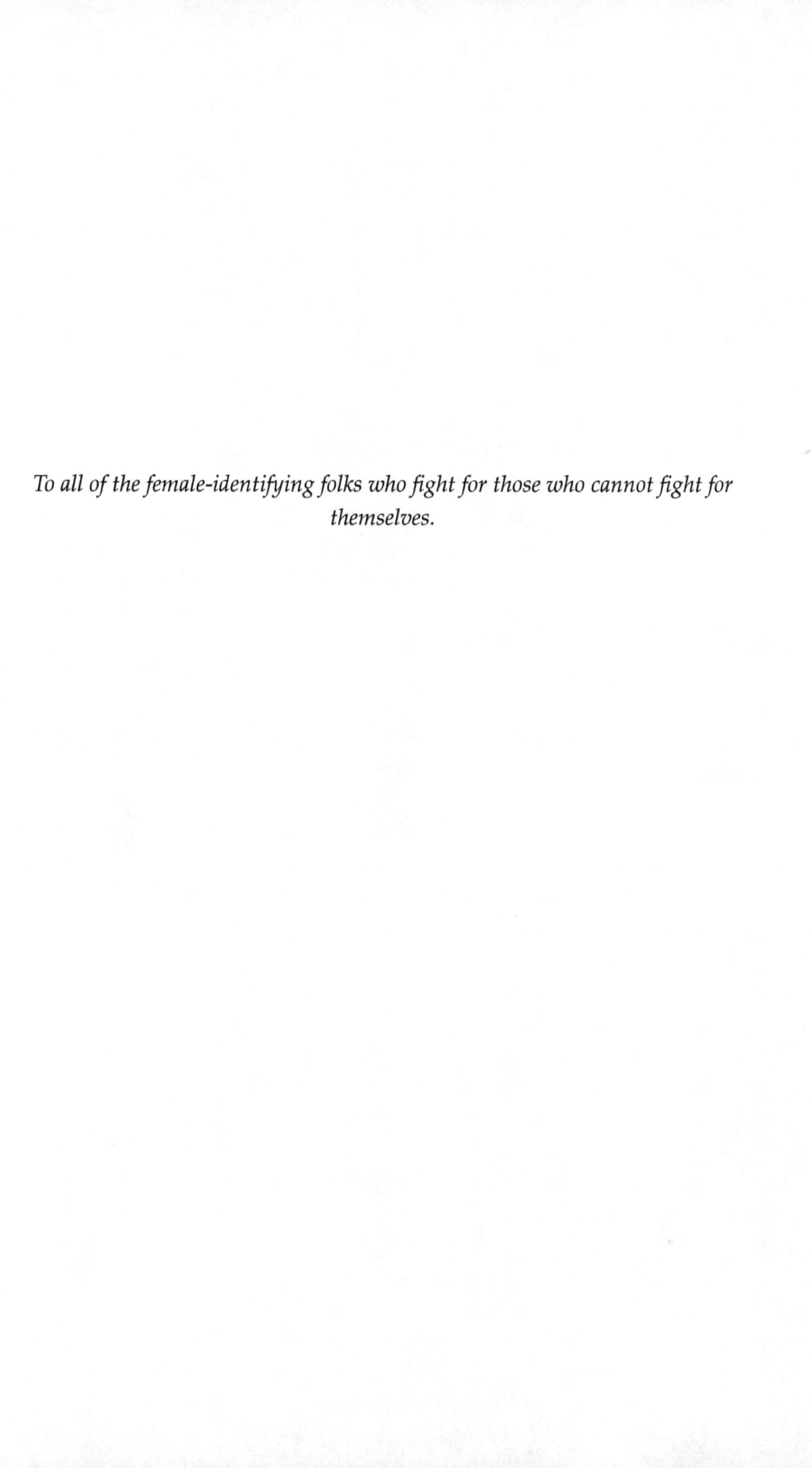

To all of the female-identifying folks who fight for those who cannot fight for themselves.

Chapter One

Procrastination will probably be listed as my top skill on my curriculum vitae…that is, if I ever complete my graduate degree in Women's Studies. Procrastination made it necessary to extend my degree an extra semester, and then an extra year. Procrastination had me sitting in front of my advisor's office the Thursday before spring break, pleading for help with a final project. I should be finishing grad school in June and entering the world of academia in the fall, but my faculty position would soon be gone if I didn't finish this one last paper to complete my master's degree.

"You've really backed yourself into a corner. Even considering you have a break coming up, you need to have this practicum finished in the next six weeks, or you're looking at summer, or fall—"

"I'm literally out of money. If I don't finish my degree, there goes my position in the fall, which is the only way I'll be able to dig myself out of this hole of debt…"

"Have you thought about why you're so resistant to moving forward with your study of the archetypes?"

I liked Kimbra Moriguchi a lot. She'd held my hand through all of life's ups and downs over the past three years. But she never let me skate past accountability.

"Yeah, I've thought about it. I can't *stop* thinking about it, and now I'm stuck. Frozen. As a woman in the tail end of her maiden phase, according to the literature anyway, I'm supposed to be excited about creating and preparing myself to move into the mother phase. I can't get past my own bullshit to create, much less consider nurturing anyone else. I'm a lesbian who doesn't want children of my own, so what does that say about the next stage of my life? I think I'm having an existential crisis way before my time."

Kimbra gave me a sad smile. "I know it's overwhelming. You're about the fifth student I've had in this semester who's going through the same stuff. How about this? You're going home for break, aren't you?"

"Yeah. My aunt and uncles are expecting me." And expecting answers to the "what the hell are you doing with your life" question.

"Your aunt is still raising children, correct? So, she could be your interview about the mother phase of the feminine archetypes. Are there any women in your hometown you'd consider part of the crone archetype?"

And then, inspiration hit. *Finally.*

"You know what? We had the strangest thing happen last summer, right before I came back to school." Kimbra had always loved to hear my tales of small-town America. To her, a born-and-bred city girl from San Francisco, my life experience was almost mythical in its cliched existence.

I'd had to vigorously defend my first grad-level paper on the survival of the small-town lifestyle because I'd argued that there were still places in America where you could find the farmers chatting on a bench in front of the drug store, no traffic lights, barn-raising parties, churches full on Sundays, and homes where folks never locked their doors.

I went so far as to create a whole multimedia presentation of life back in Calaveras, and my class had gotten a kick out of it. It also cemented me a place in Kimbra's good graces.

"Do tell," she said, sipping her herbal tea. She loved to share her latest concoctions with me. Her office smelled like brown sugar and lemon, and knowing she'd have a warm drink for me and a place to talk made this harrowing phase of my life a little easier.

"So, you've seen those Rowdy Real Estate posts, right? The ones where they show these homes that are outrageous? Well, Calaveras happens to have one of those. You ever heard of country singer Owen Buckley? Well, after he made gazillions of dollars off that one song, 'Boots and Booties'—"

"Which seems to have finally died a death of obscurity. That song was the most painful earworm."

"It was, but it made him stupid rich, and he built a massive compound in Calaveras. A huge house on seven acres. It did a lot for our little town. Tourism picked up, and Buckley donated money to build a youth community center and then a skate park. Can't say I was mad about it. But anyway, he built this big ole funky house, filled it with all kinds of bizarre things supposedly, although I've never been inside. He ended up moving to Nashville, though, after only living there two years. Commuting was too much of a pain because he had to drive two hours to the nearest airport.

"Anyway, the house has been empty for about six years and someone bought it over the summer! An older woman, single. No one knows much about her. She moved in and barely anyone has seen or talked to her. She gets all of her food and supplies delivered, and what she can't, she buys at the local drug store, but she goes in right before closing or when the store opens to avoid running into people."

"If that's the case, how do you know if she's a crone?"

My cheeks flushed. "She's got silver hair? Like, wild silver hair. That's practically all I know about her. Well, that and she's armed. Mr. Tompkins, whose property is adjacent to hers, kept complaining to my uncle—he's one of five police officers in town—that he hears gunfire from her property, but my uncle Ernie said she's within her rights to have a gun range on her property. Anyway, the whole town's been titillated about her since she arrived, making up stories. There's even an Instagram account that posts sightings of her."

"Sounds like a nightmare for her," Kimbra said, and that made sense, but Kimbra had repeatedly explained that she lived in a place where new people came and went, and most people didn't know their neighbors.

"All part of small-town living, even if one buys a wacky mansion and wants to be a recluse."

"If you're going to make your deadline—and you know I believe you can do it—you need to get her to talk to you. You have a way of disarming people with that folksy charm you can put on like a uniform for a tour guide at a national park." She snickered as I sputtered in protest.

"Folksy charm? I'll have you know that the panel for my thesis presentation on the role of true crime aficionados in female-presenting empowerment would disagree with me being charming at all."

Kimber laughed heartily. "Because you invited a panel of old white men in law enforcement and then belittled their attempts at justifying their lack of meaningful action regarding victim advocacy. *I* was cheering you on, but I think the balls of every man in that packed hall shriveled a little."

"I was pretty damned proud of that presentation. Too bad I haven't found any police departments willing to take a look at my ideas."

"Patience, grasshopper," she said. "Don't give up just yet. I think you should take your presentation on the road. Speak at law enforcement conferences and public health forums. Someone is bound to see your proposal as viable."

My thesis project, which focused on the need for more entry points for victim advocacy in crimes against female-presenting persons, was the culmination of my grief after losing my mother. I could talk about the Violence Against Women Act all day long, but it was still incredibly painful to discuss how it felt to hold my mother's hand as she bled out on the floor of her living room after an ex-boyfriend got out of prison, returned to Calaveras, and showed up at our house.

"Go home and use that fire to ignite your passion for deconstructing the feminine archetypes." She snorted at my expression. "Don't let a little old lady keep you from your degree, huh?"

Chapter Two

Turned out, Rosalind Ford was no little old lady.

As I stalked her through the aisles of the local CVS just before closing, I couldn't help but notice several pertinent details:

She was not old, despite her wild mane of long, curly, silver hair.

She was ripped, her arms and shoulder muscles perfectly toned beneath her tank top and the stretched-out and frayed, knitted sweater that hung off her shoulders. She wore cut-off jeans that hit her mid-calf and were more a tangle of loose threads than actual denim. Her outfit was finished off by a pair of ratty black work boots that were unlaced at the tops and looked too big for her.

In my hurry to make the four-hour drive home in time for my aunt's Saturday night dinner, I'd forgotten my facewash and moisturizer for my eczema, which was threatening to take over due to my current stress level. Instead of rushing, I took my time watching Rosalind cursing to herself in the stationary aisle. She wore dark glasses despite it being 8:47 p.m.

"Brandon, I thought you ordered more Post-its for me," she hollered to the assistant manager. I used to babysit Brandon, and I was trying really hard to avoid him seeing me.

Her voice was Angie-Harmon-deep and husky. It curled my damn toes. Her olive complexion was darkened by the sun and smooth. She had faint tan lines on her shoulders, a few lines on her face, and thin lips…but man. She was gorgeous.

"I did, Ms. Ford. They're in back. Hold on, I'll grab them for you."

I was so busy watching her, I didn't move in time, and when Brandon barreled around the corner in a hurry to fetch the mysterious woman's supplies, he ran right into me.

"Aurelia Muse! Boy, it's been a while. How are you?"

The gangly teenager pulled me in for a hug, and I stumbled forward into him.

"Brandon. Hi." I patted his back clumsily.

He pulled back with a smile. "I didn't know you were in town! Let me grab Ms. Ford's items and we can catch up."

"That's all right, I—"

But he'd already trotted through the doors to the storeroom.

"Muse? As in Deputy Sheriff Muse?"

"My uncle," I said, turning to face her. My…*crone*? She was a little taller than me, slender but strong, as opposed to my soft, academic body. Drop-dead stunning. "I'm Elia."

I held out my right hand, all polite like the small-town girl I'd been. In the before-times.

She looked down at my hand, then at the load of notebooks, Post-its, Sharpies and tape she had clutched to her chest.

"Tell Ernie I said to come by tomorrow."

I started to ask her a question…but what would I say to her? "Hey, you're a woman of a certain age, can I interview you about being a crone?" I hadn't mapped out how I could get her talking, but that sounded hella rude. Should I tell her what I was doing, or maybe just try a normal conversation? Should I ask on a curious getting-to-know-you premise? You know, two single women becoming acquainted over coffee? Or drinks? God, that would sound like I was hitting on her. Was she even gay? Sometimes I was a disaster at peopling.

And what did she want with my uncle? My mother's youngest brother, Ernesto Muse was one of the last innocent good ole boys left in this world. One of the last optimistic and generally positive cops left in this world. He'd spent four years working for the Stockton Police

Department before coming back to Calaveras to take up the small-town cop life.

"Here you are, Ms. Ford. A case of rainbow Post-its. That's a lot of—"

"Thanks." She cut him off and frowned at me before she carried her load over to the check stand by the front door.

"Just let me know if you need more. I can put in orders at any time. We usually get the stuff in within a couple of days—"

"Thanks. I'm all set."

Brandon continued to attempt conversation with her, but she was on her way out before he could even thank her for shopping at CVS.

"Man, she's a tough nut to crack," he said to me as he reached for my items. "She comes in at least once a week and cleans out the stationary aisle. What could she possibly need to do with all that stuff?"

"Some people prefer that analog life, what can I say?"

He grinned at me. "You look great. How's the big city treating you?"

I laughed. "If by big city you mean graduate school, it's kicking my ass. I'm almost done though."

"Oh yeah? Then what?"

I blew out a breath and went to slide my debit card into the kiosk… where I found hers.

"Oh no," I said, pulling hers out. "Let me see if she's still here." I left my things with Brandon and ran out to the parking lot, but there were no cars there besides mine. I walked back in.

"I can take this to my uncle," I said, suddenly realizing I'd found my way into a conversation with her. "Since apparently he's going to see her tomorrow?"

Brandon was just at that young enough age that he didn't question me, the deputy's niece. It was a good thing for Ms. Ford that I was only a nosy, desperate grad student and not a dangerous person.

I finished purchasing my things, promised Brandon I'd say goodbye before I left town, and pointed my old Ranger pickup to Uncle Ernie's house. I arrived in the middle of poker night with his buddies.

"You bring beer, kid?" He pulled me in for a hug and kissed my hair.

"Of course. I grabbed some of that hard cider from Fieldwork that you liked last time you came to visit me." I'd packed up a case in a cooler before leaving my San Leandro apartment that morning for the drive up to Calaveras. It was my ticket to the guys' card game, and I didn't want to miss out on all the gossip, especially now.

"Good girl," Uncle Ernie said, tugging on my longish dark brown hair. Ernie was more like a big brother than an uncle. He was only eight years older than me. He'd lived with Mom and me when he was a teenager. Their parents thought he should be helping his sister and his niece. He didn't mind one bit. Despite being a teen single mom, Cristina Muse had things under control, so while he did watch me occasionally, he ended up with more freedom than he would have had with his Mexican mother—my abuela Bonita—watching his every move.

Papa Herman was a white man, a retired career Marine, so that meant their house was full of rules growing up and both kids had been ready for freedom by the time they hit their teens.

Mom may not have planned on having a baby at sixteen, but she graduated early, got a good job working for the County of Calaveras, and Abuela watched me during the day. As much as Papa was frustrated with his children's choices, he loved me. I could do no wrong in his eyes, unlike Mom, Uncle Ernie, and Uncle Teddy.

"Girl, where's that beer?" Uncle Teddy called out from the poker table, where he was shuffling the cards. "You know your Auntie Rachel won't let me have it at the house."

Auntie Rachel ran her teetotaler home with the efficiency of a practiced stay-at-home mother of four. Teddy followed Papa into the Marines, but an injury in the line of duty sidelined his military career. Now he spent his days giving tattoos and selling his art in his busy shop downtown, sneaking beer wherever he could get it.

"I know. I gotchoo." I'd moved in with Teddy and Rachel after Mom died because they had the space—a converted attic in their turn-of-the-century home—and they wanted me to have a home base in

Calaveras. You know, in hopes I would return after I finished school. That wasn't likely to happen, but I appreciated the effort.

I wheeled the cooler into the kitchen, pulled out four of Fieldworks' best brews, and brought them in for Ernie, Teddy, and their two buddies, Tony and Angel.

"Órale, Elia, ven aquí con las cervezas!"

"Yeah, yeah." I was used to the razzing I got from these guys.

"Looking good," Angel said as he stood to hug me and accept a hard cider. "Still gay?"

"Lo siento, Angel. Sí. I still love women."

He made a ridiculous show of being disappointed as I hugged Tony and handed him his cider. "Rainbow shit? Do they only have gay beer down there in the Bay? Maybe if you drank some tequila it would straighten you out."

I groaned as he winked at me. "Thanks, but can you blame me for only liking women? If I were into guys, I'd be sitting home alone on Saturday nights while you fools play cards."

Their razzing was the only negativity I'd experienced coming out, and it never felt negative. During my college visits—especially after losing my mom—they'd all stepped up and made me feel like one of the guys.

They all laughed as I perched on the arm of the couch, the movement reminding me of my stolen property. I reached into my hip pocket and held the card out.

"Ernie, I'm supposed to tell you that Ms. Ford would like you to come see her tomorrow."

"So she gave you her credit card?"

"No, she told me to tell you, then she left the card in the slot at the store. I told Brandon I'd give it to you."

Ernie frowned. "He should have kept it, locked it in the store safe, rather than trust some random chick—ouch!"

I didn't care if he was a deputy or the damn king of Spain, I smacked him upside the head. "I'll have you know I used to babysit Brandon and his little sisters. I'm trustworthy."

"Man, that vieja loves you, Ernesto," Tony said. He made kissing sounds at Ernie, who flicked a cashew at him.

"She's a lesbian, dumbass." Ernie ran his thumb over the credit card numbers and frowned. "She's a former cop, you know that?"

The guys got quiet around the table.

"No shit," Teddy said. "I knew you'd been up there a couple times talking to her. Is she loca like they say?"

"Nah," Ernie said, taking a drink of the cider and giving a groan of approval. "I won't say a whole lot, cause it's her business, but let's just say she's been through it. Sucks that people here are treating her like a freak show rather than a neighbor, you know?"

"She's always cool when I see her, like she says, 'thank you' when I drop off her mail and shit," Tony said with a shrug. "Saw her out there cleaning spray paint off her wall the other day."

Ernie swore under his breath. "Some asshole kids tagged her place, calling her a bruja."

"A witch?" I felt for the woman. There were a lot of kids around Calaveras with nothing better to do, but that slur hit close to home. In my studies, I'd done a lot of research on how that particular label was used to control women, take power from them, and how many women had started to reclaim it, practicing various forms of witchcraft as an act of defiance. A way to take their power back. I was all for that type of empowerment. Fuck the patriarchy.

Well, my brothers and these two weirdos were okay, but the rest could kiss my ass.

"It's bullshit," Teddy said, dealing the cards. "You want in, Elia?"

I held up a hand. "I promised Natalia and Miguelito I'd tuck them in tonight." The eldest two of Rachel and Teddy's kids knew me the best, as I'd been around when they were little. Lealie and Oscar were born after I left for college. I hated missing out on the early times with them. I loved the littles so much, which was another reason I was torn about finishing my degree program and taking a faculty position. I'd only see them over breaks. I'd miss out on so much.

"They love it when you're home," Teddy said with a warm smile. "We all do. Especially when you bring the good brew. If you'd just come home, we could make it ourselves."

"You know it." *And I would love to spend time with you.*

We toasted each other, and I watched as they all played shitty hands. In all these years, they were still the worst poker players I'd ever seen. "Maybe y'all should go out to the casino and take some lessons," I finally said after five hands of trash.

"What, you can play better? Bring it," Angel said, but I took one last swig of my cider and stood from the couch.

"Not tonight. The kids are waiting on me. You guys still play Wednesdays too?"

They grumbled that yes, they did, and then got back to shit-talking each other. I said my goodbyes a few minutes later and Ernie followed me out.

"I don't suppose you'd take me with you when you go out to her place tomorrow, would you?"

Ernie raised an eyebrow. "She's a little old for you, don't you think?"

I socked him in the gut, and he laughed. "I'll tell you why, and then you tell me if I should go or not."

He crossed his arms over his chest in his cop stance.

"I need to interview a woman of a certain age for my very last practicum. I have to do this for my degree."

"Why her? Aren't there other old women in town?"

"I don't want it to be tainted by my history with them. I'm already talking to Auntie Rachel, but I need someone…beyond childbearing years. That doesn't mean old. I don't know if she'll even talk to me, but—"

"She might. She's really cool. Been through hell, though. Her fiancé disappeared while she was in the middle of a wrongful termination lawsuit, I can tell you that much, as it's public record. But Elia, I'm the only person in town she talks to, so I don't want to upset her. She's had enough people be assholes to her since she came to town."

"I swear, I just want to meet her. Make the introduction and then if she wants me gone, I'll leave her alone and go talk to one of the old women at Casa De Oro. Auntie Rachel volunteers over there, she'll know someone." But I didn't want to talk to some random old woman.

I wanted to talk to *her*. Rosalind Ford.

"All right. I'll pick you up at ten. She doesn't get up early. She's kind of a night owl."

"Great. Should I bake for her? Take her some of abuelita's mole sauce?"

"Nah, then she'll be suspicious. I'll tell her the truth, that you're doing a ride-along with me, you know, what you need to be doing for your *other* project." He raised an eyebrow. "You're still working on your proposal, aren't you? It's such a good idea."

"I am, I swear. After I graduate, I'll have more time."

"All right. I'll pick you up in the morning."

"Thank you. Want me to make you breakfast?"

He gave a sheepish grin. "Please?"

I shook my head. "Someday you need to find someone to cook for you."

He shrugged. "But you're so good at it."

"Wow, what, are we going to be the old spinsters together?"

His eyes widened a little too excitedly. "We *could*...if you came home. Man, I miss you. It's not the same without you here."

I sighed and hugged him tight again. I did miss my family, but I'd worked so hard for a career in academia. *Shouldn't I see it through?*

"I don't know what I'm doing. I'll be screwed if I don't finish this practicum though, so please, help me talk to her?"

"All right, but watch your step. She'll freeze up quick if she thinks you're like everyone else."

"Like *what* like everyone else?"

"Nosy."

Chapter Three

I got up early, made chocolate chip pancakes and bacon for the littles, and then made a big batch of breakfast burritos for Ernie, as well as some to take to Rosalind. Food helped people open up, no matter what Ernie said. At least that had always been my experience, and I was a damn good cook. I learned from my abuelita.

I showered, straightened my naturally wavy hair—which brought out the auburn highlights, thanks to my mixed heritage—and dressed in tan leggings, a long, white, sleeveless shirt, and Chucks. My skin was so pale, though. I needed some sun this week, that was for damned sure.

"Auntie Rachel? I'm headed out with Ernie for a bit, but I'll be back later in case you and Teddy want to go out? Catch a movie?"

Rachel sat on the couch with her Kindle and a cup of coffee. "Maybe. But the thought of getting dressed today seems like too much work. I kinda want to read all day."

I laughed. "Then you should do that. Teddy will keep the kids busy, and I'll cook dinner."

She smiled up at me. "I'm so glad you're here. We all miss you."

I squeezed her shoulder. "I've missed you too. And the kids. Man, they change so much when I'm gone."

She raised an eyebrow at me but sipped her coffee.

"I know, I know. I'll be back later."

I grabbed the bag with the burritos and mole sauce and met Ernie on the street in front of the house. Rachel and Teddy's place was two blocks off the main street of the town, which had been around since the gold rush. Many of the houses and buildings downtown had survived, but the population had only made a comeback in the past twenty years from its heyday. It was less touristy than neighboring towns, like Murphys or Angels Camp, which had become popular for their wine-tasting offerings from local vineyards, but it had an equally rustic charm.

I did miss that charm when I was in the Bay Area. I loved knowing that everyone here knew me, even if that meant they knew the worst of my life. I sometimes wondered why I'd been in such a rush to leave.

"Oh, man, that smells so good," Ernie said as I climbed into his cruiser.

"You want yours now or are you going to sit someplace and eat this like a civilized person? I made the mole sauce, so—"

"I got this."

He drove us across town to Mark Twain Park, where our little community gathered for all kinds of festivals that we've been cele-brating for at least a century. Snail races, homely dog pageants, and Halloween parades, along with Octoberfest, Fourth of July, Frog Jumping and on and on. The picnic area was well-maintained and fairly empty, since the various church congregations in town were still in session. Ernie carried his burrito over to a table in the sunshine, and I sat across from him.

"So how is it that you've struck up a friendship—"

"An acquaintance. I told you that Mr. Tompkins kept complaining about her shooting, right? Seriously, she's using the area farthest back on her property and well away from him. She's within her rights, and it's not like she's doing it every day or anything. When I went over to talk to her the first time…" he began with a smile. He took a bite of the burrito and his eyes rolled back in his head. The sounds coming from him were ridiculous. "She was real short with me at first, but then she was like, 'I've been where you've been. I'm sorry this is creating more work for you.' I reassured her that Tompkins complained about Buckley's noise way more often, which led to her asking about Owen Buckley, and letting me know about some of the more bizarre things she'd found in the house."

"Oh my God, did she give you a tour? I've always wondered about the bits of the house that weren't shown in the magazine spreads."

He laughed and finished chewing. "Yeah, she showed me around. Not all of the place. She said there were still rooms she hadn't spent any time in. She signed an agreement with Buckley's manager that if she came across any intellectual property, she'd pass it along. She also said that if there was anything they wanted, they had six months to claim it, or she was going to auction it off for charity."

"That's so wild! I can't imagine living someplace where you don't know every last thing you have in your house. Mom...well, she kept our place sparse, never liked clutter, and Auntie Rachel is like that. My place is miniscule. There aren't any hiding places."

Ernie took a sip of water. "Think you're going to stay there?"

I slumped in my seat. "I don't know. I thought I would. I was offered a faculty position in the fall, that is if I finish my damned degree on time."

"That's great, mija. But?"

"But...I don't know! I feel like I'm still learning, you know? Growing. I don't know that I'm ready. I'll be like all the profs in undergrad that I couldn't stand because they'd been in their positions for decades and hadn't had actual contact with the subjects they were teaching. And like, what does a twenty-five-year-old have to offer to people who've been out there living their lives?"

"Not to push either way, but you *have* been through more than the majority of students you'll be teaching."

Had I, though? Sure, I'd been a victim of trauma on more than one occasion, but so had millions of other people, especially those who identify as female, trans, or non-binary. I was no one special. Perhaps I'd thought that by allowing my trauma to fuel my fire in academic pursuits, I was using my pain to bring about good, but was that true? Or was it a way to hide?

"Maybe my experience and skills could be put to use in a better capacity. Maybe I should wait until *I'm* a woman of a certain age and have a bit more life experience under my belt. Then I'd be a better candidate."

He shrugged and finished the last of his burrito. "Sounds like the school thinks you're a good candidate now if they offered you the position."

"Maybe."

"And maybe you're having a bit of imposter syndrome."

"Maybe."

He laughed. "And maybe I still want you to come work with me."

"Ahhhhh, the truth finally!"

He threw his wadded-up burrito wrapper at me. "Come on, you know you'd be a great cop, and we could use a female-identifying officer. And I could use someone I trust at my back." He gave a small shrug. "I want you to do whatever is going to make you happy, El, you know that. No harm in keeping your options open."

"I know. You know Abuelita would have had a cow."

His smile turned sad. "Your papa too. But they'd be proud of you no matter what you do. We're all proud of you. You're a survivor, El."

I rolled my eyes at that. "Enough, already. Now, how should I play this visit? Should I come right out and ask if I can interview her?"

Ernie polished off his can of water and his brows met in the middle. "Let's see what mood she's in today."

And with that, he cleaned up his mess and radioed that he was code 10-62—meeting a citizen—at the Ford place.

At which point the dispatcher asked, "Which place?"

Ernie heaved an exaggerated sigh, gave the proper address, and the dispatcher answered "10-4."

"They'd prefer to still call it Buckley's house, but he's long gone. Roz deserves better than the town treating her like some freaky shut-in or a witch."

"I'm sure you're right," I said. I couldn't wait to meet her for real, on her own somewhat-legendary turf.

Chapter Four

Like everyone else in Calaveras, I'd ridden my bike by the Buckley house during construction and after Owen Buckley moved in. We'd been told by our parents to stay away, to give the man his peace, but we were nosy. We wanted to know if it was true there was a waterslide that went from the top floor all the way down to the pool.

Sadly, we couldn't see that from the road. I knew better than to hop the fence and sneak around. Papa had warned me not to, and Mom threatened me with perpetual punishment if I put one toe over that property line, and that was enough to keep me away.

Eventually, Buckley opened the grounds to the public for a few special occasions, and we were disappointed to see that the pool was actually indoors and couldn't be seen from the outside at all. I'd fallen in love with the gardens, however, and the roses had been some of the best-smelling flowers I'd ever encountered.

Pre-teen Aurelia was internally squealing with delight that I might finally catch a glimpse inside the place.

When we pulled up to the gate, Ernie entered a code and the gates opened.

I was saddened to see that the gorgeous landscaping Buckley had kept up, even after he'd left for Nashville, was overgrown. The flowers needed deadheading, the roses were nearly overrun with passion-flower vines, and the lawns were overgrown. Poppies sprouted from every corner of the yard, brightening the space with pops of orange that gave me hope the gardens could still be saved. Angel's brother ran a gardening service. Maybe Ernie could convince her to get them out here.

Ernie parked the cruiser to the right of the house in the circular driveway, in front of the tennis courts. I could see around to the back of the house from this angle. Rosalind was sitting on a lounge chair on the back patio, which I remembered had been done in large mosaic panels. She wore a huge floppy hat like the kind you might see in a European travel brochure. When I opened the cruiser door, I could hear music pouring out of the house. I recognized The Ramones. So, she liked punk. *All right.*

"Think Mr. Tompkins can hear the music at his place?" I asked as I walked beside Ernie.

He snorted. "I'm tempted to tamper with his hearing aids, so he'll leave the poor woman alone."

I raised my eyebrows. "You wouldn't."

He shrugged. "She's got good taste in music at least. Hey, Roz," he called out, in case she hadn't heard us pull in.

She turned in her chair and waved to him.

"Hold on, let me turn it down." She pointed a remote at the window and the music faded to a low roar. "I've still got to figure out how to hook my phone up to the Bluetooth speakers that are sprinkled around the garden. The tech that country bumpkin left was just advanced enough at the time he installed it to now be barely work-able." She stood from her chair and dusted peanut shells off her knit overalls.

Then she noticed me.

"Didn't know you had a deputy, Deputy."

Ernie smiled at her and shook her hand. "Roz, this is my niece—"

"Elia. We've met." She had a blank look on her face, but something in her eyes twinkled when she said my name. I swear I wasn't imag-ining it. But it seemed like the kind of twinkle that came before mischief. The good kind of twinkle. *Hmm.*

"You left your credit card at the store last night," I blurted out. "I tried to catch you, but you were already gone."

Ernie pulled the card out of his shirt pocket and handed it to her.

"Thanks," she said, frowning at the card. "Guess I was distracted." She glanced at me and then she looked square at Ernie. "You hear anything?"

He shook his head slowly. "'Fraid not. I'll keep trying."

A crease appeared between her brows, but then it disappeared. "I need help with that other thing," she said, her eyes darting to me.

Ernie stood straighter. "Oh, well, you're in luck. I brought Elia along. She's way better than me at computer stuff."

She crossed her arms over her chest. I was momentarily mesmerized by her long fingers grasping her bronzed biceps. Her skin was so, so lovely, and her hands were—

"What makes you qualified?"

"For?" I obviously missed something.

She dropped her arms and turned for the house. "Might as well come in. I'm dead in the water unless I get this damn thing to work."

I looked to Ernie, and he simply gestured for me to follow her in.

Her bare feet slapped on the patio and then on the wood floors in the room we entered, which could, I suppose, be called a great room, only it was mostly empty. The cavernous wooden space resembled a saloon from the Old West, complete with loads of antlers mounted everywhere. I could see a modern stainless-steel kitchen through a set of saloon-type doors, but the large space was only occupied by a long solid-wood bar with about twenty stools tucked underneath.

"I know there's a lot more I can accomplish if I can just figure out how to get these extra monitors set up."

We came to a doorway with more double doors, and she pushed through. The room on the other side was a fairly normal living room, except there was deep green shag carpet all around and big, bulky leather furniture that obviously a country dude would pick out, and the wallpaper had…cowboy hats and tumbleweeds on it? Did he actually pay someone to decorate this place?

"I'm telling you, Roz, I can have the consignment shop come and pick up any of this…furniture." Ernie curled his lip. I was grateful he'd said something. If he would have complimented the room, I would have barfed all over the green shag.

She waved a hand and kept walking. "Eventually. His six months are nearly up and then I'll do something. I'd like to have an auction, but that's work I don't have time for. The carpet's gotta go, though. I bought one of those vacuum robot things and it got tangled, this shit's so tall."

"I mean, they weren't made to tackle the grasslands." *Fuck*, I didn't mean to say that out loud.

Ernie snickered. Rosalind stopped in front of a section of mirrored wall. I couldn't tell if I'd offended her by her expression.

"*You* buy a house this size and then let's see how quickly *you* address its less-than-appealing elements." She smirked and then waved her hand in front of the mirror. "Shit." She stepped two steps to the left and tried again. "Dammit." Four steps to the right, she waved her hand, and a keypad appeared to light up behind the glass.

"*Say whaaat?*" I muttered, stunned. She punched in a code, messed it up twice, and then finally got it on the last try. A seam appeared in the glass, and the wall moved back about a foot, opening up a dark hallway.

"Pretty neat, huh?" Rosalind said. "Only problem is, for a safe room, it's not practical. If you mark the spot where the keypad is, you've given away its existence. And if you have to hunt for it in an emergency, that's precious seconds lost. Eventually I'll switch out the dumb keypad. It doesn't pick up touch very well anymore. I'll get a thumbprint scanner or something. Anyway, I'm set up in here for now, but I'm gonna need more space soon."

She led us down a short, dark hallway, and I was just about to whip out my phone for a light source when she flipped a switch.

There we were, in a narrow Cape Canaveral-style computer control room. There were about twenty screens on one wall, showing views of the whole property. On the opposite wall, there was a table with three large computer monitors still in their boxes, two keyboards, three mice, and a boatload of notebooks, folders, and Post-its strewn all over the surface.

There was also a fridge stashed in here, a cot, and a wardrobe. The room, while small, was still bigger than my apartment in San Leandro.

"The operation is growing, huh?" Ernie asked her.

"Word got out. I've got a lot of former contacts who are taking advantage of my free time. The problem is that everything is much more sophisticated now, and I'm used to a more tactile approach."

"How many cold cases are you working on?"

My ears perked up.

She sighed. "I've lost count. I've got two more rooms full of file boxes and crime scene recreations, boards, you name it. I've got the space, but it's getting too big for just me. I thought putting it on the computer might help, but it's not organic for me to work that way. Plus, the fastest wi-fi is in here, but I can't stand being cooped up in here with no windows." She threw her hands up. "I can't even hook up these monitors, let alone get them all working the way I want."

"El and I can take a look," Ernie said, raising his eyebrows at me.

"Sure," I said. "I run a research program in the Women's Studies department at East Bay University. I've had to become my own IT person."

She looked between us and raised her eyebrows. "Have at it."

It took less than an hour for Ernie and me to get everything hooked up properly and for him to show Roz how she could use each monitor to run certain programs and be able to look between them easily. As we were getting things set up, my curiosity grew. She was working on cold cases? Like for actual police departments or on her own, I wondered? Ernie asked her a lot of questions, and I tried to pay attention without seeming like I was too involved.

"I've checked, there was nothing after she left. I've talked to every family member and co-worker I can come across, but no one has heard from her. It's been two years and nothing."

"Have you tried Websleuths or Reddit Bureau of Investigation? A social media scrub?"

I'd been using some zip-ties I found in a box on the floor to clean up her cords and spoke without thinking whether or not my contribution would be welcome. I crawled out from under the table to find her staring at me. I'd expected snark, but her face was soft, and she'd removed her dark glasses to reveal the most incredible blue-green eyes I'd ever seen.

"I've looked at Websleuths a time or two, but it's so complicated. And Reddit? Isn't that just for conspiracy theorists?"

"It's a mixed bag of folks. Sometimes you can find good info there."

Roz looked at Ernie and then back at me. "How do you know all this stuff?"

Ernie spoke before I could string words together.

"El did her master's thesis on resources and programs to help empower female-identifying victims of crime and their families. She's got a lot of great ideas—"

"That I'm sure were really popular with law enforcement?" Roz chuckled and set down a stack of folders she was moving. "That's the kind of shit that got me in hot water in my department."

I shrugged. "It was a strong thesis, but I could see their arguments. I'm still working out the kinks."

Roz nodded at me for several beats. "Right. Well, thanks for helping me get this set up. Maybe I'll actually make some headway. Thank you for coming out."

Ernie tipped his head to his shoulder and listened to his radio for a moment, then stepped out of the room to talk to dispatch.

I was running out of time to ask her if I could interview her for my project. I was just about to say something when Ernie poked his head back in.

"I gotta head into town," he said. "El, I can drop you back at home."

"Actually," Roz said. "Elia, would you mind sticking around for a bit? I can run you home later?"

I looked at my watch. I'd planned on helping out Rachel with the kids, but she'd made it clear she didn't want to go out. Maybe I *could* stick around. "If it's no trouble."

She rolled her eyes. "Thanks, Ernie. I'll bring her home."

He raised his eyebrows, tapped his fingers on the doorway twice. "You sure?"

It seemed like that was more for me than for Roz.

I nodded. "It's no problem. I'll text Rachel."

"All right then." He waved and turned to leave as his radio squawked loudly.

"Your uncle is the most overworked and underappreciated cop I've ever known, and that's saying something." Roz turned her intense gaze on me, and my chest fluttered. "I don't know what you know about me."

I was startled. "Uh, you were a cop? You bought this house? That's about all."

She nodded and crossed her arms over her chest again. Her hands distracted me for a moment once more, but I tried to keep my eyes on hers.

"Nothing about the money, huh?"

I shrugged. "Inheritance? Win the lotto?"

"Wrongful termination and defamation lawsuit."

"Oh. Wow. Okay."

"Yeah," Roz said. "Right. Well, here's the deal. I had a really fucked-up situation at my previous job. I was the lead detective on the case of a trans kid who was assaulted. A series of odd turns happened, and they took the case away from me. I had a little pull with command, so I kept it, but when they found out my suspects were a couple of off-duty cops and I refused to let it slide, they fired me."

"That's awful," I said, my stomach clenching. "That must have been horrible for you."

She turned to look at the computer screens showing footage from cameras set up around the property. "Horrible for a lot of people."

"I'm glad that you were compensated at least. Although, no offense, you could have gone anywhere. Why Calaveras?"

"Why Women's Studies?" She'd turned to face me, and we were standing so close, the movement stirred the air next to my bare shoulder and I broke out in goose bumps.

"Why?"

She nodded.

I stood a little taller. "Did Ernie tell you about my mom?"

She nodded again.

"Then you know."

"Maybe. Depends on what you do with it. Freaking poetry? Art? Something like that?"

I laughed at her disdain. "What would be wrong with that?"

"Nothing," she said with her own laugh. "Other than it's boring as shit."

"I'm not a huge fan of poetry, so no. My work has been geared toward helping female-identifying people overcome trauma. Resiliency, advocacy, and empowerment have been my focus."

"Interesting. I'm a fan of all three. And that's kind of the answer to your question."

"Why here?"

"I guess I, too, went through a traumatic experience after years of helping other people deal with trauma, and while I needed some time to be angry and selfish, I'm ready to get back to work."

"Yeah? As a police officer?"

She wrinkled her nose. "I think I can be of more use helping departments as a consultant. I'm good at what I do. I had one of the best closure rates of any detective in my precinct in Denver, but I decided that I'd rather do what I'm good at without giving up too much of myself."

"That's very resilient of you," I said with a grin.

"Touché," she said. "But I'm realizing I'm in over my head."

"How do you mean?"

"Exhibit A," she says, gesturing to the room around her. "I have nearly unlimited resources at my disposal, but I'm not the most organized person. I was fortunate to always have partners who were very organized, but now it's just me and…yeah. I know there are programs out there—"

Something caught her eye on the camera feed, and she walked closer to one of the monitors.

"Those little shits," she said, and she darted out of the room.

"Roz?" I called out to her. I looked up at the screen, and in the bright midday sun, there were two pre-teen boys I didn't recognize. They had ridden up to the front gates on their bikes and were pulling spray cans out of backpacks. There was no sound to the feed, but I could tell they were laughing.

"Those little shits!" I echoed.

They were just about to start tagging the stone wall when suddenly they looked up, soundlessly screamed, and then went running toward their bikes. They pedaled away as if the Hounds of Hell were chasing them.

Roz returned a few moments later, cackling.

"What happened?" I asked, as she seemed quite pleased with herself.

"I may be lousy with computers, but I did pick up a few skills in the department before being fired—including piloting drones." She pulled out her phone, tapped it a few times, and then stood next to me, holding it out. "Exhibit B."

The drone she'd used had a camera feed that she could view on her phone.

"I used a voice modifier to give them a little scare, and I attached a laser pointer to the drone…and pointed it right at their scrawny little chests."

I covered my mouth. "Oh my God." I couldn't help laughing. Served them right.

"I kinda don't blame the kids for starting rumors about me. After the first time I caught them on camera trying to climb over the gate, I started hiding out in the bushes in a skeleton mask and jumping out at them. One of the kids' parents called Ernie to complain about me. First Tompkins, then the kids. He didn't know what to do with me. He came out here all frowny, you know how he is."

"I do," I said. My uncle was a damn good cop, but if you didn't know him, you'd take his serious expression as evidence of him being an insufferable prick. He wasn't, thank God. I couldn't handle having a huge dick in the family.

"Once I showed him the footage, he just gave that resigned exhale he does. He asked me for a copy, I sent it to him, and he told me he'd take care of it. He started coming out about once a week after that, checking to make sure everyone was leaving me alone. Then he asked me for help on one of his cases, I asked him for help on another matter… He's the closest thing I have to a friend here."

I smiled. "He's pretty great."

She got that twinkle again. "He told me all about you, by the way. I told him to bring you up here sometime."

"Me? Why?"

She shrugged. "Curiosity. Guess I wanted to meet the Muse who got away from Calaveras."

I snorted. "I guess? I miss it, though."

"Your family misses you, too. At least your uncle. I haven't met the rest of them yet, although apparently, I have an open invitation to poker night?"

I laughed. "That's awesome. Just so you know, your money is probably pretty safe because they all suck at cards."

"All right then. Perhaps I'll check it out."

We stood there for a beat longer before she backed away. "Right—"

"So—"

"The thing is—"

"How can I—?"

And we both laughed.

"How can I be of assistance?" I asked, trying to enunciate slowly so I wouldn't trip over my words. We'd definitely had a moment there, but I had no idea how to interpret it.

"Sorry. I've been spending too much time on my own, I think I've forgotten how to converse. I thought I'd be living the dream, you know? By myself, no one to hassle me, well, except for the neighbor. What's the deal with that Tompkins guy anyway?"

"Mr. Tompkins has been a hundred years old my whole life, it seems. The Tompkins family has been in the area probably since the late eighteen hundreds. They used to own the whole area. The state got them to cough up the land for the town so it could be the county seat for Calaveras County. They weren't happy the town wasn't named after them, but at least they got to name a street."

"They did? Where?"

I snorted. "It leads out to the dump from the other side of their property."

Roz threw her head back and laughed. "Serves him right," she said. "I'm sorry, I don't know if you're friends—"

"No, don't worry about it. I don't think there has ever been much love between the Muses and the Tompkins clan."

"Okay. Well, I thought I'd pick your brain about some of the tools you mentioned."

"Oh. Sure. Okay."

She frowned and flicked her hand at me. "I'm not a hundred percent ready to give up my Post-its and bulletin boards, but I need… something. I feel like if I could look at these cases holistically…I don't know. I need a system, and I don't have one and it's driving me nuts. "

"I think I get it. I do. Let's sit and you can walk me through some of your needs. Maybe we can come up with something together."

Chapter Five

Three hours later, I was on my second Diet Coke, and I was surrounded by candy wrappers.

"This way you've got all the things in one place, and you can branch off from there."

We'd used a program called Notion to create a workspace for every case she was working on, and I was showing her how to access everything from a single data point.

"You can have a task list, contacts list, a calendar for each case that also links to your main calendar here," I said, clicking over to the master calendar. "You can set reminders here that will connect with the calendar on your phone, so you always have access."

"This is really cool," she said, leaning over my shoulder. "Now, how do I see the whole list of them?"

She automatically reached for the mouse and my hand was still on it.

"Oh, sorry." I pulled my hand back when her skin brushed mine. She smiled down at me. I was close enough to catch the scent on her skin. She smelled like strawberries and cream…and I needed space before I did something stupid.

"Hey, how about we take a break? Can I feed you?"

I turned to look at her and was at eye level with her rosy lips.

"My burritos! *Dammit.*" I turned the chair around, and she stood in front of me with her hands on her hips.

"Excuse me?"

"Oh, I just realized, I left the batch of breakfast burritos I made in Ernie's car. I hope he refrigerated them."

She laughed. "You better text him. It would be criminal to waste a batch of burritos." She grinned and stepped back from my chair.

"Is there…can I use your restroom?"

"Oh, yeah. Sorry. Uh…do you want to use the plain boring one in here or one of the fun bathrooms?"

I laughed. "Fun. Definitely."

She rolled her eyes. "I'm not sure what's more ridiculous, that he built this place or that I bought it. Step right this way."

She led me back through the funky cowboy living room to the saloon and pointed to the right corner.

"Some of the bathrooms in this place…you're taking your life into your hands, but the ones in here are pretty safe."

"How many bathrooms are there?" I asked as I walked toward the side-by-side doors.

"I think ten, not counting these two, but I swear there's one I found once and haven't found again."

"How is that possible?" I muttered to myself as I made it past the bar to a short hallway. There were two doors, each with stick figures of the traditional male and female variety but wearing cowboy hats. But there were also pictures taped to the bathroom doors of what I'd describe as non-binary and/or trans folks. From David Bowie, to Kristen Stewart as Joan Jett, to Harry Styles in a dress. It was the best thing I'd seen about the place so far.

Inside the bathroom was a single stall with a half door made out of wood. When I opened it, I found myself looking at an outhouse-type setup like something you'd see in a horror movie, complete with plastic snakes and scorpions on the bench, on the floor, and even hanging from the ceiling. There was an animal skull hanging over the brass toilet seat in the middle of the bench. I wondered how much of the decor came with the house and what, if any, had been added by the current owner.

Roz was such a paradox. As we worked, she was tough as nails, on task, and completely businesslike in her approach to the cases she was working on. She was mostly focused on missing persons involving women, children, queer and trans folks. We hadn't talked a whole lot about what she was going to be doing, exactly, but I got the sense she was trying to establish her own ways of examining the cases because she didn't trust the systems in place for law enforcement.

But then I recalled the stories she told about messing with the nosy kids, and she seemed like she had a mischievous streak, like she knew how to have a good time. I knew from Ernie that cops tended to goof off when they were between calls, and I'd seen some of their hijinks for myself when I'd visited the station. Roz did not seem like the kind of person who didn't like people and wanted to be isolated.

So why move into this giant house by herself? What happened to her must have been so awful to make her want to literally leave everything behind.

My project loomed, so sure, my internal interrogation had to do with that, but I also wondered on a human level…what was driving her? Helping her just little bit had me wondering, what would it be like to know your purpose and be so good at it, embrace it, and run with it? Maybe that was the major difference between the maiden archetype and that of the mother and the crone.

I washed my hands in the trough sink and looked around. There was a stack of cloth hand towels, and nearby, a small card that said, "Use Me," written in Sharpie. After use, I spotted a hole in the wall with a similar sign that said "Abuse Me." I reached out to put the towel into the hole and it was sucked right out of my hands, causing me to shout in surprise.

When I came out of the bathroom, a little shaken, Roz was standing at the end of the hallway laughing.

"Gotcha! I swear, I thought that whole laundry-sucking thing was bullshit when I saw the ads on social media, but it works! I had a system installed when I moved in. You'd think I'd have bigger priorities, I know, but laundry is my least favorite thing ever."

"The reptiles and arthropods were a nice touch." I rubbed my hands on my leggings as I approached her.

"How could I not? If this place is supposed to be an authentic saloon, I thought I'd add some realism."

"Right? I mean, why wouldn't you?" I laughed.

"Right. Well. Hungry?"

"Sure. I don't want to put you out though."

She gave me an incredulous look. "After the work you did? You've saved me countless hours of pouring over papers and slicing up my hands with papercuts. The least I can do is feed you."

She led me around the bar and into the industrial-sized kitchen.

"Wow, this place looks like it could feed an army."

"Probably it could. There's a smaller kitchen on the far side of the house, which is kind of set up like a little mansionette? Like maybe Buckley planned on moving someone in over there at some point, or maybe he just didn't want to walk the half mile over to the saloon. I swear. I have no idea what he was thinking with this place. Which is to say, I often wonder what the hell I was thinking *buying* this place."

"Have to admit I was wondering the same."

She nodded as she opened the fridge. The door was lined with green tea drinks, sparkling water, and canned wine.

"Hmm. Right. Pasta okay? I get meal deliveries. I'm not a huge fan of cooking."

"Whatever you're having."

She grabbed two boxes and popped one in a microwave...and the other in the second microwave. Guess it made sense to have two of everything?

"There's a short answer for the question of why I bought this place and a more involved one. How much time do you have?"

A niggling feeling in the back of my mind let me know this would have been a perfect place to tell her about my practicum. It would have been. But I was riding a high of being privy to knowledge the whole damn town had been desperate for, and I didn't want her to stop talking.

Damn the consequences.

Maybe I don't actually need my master's degree?

"I'm not on a schedule." I'd texted Rachel from the bathroom. She'd told me not to worry about coming back anytime soon.

I want the tea she'd texted.

"Okay. I'll give you the middle ground. After I got fired, which devastated me, by the way. I'd fully planned to work until my pension, and even then I figured I'd still do some sort of public service work. At least I hit my twenty years before they fucked me over. I was forty-two years old when I filed a wrongful termination lawsuit."

"And that was…"

She smirked. "Three years ago. I'd been let go six months before that. Took me a while to see that it was the right thing to do. I come from a cop family. Dad, two brothers, and uncle. They were on my side as much as they could be. Dad supported me filing suit. We talked about it a lot. I showed him case after case of female cops being wrongfully terminated and winning, and my case was even stronger than most. My attorney suggested, and I agreed, that we should seek stupid money."

"The only way to change the system is to make the system hurt," I muttered.

"That's right," she said. "And it's less problematic than saying you want to burn the whole thing to the ground."

I smiled. I so got what she was saying. "Amazing how you have to choose your words carefully around things like that. So, you filed the lawsuit, it went to court…did you get stupid money?"

"Ridiculous money. Ludicrous money. And I decided to get the fuck out of Denver. I wanted to go somewhere I was not likely to be known, someplace that was tolerant and diverse and had way better weather than Denver. I sent my attorney on a wild goose chase for a preposterous piece of real estate where I could spread out, have plenty of privacy and space to do whatever the fuck I wanted, and we narrowed it down to five possibilities.

"This was the one that fit all the criteria. Good ole boy Owen was desperate to get out from under this place and accepted an offer that was sizably reduced from his original asking price. My attorney knew this place had been sitting empty for years, and that no one had offered anywhere near enough for him to sell it. It's a ridiculous house, that I bought with ridiculous money, that I received because of a ridiculous situation. I think it's all fitting."

"As long as you're happy," I said, and the moment her eyes shot to mine, I knew I'd pushed it.

"Happy is the lie we tell people who want the simple answer. I'm not looking for happy. I don't know *what* I'm looking for. Appeasement? Acceptance? Acquiescence? Fuck it. At least I'm not angry every minute anymore."

"Not every minute, but still angry?"

She wrinkled her nose and tapped a finger to her cheek. "Maybe once an hour, every forty-five minutes. Like fifteen minutes of every hour? The rest of the time, I've been working on getting this fucking work off the ground, and now that you've gotten me on the right path, I think I can finally make some progress." She took our meals out of the microwaves with hot pads, grabbed some napkins and pointed toward the silverware. "Want to eat in the saloon or out back?"

"Out back sounds good."

"Sweet," she said. "Want to grab drinks? I'll take a Peace Tea."

I opened the fridge door as directed, grabbed her a giant can of sweetened tea and, for myself, an orange-flavored sparkling water. I followed her out onto the back patio, where there was a picnic table. We sat side by side so we could look out over her sprawling piece of land.

"You definitely have one of the most gorgeous views in the county."

She chewed a bite of pasta and nodded. "If this were the good ole days, this would have been an excellent piece of land to fortify because you can see all approaches clearly. No one can sneak up on you with this slight elevation. I love the trees lining the property, they're just tall enough to provide shade but from upstairs, you can see beyond them, where the river runs along the back of the property and then meets up with the lake. You know, I've even got a boat dock out there and Buckley sold me his boats, too. A party boat, and a little fishing boat with a brand-new trolling motor."

"I love those party boats. Papa used to have one when we were kids. I learned how to swim jumping off that boat."

She frowned. "Like, on purpose?"

I shrugged. "Papa was right there. I'd been bugging him to teach me, so once we got out there, I ran past him and jumped in, and he had no choice but to hop in after me. Once was all it took."

She shook her head. "I'm not a strong swimmer. I'd like to be, but I won't be jumping into Frog Lake like a maniac."

"I wasn't a *total* maniac. I was like eight years old. Isn't that typical eight-year-old behavior?"

She closed her eyes, and I laughed at her exasperation.

"Okay, this from the woman who chases kids off with a drone."

"Yeah," she said, taking several pulls on her can. "I'm going to have to come up with something new. They'll tell their little tagger buddies what to expect. I'm thinking of ordering some of those animatronics from the Spirit store. Hide them in the bushes? Maybe those scary zombie babies or the Regan one with the head that spins around. Oh my God, what if she puked pea soup on them?" She cackled, and I almost spit out my pasta.

"How about putting speakers out there and just whispering to them? Uncle Teddy had this thing called an Eviltron that he put in my bedroom when I was a teenager. It would randomly whisper at me, make skittering noises…scared the shit out of me."

"Did you get him back?"

I grinned. "I hid in the backseat of his car at night before he left the shop. He drove home and had just pulled into the driveway when I started talking to him. He almost drove through the garage door! It was great. He checks his backseat every time he gets in the car to this day."

"All right," she said with approval. "You just might make a good accomplice."

We brainstormed other ways to scare off the kids without making Ernie's job harder.

"I probably should quit with the shooting range, get Mr. Tompkins off his back. Maybe I could go to the other side, but then I'm near the winery. They'll probably complain it interferes with their wine tastings or something bougie like that."

I cracked up. "Don't get me wrong, I know the wine industry has done a lot for Calaveras, but I can't tell you how glad I was to get away from all the tourists."

She gave me a serious look and noticed that I'd finished my pasta and was now bending the foil cover into tiny pieces. "That all you wanted to get away from?"

I sighed and slumped a little. "I needed to get out from under the watchful eye of the town. I felt like people were watching me, waiting to see if I would break. Ernie told you that I was home from undergrad when it happened?"

She nodded and then held up a hand. "Wait. Does this story require wine or ice cream?"

I frowned. "Does it require a *choice*?"

She nodded and gestured for me to follow her inside.

"Let's grab both. I'll take you to my favorite room…so far. I still haven't decided."

"Lead the way."

Chapter Six

"I'm pretty sure, last time I checked, that there was no tropical paradise in Calaveras. No ocean, no sand, and yet…"

There it was. The elusive pool we'd all tried to see all those years. It was incredible. Made to look like an island paradise, there was a whole wall and ceiling of glass, though the glass looking out over her property was frosted for privacy, so even if us bratty little kids would have hopped the fence to come find it, we wouldn't have been able to see anything.

A sound machine gave us the waves and seabirds, and some mellow music wafted out from behind the palm fronds planted around the seating area.

"What is that?"

She stood beside me and looked out into the pool, which had a dark shape in the middle. "What lagoon is complete without its Creature?"

I shook my head. "Of course."

"He's remote control, too. I can make him swim around. It's awesome."

"No doubt."

"This is probably the most ridiculous part of the house, and it's my favorite. I sit here and drink my morning tea, read for a bit, and then a lot of days I end my night here with a drink. It's pretty peaceful, and since it's a saltwater pool, there's no heavy chlorine smell. I'd have hated that. It would permeate the whole damn house."

We sat side by side on lounge chairs facing the pool, which was at least wide enough to do laps, and it had an island in the middle with a movie screen hanging between two palm trees.

"I'm not sure I'd ever leave this room," I said, dropping a foot to the sand and digging my bare toes in. Her eyes tracked my movement as she took another sip of wine from her can.

"That's good. Then we have plenty of time for you to talk." She turned her body sideways to face me, and those giant, intense blue-green eyes focused on me.

I barked out a laugh and nearly spilled my wine. "Is this a new tactic for interrogation? Get the subject liquored up and comfortable?"

"Are you liquored up after a half can of wine? If so, that's sad."

I laughed again but it wasn't free. "I *was* feeling comfortable. I don't like talking about what happened. Not that I can't relay the facts, but it always changes things with people after they hear about it."

"Of course it does—"

I held up a hand. "I'm not sure if it's that people treat me differently after I tell them because they feel sorry for me, or if they just can't relate to someone who's been through something like that. People here stopped really talking to me about more than the weather, or 'how's your grandmother' kind of conversations. At school, I channeled my feelings into rage, and I became 'too much' for my friend group." I glanced at her. "No offense, but I'd figure you'd be tired of hearing stories like mine."

"No. Not at all. A good detective learns something from every interview. Plus, I know you crawled your way out of hell and made something of yourself. I admire resilience."

I nodded and took another sip of my wine. I wasn't tipsy at all, but the combination of the beach, the ice cream, and the surreal atmosphere of the day had me ready to open up, despite the fact that I was supposed to be interviewing *her*.

Well, maybe she'd open up if I showed her my underbelly. I hated the transactional aspect of this conversation, but there you go.

"Mom started dating Armando after I left for college. He was a friend of Teddy's from the Marines who was passing through but ended up staying. It got hot and heavy real quick. I guess having the freedom she'd missed out on as a young woman with a kid made her a little wild? He was younger than her, and kind of a dick, but she always had some explanation for his behavior.

"Anyway, when I came home that summer, I stayed with my grandparents. I didn't want to live with a man. Ew. I was pretty anti-men before I went to college, but it became solidified after a few experiences at school. I'd also just broken up with my first girlfriend, who didn't want to be tied down over the summer, and I didn't want be around lovebirds. I hated the way he talked to her." I finished my can and set the empty in the sand.

"I have more behind the bar." She thumbed over her shoulder, and I laughed.

"Instead of how many bathrooms, should I have asked how many bars?"

"Four," she said around a bite of ice cream. "Want more wine?"

I shook my head. "Gives me a headache if I have more than one, thanks."

She gestured for me to continue.

"Yeah. So, we were barely speaking by the time I went back to school. I wasn't going to come home for Thanksgiving, but Ernie asked me to. He was worried about her, said she hadn't been answering his calls. When I got home, she had a black eye. She begged me not to tell Papa, but I did. There was a whole family intervention. Teddy kicked the shit out of Armando. He left. He was back when I came home for Christmas break. I had no idea. Opened the door and he was there. He told me to quit being a bitch and be there for my mother.

"We got into it, and he got in my face. Didn't touch me, but it was enough. Mom sent him packing, and I thought it was for good. We had a nice holiday, but before I went back to school, he came over, begging her to take him back. Mom sent me to my room, and I called Ernie, who was home for the weekend from his police job in Stockton.

"I walked out and told Armando to leave, that the cops were coming. He pushed Mom out of the way. She fell and hit her head. He came at me. We were going at it when Ernie got there, the cops right behind him. I didn't care if I got hurt. I knew how to fight, and I wasn't going to just take it from him. Ernie took him down. The cops arrested him. When they searched him, they found brass knuckles and a knife that he wasn't supposed to have. Turned out he was on probation. Got him for probation violation and assault. He went to prison. I thought that was the end of it. Mom spent the next year going to counseling and traveling. Things were going great."

"Until they weren't?"

"Until they weren't. I was home for summer break between junior and senior year, and Mom and I were getting along better than ever. She was talking about coming to stay with me in San Leandro for a little while. She was working from home by that point and thought it would be fun. We even made plans to go to Europe together after I graduated.

"But one night, about three weeks before I had to go back to school, I woke up to her crying. I ran into the living room and found Armando holding her by the hair as she pleaded with him. He threw her down and came at me with a knife. I fought back," I said, pointing at the backs of my forearms, which had several deep scars, "but he stabbed me in the thigh, and I fell. Couldn't get back up. He told her if he couldn't have her heart, no one could…and he stabbed her in the chest. He kept yelling at her that this didn't have to happen, if she would've just listened, and then he ran out the door. I called 9-1-1 and crawled across the room to her. I held her until I passed out, and when I woke up in the hospital, they told me she was gone."

I'd told the story so many times, including in depositions, in court, then in victim support groups and counseling. I eventually realized that telling the story let me share how strong my mom was. It was my way of keeping her alive and healing myself. And it was my way of helping others.

"The cops handled everything exactly right, which may or may not have been because they knew my family. I know a lot of victims aren't given that courtesy. But the court system failed. Armando had been let out of prison early due to the COVID release program. He'd only been charged with the probation violation, not the assault, so they let him out, not even considering the fact that he wasn't done with my mom. They didn't even tell her that he was out. Ernie still blames himself. Thought he should have known. It was part of why he decided to come back home instead of staying with Stockton PD."

"There needs to be a better way to track intimate partner violence complaints and convictions. That's a completely different set of details and concerns than a probation violation. The only way to fix it is to change legislation and work with the district attorneys on making the charges stick. I'm tempted to make that part of my post-wrongful-termination mission."

Inspiration hit, and I turned my body to face hers. "That would be huge. Are you really thinking about it?"

She sighed. "I am. Although I'm not sure I'm ready to play nice with politicians. I have before. I'm in this weird place where I have all these ideas of how to be helpful, you know, give back, but I'm also pissed as hell at 'The Man' for everything that happened."

Another opening. This time…fuck it. I went for it.

"Are you familiar with the three female archetypes?"

She frowned and looked out at the water. "You mean, like mythology? Cultural anthropology? Shit like that?"

Shit. *Great.* "The societal expectations of women at the three seasons of their lives: The maiden, the mother, and the crone?"

She rubbed her feet together on the lounge chair. I noticed that her feet had faint tan lines from flip-flops, her toenails had clear polish and were perfectly manicured. Her arches were high, and the bottoms of her feet were much lighter than the bronzed skin on top.

"You mean, like, the societal expectations that girls are virgins, mothers are only good for taking care of people, and if you're not married or a mom and you're of a certain age, you're useless or you're a washed-up old hag who eats children in the woods?"

I bent in half, curling forward on the chair with the force of my laughter.

"Well, that's one way to obliterate my entire graduate practicum, but yeah, I suppose that's it."

"I just think it's bullshit, is all. It's based on a heteronormative view of society, and it keeps the fucking patriarchy in place."

I fell a little bit in love with her right then.

"Are you willing to go on record with those thoughts?"

She frowned at me. "On record?"

"I have to complete one last practicum for my master's degree. I'm supposed to be studying the female archetypes and—"

"So what am I, the Crone in this scenario?" She shook her head and finished off her wine. "*That's* some bullshit. I'm only forty-five."

"And that's why I wanted to talk to you for my project. You're the antithesis of the traditional view of the Crone. You're beautiful." The wine must have given me courage. Her eyes widened as I continued, her lips playing with a smile. "You're vibrant, energetic, and passionate, and while you *do* fit the archetype in that you're reluctant to help, it's not because you don't want to, but more because society has wronged you and you've learned to be cautious." I shut up when her expression hardened.

"They took *everything* from me." Her voice cracked, and I noticed the slightest tremble in her chin. "My colleagues all turned their backs on me, they wouldn't respond to my calls for backup. I got jumped, did you know that?"

"No, God. I'm sorry." My heart was pounding as I thought about how scared she must have been, but she'd been unable to show it. I knew from speaking with law enforcement folks that they held in their fear, and, for many, it led to self-destructive habits.

"Sometimes I wish I *was* an old hag, with poisoned apples or evil spells. I wanted to lay waste to my department after everything happened. In addition to losing my career, I lost my friends. My fiancé disappeared, too."

"*What*? She left?"

She shrugged and looked away again. "I don't know. There were no signs of a struggle at our place, and though she took money out of her bank account, she hardly took any of her belongings with her. Part of my motivation to set all this up," she said, gesturing in the direction of the command center, "is to find her. But the longer I look, the more I think she doesn't want to be found. I know she's alive, but none of her friends and family will talk to me. I've got a couple of private investigators looking…I don't know. At some point I'll let it go. I just need to know if she left on her own or if someone threatened her."

"Do you think? I can't imagine she'd leave you in the middle of everything."

"She didn't want me to go through with the lawsuit. She wanted me to just move on, for us to start over somewhere else."

"Was she a cop?"

She shook her head. "Crime scene tech. She worked in a different department. When we got engaged and moved in together, she transferred over to Denver. I needed to be close to the department, and she didn't want to commute anymore. I think she wanted me to transfer, but that wasn't going to happen. There weren't any positions in her department, and I would have lost my seniority and had to retest for detective."

"Did she support you coming forward?"

She shrugged. "She was supportive to a point. She thought we'd had a hard enough time being accepted as a couple, and she didn't want to be in the spotlight at all. No one bothered me when she transferred, but I guess she got some grief from the techs. I also didn't give a shit, while she was more conscious of appearances.

"The case was fucking awful, and our officers did a shit job. They didn't follow procedure. The kid was being bullied and the parents had made several attempts to get help from the school and from us. Cops in my own fucking department told the kid not to press charges because the bullying would only get worse. That they needed to let it go. The kid was beaten up on his way home from school three times, the last time severely enough to go to the hospital. The kid wouldn't identify their attackers. They were too afraid.

"I tried to get involved with the investigation and when I started digging, I found out who the bullies were. I was told to drop it, that I would be reprimanded if I contacted the family. I did anyway. Still couldn't get the victim to identify their attackers even though a witness had given me their names, but I figured out why they wouldn't talk when I discovered that the suspects were related to cops in the department. I went to my captain, got disciplined, went to IA, they dropped the ball. I went to the deputy chief and got fired. God, I'm still pissed talking about it. The kid committed suicide."

I put my hands over my mouth. "Roz…"

"I know. My attorney encouraged the parents to sue the department, but they were heartbroken and didn't want to go through with it. I donated a huge chunk of my money to the Trevor Project. I set up a scholarship for his younger brother…but fuck, I felt so goddamned helpless. After my case went to court, after I won the settlement and got paid, I got the fuck out of there. Took a while to find this place, during which time I stayed with a cousin in Sacramento. I got to thinking, there's more I can do in my current situation than I could have done in one police department. Let's hope I can make it happen." She turned and wiggled her eyebrows at me. "How's that for a crone?"

"Completely bucks the archetype."

She raised an eyebrow. "Not completely."

She hesitated one second before hopping up from her chair, tearing off her clothes and running into the water. She disappeared around the island, and I was about to investigate when she surfaced and shouted, the sound echoing off the walls of the pool room. I heard her splashing, and then she came around the opposite side of the island.

"Sorry, had to wash off the heavy stuff. You should join me."

A swim did sound good, but I was still in shock from seeing her. *Naked*. I'd known this woman less than a day and she'd turned my world upside down. We'd shared our wounds and we'd laughed. One thing I knew for certain: she shouldn't be by herself here in this big house doing such a big, important, heartbreaking job. Alone. She deserved better.

I peeled off my leggings and pulled my top over my head, along with the bralette I'd worn underneath. It was quite intimidating strolling casually toward her, knowing her body was in tip-top physical condition and I…well, I could have used a bit more time in the gym, but I'd never let my insecurities keep me from expressing my sexuality.

The water was absolutely perfect. It felt wonderful on my skin. Saltwater pools really were superior in many ways.

I swam toward her slowly, taking my time, and giving *her* time to decide whether this was simply skinny-dipping or the beginning of something more. I stopped about three feet away.

"We got a little heavy. I'm sorry, but I'm not sorry."

Her big blue-green eyes were trained on me, and with her hair wet and slicked to her scalp, they seemed even more intense.

"Same. Although, I should be very clear. As much as I find you attractive and would love to fuck you, I can't."

"Okay." Her blunt admission turned my crank.

A crease appeared on her forehead, and she sighed. "Not until I know... I need to know what happened to Michelle, whether she's okay, before I can move on. If I thought she wasn't, and I..."

"I totally get it. And I'm flattered." I offered her a small smile, and she seemed to relax. "But I think you shouldn't be here alone. Doing all of this. You need help. Holding on to all of these stories as one person is too much. Let someone else bear it with you."

She swirled her arms around her a few times, staring at me. "Bear it with me," she finally said, her voice low. "Help me."

"*Me?*" I hadn't considered myself in that scenario. Everything she'd shared with me had me thinking she was onto something so important. There were myriad possibilities for making a difference. But did I have what it took to be useful to her? To this important mission?

What if this was the type of work that would have the biggest impact rather than working with undergrads?

"Yeah! I know you have school, but you're finishing this term, right? Come back. Help me. Do this work with me. Think about how many people we can help with my contacts and your computer magic. And maybe we can make something of that thesis project of yours, make it palatable for law enforcement to get onboard."

My heart soared at the thought, but I squinted at her. "How do you know I'd even be helpful? I might drive you crazy. I could be a total flake."

She rolled her eyes and splashed me. "You forget I know your uncle."

"Then I'm sure he told you I was a pain in the ass."

"And I'm not? Look. Help me this week. I'll let you interview me about your dumb archetypes, and you can help me organize all these cases. Then you go back to school, do your thing, and we talk when you graduate. Deal?"

I think I'd already convinced myself I wouldn't be taking that position in the fall. This scenario sounded way better. Plus, I'd be close to my family, and I'd finally learn the secrets about the Buckley house.

I took her hand. "Deal— *What the!?*"

The Creature had made his way between my ankles and scared the shit out of me.

Roz cracked up. "He likes you."

"I think you do, too." If we were going to do this, we needed to be honest.

"I do. You won't take my shit, I can tell. Or at the very least, you'll give it back."

"You know it." I put on my poker face. "The first priority should be finding Michelle."

She nodded, her smile gone. "Yeah. I won't be able to move on until I do...and I want to. Move on."

I grinned. "Good."

Chapter Seven

Roz and I got to work the next day, and for the rest of the week, I spent days with Rachel and the kids, afternoons napping, and evenings with Roz.

Rachel and I talked about the expectations of mothers, and how she'd gotten a lot of flak from her college friends when she chose to stay home with the kids instead of going to law school like she'd originally planned. She loved being a mother and saw her role as crucial to developing well-rounded community members. She was also the first one to support her friends who chose not to have children, and she loathed that our society makes women choose and, if they try to do both, makes them suffer for it.

I saw her in a new light after our conversations. I still wasn't ready to have kids, figured I never would, but I appreciated her sacrifices even more. I threatened Teddy within an inch of his life that he'd better take good care of his family.

"Be easier if you came back and helped."

I'd rolled my eyes at him, but he was right. It did take a village, and I missed mine.

Roz and I worked into the wee hours Monday and Tuesday before she brought me home. Wednesday, I convinced her to take a break and come play poker at Ernie's. She kicked everyone's ass. I might have let her kick mine. I hoped that if she felt comfortable with the guys, they'd be a good connection to the outside world for her after I went back to school.

I was becoming very protective of her.

And very attracted to her.

We hadn't had any more skinny-dipping excursions, but every time we touched in passing as we worked, it sent a zing to my heart like an urgent transmission from my brain saying *yes, this is where you belong, she's where you belong.*

"You weren't kidding, they do suck," she'd said on the way to drop me at my aunt's place. Teddy was staying the night so he and Ernie could go fishing early in the morning.

"But they're hilarious."

She agreed. "And damn, Angel can cook. How is it that people learn to *like* to cook? It's always felt like such a waste of time."

"Says someone who's spent years grabbing food on the go, I'll bet."

"Guilty."

"I love cooking." I smiled at her. "I'll cook for you."

So I did. Actually, we cooked together Thursday and Friday, packing up food and freezing it so she'd have some other options than her meal plan.

"You are really good at this," she said Friday, the night before I needed to return to San Leandro. I'd planned to pack up, hug the kids, and leave in the morning. I thought I'd be anxious to head home by now. The opposite was true.

We'd accomplished quite a bit over the week. I'd finished Notion templates for all of the cases she had. There were fifty-seven, from all across the country, some murder cold cases, some missing persons. She'd managed to make connection with law enforcement in several big cities and they were all chomping at the bit to get her to consult on their cases. I increased her security to keep her from getting hacked and losing vital information that needed to remain secure.

"Thanks. I'm glad you like it. If I end up sucking at this job, at least I could keep you well fed." I held up a spoon for her to taste the pasta sauce I'd made that afternoon. She backed me into the counter and closed her mouth over the end of the spoon.

She moaned and licked her lips, the movement making me shudder.

"That's incredible. Where did you learn to cook like this?"

"Abuela Bonita, Mom…I had a roommate for a while who was really good, and she showed me a few things."

She leaned forward to take another bit of sauce and pressed her body to mine. It was such a natural move after spending the past week together, and I wanted it, wanted *her*. She noticed the hitch in my breath and gave me that serious gaze of hers, the one I'd seen less of as we got to know each other.

I set down the spoon and pulled her into an embrace. She held on tightly letting me know she needed the closeness too. I buried my face in her neck and breathed her in.

"Thank you, Elia," she whispered, kissing my temple. "Thank you. You don't know how close I'd been to quitting this ridiculous idea before you got here. How close I'd been to shutting up the house and moving on. But now I have hope. I have direction."

"I'm sorry I have to leave," I said, and I was. I believed in this mission of hers so strongly, I was nearly ready to throw my stupid degree out the window.

"No, don't be sorry. Finish your degree. Enjoy the end of school. Then we'll talk."

"We'll talk before then. I'm gonna be checking on you. I don't like leaving you alone with all of this. And you need to get out more. Or… you know what? You should throw a big party. Let the town get to know you. What about something for Pride?"

She raised her eyebrows. "You mean, let everyone and their little monsters infest my safe space? That's…oh, I don't think I could do that."

"You could. And it would be great. I want you to fall in love with Calaveras. Have a real fresh start here."

She grinned. "Now who's the nurturing one? The maiden is supposed to be looking out for herself."

"And you, the crone. You are helping and nurturing too. We're both bucking the archetype, huh?"

She took my hands. "I told myself I was just going to let you go and let you make up your mind about whether to come back, but think about what we could accomplish together."

"I can't *stop* thinking about it."

She pressed her lips together. "Nope. I'm not going to say anything more. Let's get you home."

Chapter Eight

On the drive back to San Leandro, I dictated my thoughts about the archetypes and how it would serve all of society to do away with those long-held beliefs about what women should be, or what their value is. They'd only succeeded in keeping women oppressed for generations. The archetypes feed into gender roles that harm young women, making them think they have to meet expectations to have worth. I was thrilled with my thought patterns. I wrote the first draft of the paper on Sunday.

I texted Roz to let her know I made it home and that the paper was done.

I want to read it.

I was hesitant, but we'd shared so much over the week. I felt as though, during our time apart, we should continue getting to know each other. You know, in case we worked together.

Work. I started making a list of what I would need. Roz had told me to come up with a proposal, and I'd agreed, but it felt weird.

Whatever you want, whatever you need, Elia. The sky's the limit. Remember, I'm loaded, and once we get this business off the ground, there will be people willing to pay a lot of money for our services, enough so we can take on all the pro bono cases we want.

It wasn't like a faculty position would have me rolling in dough, but it was time to think about benefits and retirement, shit like that. I would be leaving maidenhood, and I'd have only myself to look after me. No husband, or even a partner, even though I believed Roz and I both were interested in that outcome.

At least I'd thought so.

Three weeks after I returned home, Roz called me on a Friday night.

"Can you talk?"

"Yeah, what's up?" I'd just gotten home from the gym and had blocked the weekend out to work on my practicum.

"I found her."

Background thoughts and noise faded. "Michelle?"

"One of the PIs I hired made contact with her, told her I wanted to talk."

"That's…she's okay?"

"I guess I'm going to find out. I'm flying to Miami to go see her. So we can talk."

I plopped down on the couch. Her halting way of speaking made her sound…thrown. Like she'd never actually expected to hear from her ex and didn't quite know how to handle it.

"That's good. You can get a sense of her…position."

"Yeah. I hadn't really thought of what I'd say to her, you know? At first, I wanted to find her and bring her home."

No, I hadn't known. Roz hadn't been real clear about whether she saw a future for them. She hadn't spoken past finding her and discerning whether she was safe. Could she be thinking of…taking her back? Was that what she wanted?

"And now you're wondering whether she might still want the future you'd planned."

"Right. No. I don't know."

She sounded distracted. I heard banging and hoped she hadn't broken any of the computer equipment.

She sucked in a breath. "Shit! That's hot."

"What are you doing?"

She was quiet for a minute. "Heating up the sauce you made. I cooked a chicken—don't get excited. I finally tried out the rotisserie oven and it's hella easy to use. Why hadn't I done it sooner?"

The thought of her eating the sauce I made…her lips on the spoon, our bodies pressed together.

I hadn't even been able to kiss her. Maybe I should have insisted. Then she would have known what she was missing. She could have made an informed decision as to whether she wanted her fiancé back or…

A twenty-five-year-old woman. With nothing to offer except mediocre cooking and passable tech skills.

"Roz?"

"Yeah?" She sounded more focused now. "Elia, I don't know. I don't know what she'll say, I can't even begin to imagine what reason she could have for being in Florida, of all places. And I'm not sure if any reason she can give is forgivable after the state she left me in."

My heart sank. They had shared history. They'd been together for six years. What if Roz decided she wanted that part of her life back after she'd lost so much?

"You have to go. You need to know what happened." I had to take myself—and my desires—out of the situation.

"Right." She was quiet, and I realized that up to this point, we hadn't really had pauses in our conversations. Once we'd climbed out of her pool that night, got dried off and dressed, we hadn't stopped talking. She was the first person outside my family that I hadn't had awkward silences with.

"Right. When do you leave?"

"Tomorrow. Ernie's driving me to Sacramento to catch my flight. I told him not to be ridiculous—"

"He cares about you." *I do too.*

"I know. Look, Elia. I don't know what's going to happen—"

"I hope you get the answers you're looking for. She owes you that."

"Right."

More silence.

"Have a safe flight."

"Right. Okay. I'll call you."

We hung up. Like strangers.

I hadn't spoken to Kimbra since I'd been back. She'd emailed me to see how my practicum went so I told her I'd come to office hours.

She had tea waiting for me.

"This one I'm not sure I like. Taste it. Tell me what you think."

I could tell by the aroma that I wasn't going to love it, but I sipped anyway. And tried unsuccessfully not to make a face.

"That bad?"

I wrinkled my nose and set the cup down. "Not my favorite."

She laughed and took a drink of hers. She *did* make a face. "So how did it go with The Crone?"

Rather than tell her I was pretty sure I was in love with her, and that she was potentially getting back together with her fiancé, I stuck to the facts.

"My platform is that we need to do more to destroy the archetypes in our thinking because they've harmed women for generations. And men, to be honest."

She sat back and folded her hands on her belly…which, if I wasn't mistaken, looked a little swollen. Could she be…?

"I love it. I can't wait to read it. You can test out your theories in your discussion section in the fall."

"About that," I said, letting my mouth take over before my brain could figure out that we were making a rash, slightly formed decision. "I am going to respectfully decline the position."

I'd expected her to be disappointed, but she just looked sad. "I thought you might."

"You did?"

"You were already wavering, and it's obvious that you had a life-changing experience over break. I can see the fire in you that's been missing since you lost your grandmother last year."

Abuela Bonita had hung in there after my mom was killed, but her heart had been broken. The stress was too much. Without Papa to hold her when she cried, she passed soon after he died. I'd felt terrible that Teddy and Rachel's kids would miss out on having their grandparents. And I knew right then, even though I was being impulsive, it was important that I go home.

"Being home made me realize how much I'm needed there, not

only for my family but for my whole community. Whether I go into law enforcement like my brother, or I get involved with another advocacy program, I think I need to have more experiences before I'll be the best teacher I can be."

She smiled. "I'm going to miss you, but I'm glad for you. I know you'll do great things."

I thanked her, but as I walked out to my car, I thought...*what a dumbass*. I'd just given up a sure thing for a maybe. Wasn't there a golden rule about not quitting a job before you had something else lined up?

Did Roz's gig count?

Would I want to be a part of it if Michelle was back in the picture? What possible excuse could that woman have for abandoning her partner at the most critical time in her career? In her life? To not stand by her as she did the right thing?

Who would Roz be if she took her back?

Then I realized, did I really know who *Roz* was? I'd thought I had a good read on her, but maybe...I'd been looking for something that wasn't actually there.

When I didn't hear from Roz the rest of the week, my heart sank. Had she taken her back already?

But then I worried...what if it had been a trap, and the people who thought Roz had wronged them were lying in wait?

Monday came and still no word. I called Ernie.

"Have you heard from Roz?"

"Yeah, she canceled her flight home from Florida. She decided to buy a new car and drive back. She didn't really say much, just said she had some stops to make."

"Okay." Odd, but then what business was it, really, of mine? "So, I gave up the faculty position. Thought I should tell you."

Ernie whooped on the other end of the phone, making a very un-Uncle-Ernie-like sound.

"Are you all right?" I asked with mock concern.

"You're coming home then?" The excitement in his voice cemented the deal.

I sighed. "I am. I'm not sure what I'm doing just yet, so don't plan my life out for me. Roz asked me to work with her—"

"Yeah, she told me. Sounds like a good deal."

I waited a few beats for my voice to be strong and not shaky. "I'm not sure, though. Can you let me know what opportunities I might have with the department?"

"Are you sure? She sounded really excited at the possibility of working with you—"

"You know why she went to Miami, right?"

"Sure. A lead on her ex-fiancé. Wait—is there more going on with you two?"

"Do you really want to know?"

"No," he scoffed. "But I want you to be okay."

"There was potential, but if she's getting back with her ex…I don't know if our plans would be a good idea."

"Say no more," he said. "You gotta do what you think is best. I'll support you no matter what. Now, you hurry up and finish. Teddy's already making plans how to embarrass you at graduation."

"I bet he is."

The rest of the term flew by in a maelstrom of papers, presentations, and forms to fill out. Then it was done. Teddy and Ernie came for my graduation and helped me pack up my apartment.

Roz and I had texted, but it had mostly been questions she had about how to use the functions of her templates, all business. She hadn't said another word about her trip or Michelle. I didn't ask. I didn't want to know. I didn't need the distraction.

We got into town late on a Saturday evening, and I'd only had enough energy to drag my meager possessions into Ernie's garage. He'd asked me if I wanted to move in with him, and Rachel was okay with it as long as I came to dinner every weekend. I promised I'd be over to help her with the kids all summer and told her she should start making plans with her girlfriends. Maybe even look into law school online. Her eyes had flared at that. She hadn't said no.

Sunday morning, Ernie was up early, banging around in the

kitchen of his three-bedroom, two-bath house. I realized there would be no sleeping in on his days off if he was going to be so loud.

"Hey, get up, sleepyhead. It's Pride today."

"Pride? What are you talking about. Calaveras doesn't do Pride." A fact that galled me.

"They do now, and it's today, so get up, get dressed in your best rainbow gear, and let's go. I'm not on duty, but I promised I'd help."

"Fine." I groaned as I climbed out of bed.

"Come on. You complained for years that Calaveras should have a parade or at least a festival. You can't be a fair-weather Pridester."

Ernie didn't talk to me about his love life, but I was pretty sure he was bisexual. We'd been out more than once when I'd seen him talking to women but watching men. I hoped he'd find someone. Being a cop alone in a small town was a recipe for loneliness unless romance novels were to be believed, and then at any moment, the right unattached person would show up. Maybe he'd thought Roz would be that for him…at least until they became friends.

There wasn't a large queer community in Calaveras, but there were a few of us, and more in the nearby towns. At least I wouldn't have dating as a distraction as I figured out my life.

I put on a pair of black shorts and a white tank from the Human Rights Campaign with a rainbow and "everyone" printed below it. I pulled my hair up into a ponytail and wore pink sparkly flip-flops. It was already sweltering at nine in the morning. I'd certainly appreciated the lower temps in San Leandro. The heat was one of the tough parts about Calaveras, but it was so beautiful in my hometown, and I was still riding the high of not being in school and not having anyplace I was required to be.

Except, apparently, at Pride with Uncle Ernie.

We hopped into his Ford pickup and when he passed by Mark Twain Park, I turned to frown at him.

He grinned. "Roz took your advice."

"My what?"

And then I remembered. I'd suggested she throw a Pride celebration party. My stomach dropped, but I recovered pretty quickly. At least my reunion with her would be surrounded by lots of other folks I knew, and if Michelle was there, I could meet her, be civil, and then I could get drunk with Ernie before signing up to join the police academy.

As we pulled onto her road, there were cars lining both sides of the asphalt.

"Looks like a good turnout," I said.

"What better way to get people to come to Pride than to offer tours of the famous Buckley house."

I stared at him wide-eyed. Man, she was really going for it.

Good for her. I was glad. I hated thinking of her alone out here when she had such a big personality and so much to offer. I cursed her former department and Michelle again for how awful they'd treated her.

The gates to the Buckley property—Roz had yet to rename the place—were flung open and there was a giant rainbow made of flowers in front of the house. She'd definitely had someone in to work on the yard, which was full of color and well-manicured. There were flags representing all of the iterations of the queer spectrum lining the driveway and before we even parked, I could hear music blaring from the backyard.

"Did she hire a band?"

"Uh-huh. A couple local bands. And she got some DJ, I think…"

I had the door to the truck open before he'd turned off the engine. I was so happy to see so many folks from town out and enjoying the festival. She had a couple of food trucks parked out back, and through the back doors, I saw the saloon was full of folks. Past the patio in back, there was a large stage set up, and I recognized a band of Teddy's pals who called themselves For The Birds setting up to play.

"How did she do all of this?"

Ernie stood next to me. "She had help." He grinned and pointed to Rachel, who was wrangling the line of kids waiting to have Teddy do their face painting.

This was good. Good for Roz. Good for the town. I wanted to tell her how happy I was.

The band started to play and people mosied over to the stage area to dance and cheer them on. Ernie and I went inside the saloon to find Angel playing bartender, along with two of his brothers.

"Hey, graduate!"

I stood on the bottom rail of the bar and leaned over to kiss his cheek.

"Hey…barkeep? This a new gig for you?"

He grinned. "Roz is keeping me out of trouble. Keeping me busy." He handed us two sodas.

I raised my eyebrows and stepped down. "Is she?"

His gaze flicked outside, and I turned to see Roz taking the stage to huge applause.

Ernie gestured with his head, and we took our drinks outside.

"Thank you, everyone. Thank you for coming! Welcome to…well, y'all know it as the Buckley House, but I want to share with you the new name in just a minute. I'm so glad you could join me to celebrate Pride. Part of the reason I chose Calaveras to be my new home was because y'all have a reputation for being welcoming, and I've definitely felt that vibe since I've been here, so thank you."

She stared right at a couple of boys, who giggled and waved.

"Some of you may know that I bought this house with money I received in a lawsuit. At the root of that lawsuit was a case involving a young man in Denver. He was bullied at school, and unfortunately, the justice system failed him. His name was Ben Aronson. I want to dedicate the work I do for missing persons and victims of crime to his memory, so from now on, I'd love it if you'd join me in calling this place The Aronson House."

There was applause all around that lasted as long as Roz took to collect herself. She looked even more beautiful after the two months we'd been apart. Her hair was a little longer, fuller. She'd definitely spent time in the sun, and she looked…excited to let these folks in.

"Thank you," she said finally, smiling at the crowd. "I also plan to make the house available for local events and fundraising activities. We're going to have a website—that is, if my helper is still available— and all of the information will be posted there. Keep your eyes on the local paper and the Calaveras website and social media pages. We'll start tours in a little bit, if you've always wanted to see the wild and wacky things the previous owner left behind. I'm going to be auctioning off a lot of stuff to raise money for The Aronson Project, so also keep your eyes peeled for that. Special thanks to Angel Guillam, Tony Barnes, and the Muse family for their help getting this event set up. Enjoy yourselves!"

There was more applause, and as she waved at the crowd, she spotted me standing with Ernie and made her way toward us.

"Great turnout," Ernie said, bending to kiss her cheek.

"Thanks to all of you guys," she said, giving him a pointed look. Then she turned toward me and held out a hand. "Come with me?"

I glanced at Ernie, who was already walking away, and I took her hand. She led me into the house, through the saloon, through the honky-tonk living room, and then to a door down the next hallway that I hadn't seen before. She turned to face me and looked to make sure we were alone.

"Hi." She bounced on her toes and squeezed my hand.

"Hi yourself, Mz. Pride. You decided to do it, huh?"

"What do you think?"

"I think you're holding my hand."

She looked down at our hands and squeezed mine again.

"I wanted to show you what I've been up to…and explain some things. Can I? Can I have a minute?"

I nodded. "Of course."

She could have anything she wanted. I just didn't know *what* she wanted.

She opened the door to a large room that now housed all of her computer equipment she'd purchased for her investigations work. She had basically moved out of the control room and created an actual workspace in what must have been a large family room or ballroom type space. There were bulletin boards all around the walls, long tables in a U-shape, two desks set up with additional computers.

"It's great! This feels way more workable than the control room. You were a little tight for space in there."

"You like it?"

I glanced at her and realized she was waiting intently for my reaction.

"Yeah, Roz. I think you'll do great things here."

She linked our fingers together and took my other hand. "Or *we* can do great things here?"

My smile fell. "Roz…"

"Hear me out?" She let go of my hands and walked over to the desks. I stepped farther into the room and closed the door behind me.

"Okay."

"I kept communication to a minimum while you were at school for several reasons. One, I needed to get my head on straight after meeting with Michelle. Two, I wanted you to be able to focus on finishing your degree. Three, I wanted you to decide whether to come back on your own, without my persuasion. And four, I was working on a proposal for you. I know I asked you to make one, but I thought it only fair that I share with you what I was hoping your position would be."

"So, you did meet with her."

"I did. She was living with college friends I'd never met, working under the table, doing everything she knew to do to cover her trail so I wouldn't find her. Me, nor any of the press who had hounded her after I got fired. She confirmed she left me of her own volition because she didn't want to be in the spotlight."

My shoulders fell a little. How sad for Roz. "I'm sorry."

She shook her head. "Don't be. Better to find out before we got married, right?"

"I suppose…"

"Anyway, she said she'd had a change of heart after talking to the PI and wanted to try again. I told her I was glad she was safe and hadn't been harmed—and that I never wanted to speak to her again. I got the closure I wanted and needed. So I could move on."

The corner of my lip curled up. "That's good."

"It *is* good, but I want to be clear with you, I needed the closure, but I'd moved on when I moved here. I don't want you to think I expected you would want to dive right in, you know? I just didn't want you to decide whether to come home or not based on whether or not we'd be anything more than potentially co-workers."

"I appreciate that."

She exhaled and swallowed. "Having said that...I really missed you."

I rolled my eyes. "I missed you too."

"Good. Now, I know you just graduated, like, yesterday...but here. This is the proposal I came up with. Look at it, take time to decide."

I walked over and took the papers from her and set them down without looking at them. I rested my hips on the edge of the desk, invading her space a bit. "I will."

I could tell by the way she was wringing her hands that she was nervous about seeing me. Seeing as I no longer considered myself the chaste maiden who kept her sexuality under wraps to remain innocent, I crossed my ankles and watched as her gaze traveled up my legs, over my shorts, across my ample cleavage on display, and my bare shoulders before resting on my lips.

"Elia, look. I'm trying to do the right thing here. You have your whole life ahead of you."

I nodded. "Mhm. I do."

She blinked. "And I'm the crone, you said it yourself."

"We both said the archetypes were bullshit."

"I...I want to earn it. I want to deserve a shot with you."

"Good."

She sputtered. "Elia!"

"Look, you said you needed closure with Michelle. You got it. You said we'd talk after I graduated. We are. But now? I just want to—"

She grabbed my face with both hands and kissed me like I was the cool sip of water she needed on the hottest day of her life. She sucked in a breath, and she moaned when she kissed me for the second time. She stepped over my crossed ankles and pressed her body against mine, her high, small breasts brushing against my larger ones. I grabbed her hips and pulled her in tight, ready to show her she'd already earned it. I wanted to give it. Wanted to take it.

"Oh my God. Girl, you can kiss," she whispered, licking my lips. "What the fuck am I supposed to do with all these people outside? I gotta give tours and shit and all I want to do right now is get down on my knees for you."

I let my hands slide around to her ass and grinned. "Plenty of time for that later. You heard I moved back, right? That I'm not going anywhere? Is that good enough for you?"

"God, yes. Come here." She ran her hands over my breasts and sighed as she kissed me again, this time tasting every inch of my mouth until I was the one who wanted to get down for *her*. She nudged my thighs apart and pressed hers into my core, making me gasp. We were going to have each other's clothes off any second.

"We have to stop. You're so fucking hot, Elia."

"Happy Pride," I said in a singsong voice, and then chuckled as I kissed her one last time. "You can have whatever you want. Later."

"Good. I know just the room we should christen. I had the movie room furniture reupholstered. I didn't want to think about what that cowpoke got up to in there."

"You mean, you had an idea of what *you* wanted to get up to in there."

"Fuck yeah. Wait till you see it."

"I can't wait."

Stay Tuned for More…

For The Girls: A Paranormal Sapphic Romance Collection Available Fall 2025

About the Author

Award-winning author and Bay Area native R.L. "Ro" Merrill (she/her) is an advocate for social justice, a sucker for rescue pets, and a spinner of compelling stories. A veteran public school educator, parent of two brilliant young adults, and wife of a patient collector and fellow bookworm, she was raised on a steady diet of eclectic music and campy horror. She writes quirky and relatable queer and heterosexual characters that know how to use their words and are willing to work hard for their happily ever afters. Readers who dig swoony contemporary romance or shivery supernatural suspense will find themselves right at home in her extensive catalog. Her books contain killer soundtracks, generous amounts of spice, and enough laughs to get readers out of their heads and into their feels. When she's not writing, you can find her cruising in her Bronco, adding to her vinyl and skull collections, or head-banging at a rock show. ***Stay Tuned for More...***

facebook.com/rlmerrillauthor

instagram.com/rlmerrillauthor

amazon.com/stores/R.L.-Merrill/author/B00PI6Q1LI

bsky.app/profile/rlmerrillauthor.bsky.social

tiktok.com/@rlmerrillauthor1342

goodreads.com/rlmerrillauthor

Road Trip

You Fell First

The Heart Knows (Re-Releasing Spring 2025)

A Match Made in Spain

LGBTQ Romance

Pinups and Puppies (Originally in Love Is All Vol. 2)

I Want, More – Bolder Breed Studios #1 (Originally in Love Is All Vol. 3)

Love and Pride – Bolder Breed Studios #2 (Originally in Love Is All Vol. 4)

Everything's Better With You: An MM Sports Romance

All I Wanna Do — Bolder Breed Studios #3 (Email Ro for your copy)

Under His Sheets: Accidentally Undercover – Out April 9, 2024

Feuds and Interludes: Road To Rocktoberfest 2024 - November 2024

The Banes of Lake's Crossing (Historical Horror Romance)

The Fourth Man (The Banes of Lake's Crossing) (Historical Horror Romance)

The Redemption of Nathaniel Bane

The Absolution of Jonah Bane

The Gifted Series: (Supernatural Suspense/Paranormal Romance)

Healer

Connection

Protector

Sundowners (M/M Paranormal Romance

Sundowners Book One

Sundowners Book Two (February 13, 2025)

Forces of Nature Series: (Gay Contemporary Romance)

Hurricane Reese

Typhoon Toby

Earthquake Ethan

Summer of Hush Series: (Gay Contemporary Romance)

Summer of Hush

Brains and Brawn

Carnival of Mysteries: (Gay Paranormal Romance, connected to Summer of Hush series)

You Can Do Magic: Carnival Of Mysteries (Season One, Book One)

You Can Save Me: Carnival of Mysteries (Season Two, Book Two)

You Can Make Me: Carnival of Mysteries (Season Three, Book Three Out September 13, 2025)

Anthologies:

Thanksgiving Day Parade From Hell (Worst Holiday Ever) (Gay Contemporary Romance

Valentine's Day From Hell (Worst Valentine's Day Ever) (Gay Contemporary Romance)

Salty and Sweet (Summer Fair) (Lesbian Contemporary Romance)

The Fourth Man (The Banes of Lake's Crossing) (Historical Horror Romance)

A Piece of Him (Gone With The Dead) (Horror)

Breaking Bread—Dark Divinations from HorrorAddicts.net Press (Horror)

Exchange (Renewal) (Science Fiction)

Tap-Tap-Tap (Impact) (Horror)

Human Sacrifice (Innovation) (Horror)

The Sitter (Clarity) (Horror)

Joy Is A Phone Call Away – A More Perfect Union (Lesbian Contemporary Romance)

The House Must Fall – Haunts and Hellions from HorrorAddicts.net Press – May 2021 (Horror)

A Kept Woman – BAQWA Presents: Horror Show 2021(Lesbian Horror Romance)

Gods of Rock 'n' Roll (Free on Wattpad)

How Bittersweet is Karma? (Free on Wattpad)

Let Me Stand Next To Your Fire (Queer Cheer)

Midnight in the Renaissance Elevator

Holiday Romance

A Peace Offering (Re-release)

Love and Pride – Bolder Breed Studios #2

Once Upon A Goth Dog Solstice

Audiobooks

The Rock Season (Kiss App)

Brains and Brawn (Kiss App)

Teacher (Kiss App)

Hurricane Reese (Kiss App)

A Match Made in Spain (Audible)

Healer: Gifted Book One (Audible)

You Can Do Magic: Carnival of Mysteries (Audible)

You Can Save Me: Carnival of Mysteries (Coming to Audible Spring 2025)

Road Trip: A Rock 'n' Romance Story (Audible)

You Fell First: A Rock 'n' Romance Story (Coming Soon to Audible)

Under His Sheets (Audible Coming Soon)

Non-Fiction

Horror Addicts Guide To Life Volume 2 - Edited by Emerian Rich

Death's Garden Revisited - Edited by Loren Rhoads (Out Fall 2022)